THE PERFECT CANDIDATE

Also by T. Dasu

The Waiting Wife
(Book 1 of the Spy, Interrupted trilogy)

THE PERFECT CANDIDATE

Book 2 of the
Spy, Interrupted trilogy

T. Dasu

All people, places, situations, and incidents described in *The Perfect Candidate* are completely fictional.

ISBN-10: 0692510370
ISBN-13: 9780692510377
Library of Congress Control Number: 2015913140
IndiaWrites Publishers Inc., New Vernon, NJ

For Kumar

ACKNOWLEDGMENTS

I would like to thank former congressman Scott Murphy for sharing the inner workings of an election campaign with me. Several details in the novel are a result of discussions with Stephanie Johnson, Angus Maclellan, and Simon Byers.

I would like to thank Tara Sarath of Barefoot Publicity, who not only read the manuscript but also truly understood the characters and made many insightful suggestions. She persuaded me to add campaign tweets to the manuscript—a nice touch.

My family merits special mention for their support and patience while I let things slide. My love and gratitude go to my father, my mother-in-law, my husband, and my son.

CONTENTS

THE CANDIDATE

A tall young man stood curbside at Boston's Logan International Airport and tapped impatiently on his phone. His jacket lay neatly draped on the big suitcase between his feet, where his shadow, cast by the midmorning sun, crept halfway across the road in front. He glanced at the police car standing watch a few feet away. It hadn't budged since arriving within seconds of his appearance.

A black SUV cruised past, reversed, and stopped in front of him. The driver leaned across the passenger side and called out, "Wasim Raja?"

Wasim bent down and looked in. "Doug?"

"Hey, Wasim! Great to meet you at last! How are you?" Doug, a compact man around the same age as

Wasim, jumped out of the vehicle and came around to shake hands.

Wasim grinned and pumped his hand. "Pleased to meet you too, Doug!"

"Need help with anything?" Doug looked around for other bags.

Wasim shook his head and heaved his lone suitcase and laptop into the trunk and placed his jacket on top of the luggage.

Doug returned to the driver's seat and watched his new acquaintance slam the trunk shut, walk to the passenger side, and open the car door.

Wasim climbed into the seat and snapped on his seat belt.

"Thanks for the ride, Doug." In the rearview mirror, he saw the police car slip away in the opposite direction.

"No problem."

Doug Mayhew and Wasim Raja were the first wave of party operatives sent by the Republican Party to run the Senate campaign of Stephen Edward James, scion of the once-legendary James clan of Massachusetts. The reclusive Mr. James had decided, seemingly on a whim, to contest the special Senate election brought about by the death of the incumbent, Senator Jonathan Kirk, a Democrat.

The car slid into traffic, and Doug's attention was taken up by the manic crisscrossing of cars ahead. He clutched the wheel and leaned forward fiercely.

Wasim squinted into the bright summer morning and tried to untangle his sunglasses from his pocket. "Is it a long drive?"

"No, not really, it should take about an hour."

Although Doug and Wasim each had several campaigns to their credit, this was their first time working together. The GOP had scrambled them together at short notice to get on board the campaign. Stephen James had gone from primary contender to being the Republican Party nominee in the course of a week.

Doug looked over at his colleague. Wasim was distractingly good-looking, with a high-beam smile and natural physical grace. According to his bio, he had played basketball for a Michigan high school famous for producing NCAA stars.

Wasim pushed back his seat and twisted around to the side to get a better view of Doug.

"I tried to read up on our candidate. There's really nothing much out there other than the papers he filed. Very strange."

Doug didn't answer immediately, as he was focusing intently on changing lanes. Once that was done, he leaned back and tilted his head toward Wasim. "You thought that too, huh? He doesn't even have a Facebook page, and neither does his wife. Even my *grandmother* has a Facebook account."

"Well, on the bright side, there is no embarrassing digital trail to worry about."

Doug swore at a car that cut him off. He added in a calmer tone, "I have friends in this neighborhood. I asked around to see what I could dig up."

He now included Wasim in his cyclical monitoring of the car mirrors—left mirror, rearview, right mirror, Wasim. Sunny Wasim, with his halo of black wavy hair, disconcerting baritone, and the slightest hint of an exotic accent behind a Michigander's dropped *T*s.

Doug waited for the traffic to settle before beginning. "Our candidate inherited a shitload of money from Grandpa James, the robber baron turned banker turned philanthropist. Dad killed himself. Grandpa blamed Mom's infidelities, and Mom and two older siblings fled to Cyprus, leaving sixteen-year-old Stephen Edward James, the sole heir-to-be, to deal with Grandpa's illness and looming death. He grew up to be some kind of an eccentric horticulturist and madcap inventor. He runs an engineering company now—Bay State Consulting. The Department of Defense is his only client."

"I read about that consultancy in his application. Is it any good?"

"Apparently. They work on classified stuff, very hush-hush." Doug laughed. "And here's some personal gossip."

"Go on."

"When he married this Indian American woman five years ago, the whole town went nuts. Rumors flew thick and wild. Kinky stuff, they said he must've joined a cult."

"I'm not surprised." Wasim shrugged. "People make up all kinds of crazy stuff. How do *you* know all this?"

"My roommate from Georgetown works for the James family's attorneys."

They left the highway and veered off onto a country road that ran along the coast. Imperious homes peeked from behind high compound walls and hedges. Occasional gaps in the fences gave tantalizing glimpses of docks, private beaches, and shimmering water.

"I'm starving," Doug said. "I hope they feed us. My last candidate was so cheap he never bought us a cup of coffee on his own dime. Ever."

"I have some granola bars if you'd like."

"Seriously?"

"Hey, my ma taught me never to be without food—it's a third-world obsession."

"Your parents are from Pakistan, right?"

"Yes." Wasim looked at him. "Is that a problem?"

"Of course not. Wasim, c'mon."

"Sorry."

They drove in silence. The road narrowed further. To their right, large estates barred access to the ocean. On the left, the land was mostly woods, farms, and marshes—a vast land trust created to keep the tony community beyond the grasp of developers and interlopers.

The GPS announced cheerfully that they had arrived. But where? All they could see was an artfully landscaped ten-foot concrete wall shrouded in flowering vines. Doug slowed down and stopped in front of a solid metal gate embedded in the concrete. It had no markings. A gaggle of surveillance cameras was clustered on top, glaring every which way.

No sooner had their car stopped than one of the lenses slid down on a telescopic arm and peered at Doug. He stared back. The electronic eye retracted with a snarky little hiss, and the gate split in the middle to let them in. They drove through, and the metal panels slid shut behind the car with impressive speed.

"How very James Bond." Wasim raised his eyebrows.

Doug wasn't too happy. He muttered something incomprehensible.

They bumped along a paved driveway that meandered through the woods and took them deep inside the property. Flashing red sensors mounted on trees signaled the progress of the car to an unseen master. The road took a sharp turn and brought them face-to-face with a surreal hangar-like structure in a clearing. The dome yawned at their approach and swallowed them into its brightly lit interior. A bank of screens, electronics, gauges, and controls huddled to their left. No signs of life anywhere.

Doug looked around and blinked. A synthesized voice clicked to life.

"Please exit the car and cross to the other side of the yellow line in front," it instructed pleasantly.

Wasim got out first. He examined the floor, the yellow line, and the wall beyond. Doug was still seated inside the car and looked uneasy.

"It's OK," Wasim said. "Come out, Doug."

"Are you sure we have the right house?"

"Yes, don't worry. It's OK."

Doug emerged from the car and slammed the door behind him. They crossed over in lockstep. Immediately, a metal grill descended behind them onto the yellow line, cutting them off from their car, while the wall in front of them slid aside.

They had been disgorged at the head of a gravel path. It cut across a vast lawn in graceful curves to a stone terrace at the foot of a magnificent Victorian mansion. A garden enveloped the house and the terrace and ran alongside the broad stone steps that led down from the terrace to the glittering water of the Bay. Doug and Wasim stopped, taken aback by the beauty of the scene. It was straight out of a cinematographer's dream.

A large wooden pergola festooned with white wisteria blooms occupied the center of the terrace. The cloying scent of the flowers hung heavy in the humid August air. Underneath the pergola, a man sat at a long wooden table, poring over papers, a laptop open in front of him. He heard their footsteps and rose, giving them the first glimpse of their candidate.

Stephen Edward James III looked nothing like his application photo. Despite the heat he was dressed formally in a tailored suit, complete with tie. Soft chestnut curls, cropped close to his head, tried desperately to mitigate the severity of his expression. Steel gray eyes scrutinized Doug and Wasim through round metal-rimmed glasses. There was no hint of a smile, even when the two men came within feet of him. He seemed older than the thirty-eight years he had listed on his application.

After the introductions and handshakes, he said abruptly, "Let's go inside. It'll be cooler." His words were clipped, pinched off by thin lips precisely after the correct interval of time.

He packed his papers in a briefcase, snapped the laptop shut, and led the way across the terrace to the porch.

The young men looked at each other. *Going to be a tough sell*, Wasim texted to Doug.

Now, now, let's not jump to conclusions, Doug texted back.

Stephen took the porch steps two at a time. He glanced back at the campaigners trailing behind. They were busy with their phones, totally unaware of their surroundings. His own life had forced him to the paranoid end of the spectrum, and he envied their innocence.

They entered the home through gleaming glass double doors, walking into an expansive, airy room that occupied an entire side of the house. It was cool inside and uncluttered, with a stunning view of the garden and ocean outside. Comfortable sofas and chairs were clustered in groups, each arrangement configured for the enjoyment of a different slice of the vista. In the corner with the best view of the ocean, a square table draped in white was set for four. The room smelled of fresh lilacs that were arrayed in vases all around the room.

"Where *is* she?" Stephen frowned and pulled out his phone. Right on cue, the wooden double doors on the far side of the room opened and a woman entered.

"Thank you. I'll take it from here," she said to an unseen person behind her, pulling in a steel food cart before the doors closed.

"Hello!" She turned around and smiled.

Wasim had expected a Padma Lakshmi, a leggy bombshell trophy wife, the kind that rich, old men married, not that Stephen was old. The young woman was nothing like that, with a petite frame and the same formal manner as her husband. In her pale silk blouse and black pencil skirt, with her long black hair tied in a prim ponytail, she looked ready for a board meeting.

"Nina, meet Doug Mayhew and Wasim Raja. Gentlemen, my wife, Nina Sharma."

She shook hands with them and pointed to the table. "Please sit. Let's have lunch first. You must be hungry."

Stephen steered the cart to the side of the table. It was laden—sandwiches, salad, olives, cheese, cookies, fruit, wine, juice, and water.

"Help yourselves," she said.

The young men murmured thanks and piled food on their plates hungrily.

Stephen held the chair for her. Once she took her seat, they settled around the table, one on each side.

"Beautiful place," Doug remarked a few minutes into the meal, after the initial surge of food had calmed his hunger.

"Thank you." Nina looked up from her plate with a smile. "We remodeled it last year." She looked at Stephen, but he didn't say anything.

"Where are you from, Doug?" Nina asked.

"I am from New Orleans. I went to Georgetown University, and in my senior year, I was selected to help with the Louisiana gubernatorial race. That's how I got sucked into this business."

"Nice! How about you, Wasim?"

Stephen ate silently and watched the speakers or checked his phone for incoming messages. He didn't make any attempt to join the conversation or even look friendly. As a result, Nina smiled twice as bright and doggedly kept the conversation moving.

Wasim swallowed his mouthful and said, "I grew up in Michigan and went to the University of Michigan at Ann Arbor to study political science."

Doug waited for a minute and jumped in. "Wasim's being modest. He ran the first-ever nationwide online political campaign. Social media and all that is commonplace now, but in those days, it was radical, particularly for the GOP. It mobilized young voters and raised a significant amount of support and money…and almost certainly won the election." He looked over at Wasim, who looked embarrassed. "He was barely twenty at that time. We were all very envious."

In fact, when the senior GOP brass had approached Doug, he had specifically asked for Wasim because he knew that, given Stephen's lack of experience, they'd be leaning heavily on social media and data science. And after the GOP's drubbing in the last election cycle, the party was eager to embrace any edge they could get.

"That's amazing!" Nina glanced at Stephen and tried to include him once more, but he was impervious, busy with his phone.

"So what do *you* do, Nina?" Wasim asked and immediately regretted it, because it had caused Stephen to look up sharply.

"Nothing at the moment."

Her husband cut in. "She runs our foundation to promote K–12 education for girls in third-world countries."

"Oh wow! Tell me more." Wasim set a recorder down in front of her on the table. "I am looking for material to put in Stephen's launch announcement."

"Please don't record it," she said and looked at Stephen to see what he thought of it.

Wasim switched it off. "Go on."

"We want girls in developing countries to get into schools at an early age and stay there until they learn the skills to make a living and have control over their reproductive choices."

Wasim and Doug waited for her to continue, but she stopped and shrugged.

"That's it."

There was a knock at the door. She got up and crossed the room, conscious of the three men watching her, or rather, her husband watching the two men watch her. They heard her talk to someone on the other side. After a minute, she closed the door and returned with a tray bearing coffee paraphernalia. Doug got up to help her set it down on the table.

"I'll leave you guys to get on with your work," she said.

"Could you stay?" Stephen asked without looking at her, suddenly absorbed in his papers.

Nina frowned at him. It was a maddening habit of his, not to look at her when making a request, as if looking at her would obligate him for the favor. She sat down vehemently to get his attention, but he didn't raise his head.

What a strange couple, Doug thought. Stephen was stillness itself—watchful, wary, and economical in movements, emotions, and words, with an unnerving intensity when he deigned to look at you. Nina couldn't take a step without laughing or gesticulating dramatically with her hands. How did they meet? Get married? Stephen didn't seem like the marrying sort, and she seemed too bookish to have ventured into such an adventurous alliance across cultures and temperaments. What's their story? He leaned forward, glasses gleaming with the reflection of the ocean outside.

"We want to go over some basics with both of you," he began. "Tell me in one sentence, Stephen, why you want to run for the US Senate."

Stephen leaned back in his chair and fixed him with a stare.

"I want to influence foreign policy and restructure intelligence agencies to better serve national security."

Doug had not expected something so specific.

"Why? What is your experience in that area? How are you qualified?"

Wasim looked up from his laptop to hear Stephen's answer. The man was hard to read. Nina, on the other hand, was trying hard not to smile.

"Because I was recruited by the CIA straight out of college and retired a few months ago after fifteen years at the Agency. I served as an undercover officer in India, Pakistan, and Afghanistan, and during the last two years, I ran all South Asia operations for the CIA. Of course, this is strictly for your ears only."

Doug listened, slack-jawed. Wasim wasn't *that* surprised, given the outlandish security measures around the property.

"I have firsthand experience and understanding of the geopolitics of the region." Stephen paused and looked around.

Wasim remained impassive. As a nonpracticing Muslim, he was an outsider in his own community and an enigma to his father. But society did not see him as the all-American he was. Instead, he was treated as a young Muslim man, singled out for special scrutiny everywhere, part of a community that was under constant surveillance from inside and out. Part of his reason for taking up the messy business of politics was to make the mainstream flow closer to his people and vice versa.

Stephen's eyes lingered on Wasim.

"I have very specific ideas on what needs to be done and how to accomplish it. And I am uniquely qualified for it. I don't think there is anybody out there with my experience or ability."

He said the words matter-of-factly, oblivious to any appearance of arrogance or conceit.

"The challenge is…" He paused. "Your challenge, that is, is that none of this can be made public. I am trying to get clearance to mention my employment, but I doubt it will be granted. Too recent."

He stood up and pushed back his chair. Nina sat still and stared demurely at her hands. He walked behind her chair and looked at the two campaign pros.

"You have to sell me to the electorate without violating the Espionage Act or the Intelligence Identities Protection Act. I am sure you know what they are."

By this time Wasim and Doug had coalesced around the laptop on the other side of the table and were poring over the screen together while Wasim hammered away furiously. They conferred and whispered, all the while talking to Stephen.

Nina made herself a cup of coffee only to have Stephen swoop down and steal it from her hands.

"Did you meet your wife on the job?" Wasim asked conversationally, encouraged by the unexpected domestic gesture between husband and wife.

"No."

Wasim looked at Nina in the hope that she'd chime in, but she was absorbed in the coffee cup that Stephen had handed back. Wasim waited. He looked at each of them in turn, until Doug nudged him under the table—*drop the topic.*

"Do you have enough funds? Will you write a check for your campaign?" Doug asked.

"No. I intend to raise money like everyone else."

"Do you have a list of potential donors? We can start you off with a list from our database."

"Yes, I have a network I can tap into, but keep that list handy, just in case."

"Do you have a super PAC that supports you?"

"No."

"That's fine. Our finance director will be here soon. She will talk to you about fund-raising and donor lists."

"What do you know about your opponent?" Wasim asked.

"Her name is Katherine Collins. She was a House member for two terms but lost the previous election.

Before she was elected to the House for her first term, she served on various local committees and boards. She has three sons and ten grandchildren, was a professor at UMass, and is a practicing Catholic. The unions are solidly behind her." Stephen recited the facts in a monotone, hands planted on the back of Nina's chair.

"What's her platform?"

"I know only what I have read in the news and on the Internet. Education, environment, and economy—the three *E*s."

"We'll need opp-research." Wasim turned to Doug, who had just returned from dealing with his phones. "Right?"

"Yes, thanks to the super PACs, everything's more expensive now. We have a few consultants we work with. I'll send you the information. You can pick one."

Stephen returned to his chair and started taking notes.

"There are a couple of things I'd like to mention," Wasim said. "I'm going to be very frank. Don't take it the wrong way. This is purely in the interest of getting you elected, nothing personal."

"I understand," Stephen replied with a faint smile. He had taken off his jacket at the start of the meal. Now, he rolled up his sleeves.

"First, you have to project a more open and approachable persona. Smile, hold your wife's hand, wave, look young and energetic—that's a huge advantage you have over Grandma Collins."

"That's not a problem at all."

And suddenly Stephen became a different person. His face melted into a boyish smile. He nodded happily at Nina and slapped Wasim on the shoulder. "We should meet up for a beer this evening, guys!"

For the second time, Doug and Wasim were dumbfounded. Nina smiled at the looks on their faces.

And equally suddenly, it was gone.

"Good enough?" Stephen asked.

When the two men couldn't muster a response, he laughed. "Bread and butter of my trade. Don't worry about my image. I'll be very likable."

"That's a little bizarre," Doug muttered out of the corner of his mouth to Wasim.

"The second thing then," Wasim continued, "you need a better, broader, more populist platform. You can't run a Senate campaign on national security and foreign policy, as you well know. You have no experience in political office...we can't cite your CIA background...we'll have to find ways of strengthening your message, particularly with respect to Grandma's three *E*s."

He looked at Doug for ideas.

"I don't know," Doug replied. "We'll have to play up the philanthropy. I know that you've given away a big part of your estate to the Public Gardens and funded sustainable-cultivation research. We can use that. We can mention jobs that will be created by the foundation. I am sure we can hint at the work done by your consultancy for the Department of Defense—how it has given you a special insight into issues that threaten our national security." He looked at Wasim. "Let's get a focus group together to see what works."

Stephen looked up from his laptop. "I'll talk to my ex-boss and see what kind of language I can couch it in…to make it public."

Wasim resumed. "We'll have to cover for your lack of experience by campaigning like crazy and putting you in front of the public at every opportunity. Project you as a young entrepreneur, job creator, problem solver, and die-hard patriot."

"And, we will need to play him as a moderate," Doug said. He turned to Stephen. "How would you describe your leaning?"

Stephen replied after a brief pause. "I would say I am a conservative but not opposed to reasonable taxes. I will not compromise on national security. I will do whatever it takes."

Wasim shivered at the hardness in Stephen's voice. "And social issues?"

"Not a priority."

"Well, that won't do," Wasim interrupted. "You'll have to have a position on issues like abortion, same-sex marriage, and so on, but that reminds me, what church do you go to? People will want to know. We might even need a picture with the head of your church." He waited, ready to add the name to his address book to set up a photo op.

"I don't go to church."

There was a bewildered silence. This was another first for the campaign team.

Stephen shrugged. "Nobody who has seen the things I have could believe in a benevolent God."

Wasim turned to Nina for help.

"We occasionally go to the Presbyterian church on Main Street."

Doug said from behind his laptop, "According to Google your grandfather was instrumental in getting the church rebuilt after it was destroyed in a fire. Let's leverage that. If anyone asks, you belong to the First Congregation Church. And avoid words like *atheist* and *agnostic*."

"What about you, Nina?" Doug asked.

"I am a Hindu, and yes, I do go to the temple."

They waited for Stephen to finish his notes. When he was done, Wasim said, "I guess we should get started on the announcement. I'd like to send out a media release. We'll schedule a press conference this Sunday at four, just in time for the Sunday evening news."

"That's in two days!" Nina jumped up from her chair.

Wasim smiled. "What did you expect? This is a special election. We only have eighteen weeks. The first thing we need to do is set up a website. I'd like to post homely pictures that say *family man*."

He opened his briefcase and took out a camera. His eyes scanned the room for a photogenic spot and good light. The large window behind Nina was perfect.

"I'd like to get a picture of the two of you there." He pointed.

"Is it necessary for her to be in the photo?" Stephen asked.

"It's not necessary, but it would help a great deal, especially since you are running against a grandmother of ten."

Stephen wasn't convinced. He was about to veto it when Nina interjected.

"It's OK. It can't do any harm. I am sure if someone's determined to hurt us, they'll find a way, with or without the photo."

"Who'd hurt you? Why?" Doug looked up from his laptop.

"People from my past," Stephen said.

Victims of my excesses, he thought, who will not stop until they have destroyed everything I have. She has paid the price too many times. He was about to object, but Nina had already arranged herself near the window.

Wasim fussed around, moving furniture and the reflectors and lights he had pulled out of his suitcase.

"Our professional campaign photographer will arrive tomorrow, but I'd like to get started with a few simple pictures now and get the website up as soon as possible."

He had Stephen sit in a high-backed chair and made Nina lean against the side, almost sitting on the armrest. "OK, smile," he said. "Nice, nice, one more. Move to your left please. Nice, great! Move closer to her, perfect. Tilt your head a little! Hold it...hold it... smile. OK! All done."

Nina and Stephen drifted away in different directions, she to the coffee table and he back to the dining table where Doug sat.

"Urgent question, where can we house our team? Cheaper the better," Doug said.

"We have a large guesthouse in the botanical garden adjoining our compound. You can use that."

"I'll let the team know. They'll be arriving in a few hours." Doug tapped rapidly on his phone. "Wasim, why don't you continue with Stephen?"

Wasim nodded and turned to Stephen. "Here is a draft announcement. Also, you'll need a brief, five-minute stump speech that introduces you and your platform. I can help you with that."

Stephen took the document from Wasim's hand.

"Make a list of donors, and we will merge it with ours to form a master list. We'll need to start calling almost immediately. Prepare a succinct pitch. I can help you with that as well. Here are some samples from other campaigns."

Wasim and Doug kept up a stream of instructions and peppered Stephen with mail, links, documents, and checklists.

Stephen listened calmly, nodded, and made notes. Doug and Wasim were impressed. By this point in the proceedings, most first-time candidates were overwhelmed and frazzled.

"A few more things," Wasim said. "Nina! Come over here, please. You might want to hear this too. From now on, assume that the minute you step out of the house, you will be on camera. Someone somewhere will pull out a cell phone and catch you yawning or picking your nose. There is nothing worse than looking ridiculous. So, no dancing, no goofy poses, and no T-shirts with racy slogans. Dress well, even if you are going out to walk your dog. No excessive drinking or stuffing yourselves with food in public."

He looked at Doug. "Anything else?"

"Don't lose control—no temper tantrums or angry outbursts. If you see someone coming up to ask pesky questions, pretend to be on the phone and wave them off with a smile."

"That's true...they will probably put a tracker on you," Wasim said.

"Tracker?" Stephen looked up.

"Yes, someone who will follow you and film you constantly, to catch you in a gaffe, a factual mistake, or outburst. We'll stick a tracker on them too."

"Good God, that's terrible," Nina exclaimed.

"Oh, and from now on, only American cars."

Nina listened in wide-eyed alarm. Wasim grinned at her. "You didn't know quite what you were getting into, did you?"

"I intend to keep her exposure to the minimum," Stephen interjected with unexpected belligerence.

Wasim looked at him in surprise. Doug stepped in. "Sure, sure. Anyway, we should probably go to the guesthouse now and set up for the team. They'll start arriving soon."

"I'll drive you down." Stephen rolled down his sleeves and put on his jacket. "I'll send someone later to help you stock up on necessities."

He joined Wasim near the table. They stood for a few moments, waiting for Doug. He was packed and ready but showed no sign of moving.

This was always a delicate point in the proceedings for Doug. He had no choice but to bring it up now, even though it was public knowledge that he was gay. In fact, Doug was the founder and president of a prominent if somewhat small organization of gay Republicans in DC.

"You need to know that by hiring me, you are opening yourself to a certain type of attack. Your own party members will pressure you to get rid of me, particularly if you are successful. If you have a problem with my being gay, I need to know now, before I get too invested." He looked at Stephen.

"Your personal life is of no interest to me," Stephen said.

A little too brusque, Nina thought.

But Doug was relieved. He didn't care. Stephen shook his head, but Doug persisted.

"A congressman dropped me a week before the election, after I had put in a year of eighteen-hour days, because his pastor told him to. Even though he knew I was gay when I came on board. He took advantage of my expertise all year long and then dumped me at the very last minute to score points."

"That won't happen," Stephen said. "Besides, it's hardly an issue now. Same-sex marriage is legal."

"You'd be surprised. Some of the biggest party donors will withhold money. Giving you fair warning, that's all."

"I stand warned," Stephen replied. He turned away as if to say he was done discussing the matter. For exactly that reason, so as not to be manipulated by the party power brokers, he had wanted to run as an Independent, but his former boss and mentor, George Applegate, had advised him, and correctly so, that he needed the party machinery to have any impact in a blue state like Massachusetts.

Meanwhile, Wasim stood, staring at Doug with an odd expression. Doug couldn't decipher that look; it wasn't the usual fear, embarrassment, or hostility. Anyway, it couldn't have been a surprise to Wasim. He must have done his homework on Doug before he agreed to join the team.

"Do *you* have a problem?" Doug asked pointedly.

"No, no," Wasim replied hastily. He looked away and pretended to adjust his jacket.

THE TRACKER

S tephen walked back to the marina from the repair
shop. His crew had just finished fixing the broken
radar on his boat. Normally, he'd have paused to appre-
ciate the scenic jumble of white sailboats bobbing in the
blue waters. Today, his attention was focused entirely in-
ward. He had slept badly the previous night, awakened
every hour by dark bubbles from his subconscious.

Last night, just before bed, Nina had sprung it on
him that she might be pregnant. It had unsettled him,
even though they had been expecting it. All through
the night, memories of Nina in blood-soaked pajamas,
doubled over in pain, flashed before his eyes. That was
how the previous pregnancy had ended, barely days after they had received the welcome news. And it was his

fault. They, the monsters he was after, had crashed the taxi she was in, an "accident," and he and his precious bodyguards had not been able to stop it. Now, he was suddenly unsure about this whole Senate-race thing. Was his ambition endangering his hard-won idyll? But he wanted real political power, not the bureaucratic power offered by his former bosses at the CIA.

He kicked aside a pebble with unnecessary violence.

"Mr. James?"

Stephen looked up.

A man in a T-shirt and jeans stood a few feet away, holding up a cell phone, filming the encounter. He looked tired and crumpled, his eyes rimmed with red. Limp strands of dirty blond hair fell past his grizzled chin to his shoulders.

Already? Stephen wondered. He hadn't formally announced his Senate run yet. A press conference was scheduled for later that afternoon, along with a media release.

"You are?" Stephen asked.

"Dave Tyler, political analyst," the man replied without moving the cell phone out of the way.

"Please stop recording. This is a private venue. I am here as a private citizen."

Tyler put away the phone. There were quite a few people around, even though it was very early in the morning. Some of them were beginning to give Tyler unfriendly looks.

Stephen turned his back on Tyler and walked quickly toward a gravel path leading to the woods on the other side of the road. Tyler fell in step beside him.

"Is your wife a Democrat, *sir*?" Tyler managed to make the honorific sound like a four-letter word.

Stephen didn't answer, just quickened his step. The man was older than the normal trackers, who were usually college students or recent grads. And the kids were usually polite, at least in the video clips that Wasim had shown him. This man was quite uncouth.

Anyway, his opponents had beaten Nina's party affiliation to death during the brief primary. Doug and Wasim actually thought it would help portray him as a moderate and bipartisan "bridge builder," a convenient contrast to the entrenched left-wing stance of his opponent, Ms. Collins.

"Will she vote for you, *sir*?"

Before he could snap at the man, Wasim's voice echoed in Stephen's ear: "Don't talk to anyone, ever, unless we have rehearsed exactly what we are going to say, no off-the-cuff comments, just smile and walk away." Stephen was in no mood to smile, but at least he could walk away. He made for a tall hedge pockmarked with large, orange No Trespassing/Private Property signs.

Tyler did a quick jog around Stephen and came face-to-face with him, forcing him to stop.

"Really, will she vote for you?"

The two men were the same height, at 5'11 tall enough not to be short, their eyes level like well-matched boxers.

Stephen's temper was always ready for a fight. But he pursed his lips tightly to avoid saying something he'd regret. The man was rude and aggressive and smelled of cheap alcohol and bad digestion. His interest in Nina was beginning to annoy Stephen.

The sun hit Tyler right in the face and flecked the stubble on his cheeks with silver. He squinted, unable to look directly into the sun, ruining the effect he wanted to have. There was something about Stephen that reminded him of his soon-to-be ex-wife—a tight-lipped disapproval, an unspoken superiority implied by a slight tilt of the chin. But Tyler stood his ground and tried to disown the nasty smell that rose from his sweat-soaked shirt.

Stephen gave him one final look and, with a graceful move, sidestepped Tyler and disappeared through an opening in the hedge.

Tyler was startled by the maneuver but recovered quickly and climbed a nearby rock to peek behind the hedge. Stephen was loping down a gravel path, his gym bag swinging rhythmically in his right hand. The path took a sharp turn toward a dense thicket of trees and abruptly carried him out of sight.

With a sigh, Tyler clambered off the rock and walked back to town. He had been on his way to the campaign headquarters of Katherine Collins and had stopped to check out the hometown of her opponent, Mr. James. And as luck would have it, the man himself was strolling on the marina, deep in thought. The encounter hadn't gone as well as Tyler had hoped. The candidate had kept his cool and provided no fodder.

Tyler retraced his steps to a local coffee shop that he had stopped at earlier. And lo, it was attached to a diner at the back. The day seemed to be blessed with luck; anything he wanted materialized as soon as he wished for it—first the candidate and now the diner. He should run out and buy a lottery ticket.

"You're back!" The waitress from the morning greeted him. She was an elderly woman, all mother hen. "Did you find Mr. James?"

"Yes, I did," he replied and followed her to the booth. It was large, well lit, and sparkling clean.

"What can I get you, hon?" She bowed her silvery crown of hair to take his order.

He was too hungry to read the encyclopedic menu and asked for an omelet, home fries, and a pot of coffee.

When she brought his coffee, he asked, "Does he come here?"

She plunked down the milk for the coffee and a glass of water and said, "Who does?"

"Mr. James."

"He stops by once in a while to pick up apple Danishes for his wife. She's really fond of ours," she said with pride. "We always make them fresh for him."

"Really! What's his wife like?"

"She's Indian. I've seen her only once, and she seemed like a very nice young lady. We were so shocked when he got married. We had no idea that he was see-ing anyone! You know how people are." She shrugged. "They said all kinds of nasty things."

"What did they say?"

She didn't answer but got busy moving the sugar bowl around.

"You mean he married her because he *had* to?" He winked at her. She nodded but was clearly uneasy at the turn of the conversation. She shuffled off to get the rest of his order.

"Mmm, smells good!" he said. "Could I get one of those apple Danishes you mentioned?"

"Sure, hon, I'll be right back."

He let her make a couple of trips without grilling her further—she filled his water glass, brought him ketchup, and asked how he was doing with the food. When he saw her coming with the bill, he leaned back, closed his eyes, and pretended to be tired.

"You OK, hon?" she asked.

"Yes, of course." He opened his eyes and smiled at her. "I am writing a piece on Mr. James for his election. I have to finish it in an hour, that's all."

"He's a good man, and a brave man. Put that in," she said.

"I will. Anything particular you want me to mention?"

She thought for a bit. "You know, soon after he got married, there was a robbery at his neighbor's. He went over and stopped it. They caught the bunch of them, I heard. He got shot and almost died, but that's the kind of man he is."

"That's amazing! Who's the neighbor? Maybe I can speak to him."

"Some Pakistani man. He was married to that flighty Connor girl from around here. They'd lived here for...I don't know, maybe a year, two years, when this happened. They left town right after the shooting. Later, Mr. James bought that property for the Public Garden."

Tyler was dying to ask more questions, but she gave him the check and went away.

The diner began to fill with locals, an all-white, nautically themed crowd. They stared at Tyler before moving on to their seats. He paid his bill and left.

The sun hit him like a paddle. His little Miata waited in the parking lot, glinting and shimmering in the heat. But he decided to take a walk, to settle the vast quantity of food inside him and to sort his thoughts before he blundered into the Katherine Collins campaign headquarters twenty miles away.

The town square was compact and very pretty, with waves of flowering plants around a patch of green with a fountain in the middle. All the town's landmarks were clustered around it, all within a minute's walk. He checked the waitress's story at the police station, but they had no record of such a robbery. Neither did the swanky Edward W. James Memorial Library, the town's spanking-new public library.

Tyler debated what to do next, whether to pursue the matter of the armed robbery or proceed to the Collins HQ. Perhaps it was best not to complicate matters, just stick to the simple plan of tracking Candidate Stephen James with a camera.

What did *he* know about politics? He was an electrical engineer, not an investigative reporter. Then there was the CIA angle. Jimmy, Tyler's friend, had warned him that Mr. James was rumored to be former CIA. "It's not clear how 'former,' so be careful," Jimmy had said. "The guy is trying to reinvent himself now."

Tyler bit his lip in exasperation. He had never imagined that at the age of forty-two, he'd be standing forlorn and lonely in a strange town, trying to figure out what to do with his life. He'd thought he had it all figured out—a wife, a career, a house, and a solid bank account. Until a few months ago, he'd been the top dog, a research engineer heading a team of bright-eyed, eager, young PhDs.

But then he'd come home one day to find Claire, his college sweetheart and wife of twenty years, packed and ready to leave. "I want a divorce," she'd announced and walked out.

"Why, why, why?" he had spluttered, but she was gone. In addition to cleaning out their joint accounts, she'd left cruel clues for him around the house—tokens from lovers, rendezvous scribbled on yellow Post-its stuck inside her closet, e-mails left undeleted on the communal PC.

Jimmy, a political strategist, had been on his way to the Collins campaign when he'd heard the divorce news. He had texted, *Come along, be my opp-researcher, tracker, whatever.* And so Tyler had spent the last few days in his friend's condo, eating his frozen TV dinners and reading about the Senate race, the opponents, and the process. The world of political campaigning was harsh and fast-paced, like fighting a wildfire stoked by high winds, like stepping into a torrent of sewage—it was blood sport. Tyler had been drawn to it instantly. He had jumped into his Miata last night to meet Jimmy at the Collins HQ.

Locals stared at Tyler as he walked by the water's edge, hands thrust deep in his pockets. He didn't belong in the immaculate landscape, with his crumpled and stained clothes and pale indoor complexion. He returned their stares with a solemn bow.

His cell phone pinged with an incoming message. He shaded it from the glare and read the message.

Couldn't be, he thought, suddenly weak-kneed, and looked around. A stone bench sat under a cluster of trees, right by the water. He stumbled to it, and after a deep breath, reread the message. It was from his lawyer, Josh. That genius of a man had just wrested more than a million dollars from his soon-to-be ex-wife's agency. Tyler had funded his wife's company during the early years of their marriage and had used his connections to drive business her way. And now, he thought bitterly, he was about to reap the return on his investment.

He dialed. "Josh!"

"Mr. Tyler!" his attorney responded.

"You are a genius! Thank you! Thank you!"

"You are welcome. You deserve it."

"Your timing is perfect, Josh. I am down to my last thousand dollars!"

"I am glad I could be of help. I'll send you the settlement papers. Bye!"

Tyler looked at his phone. The gleaming technological marvel had finally buzzed good news, after months of pouring misery and more misery on him.

He leaned back on the bench. The sun had moved out from behind the trees and now beat down on his virgin skin. A happy delirium bubbled inside, even though his face was getting scorched. Psychedelic amoebas swam behind his closed lids, and a word slowly drifted in and out of his consciousness, tentatively at first but then with increasing assertiveness—*reinvention*.

He sat up. Stephen Edward James was trying to build his Camelot and reinvent himself. Why shouldn't Tyler do the same?

Tyler leaned back once more, ignoring the nagging voice that said, *Your skin's going to peel off soon.* He had a good, good feeling about the new direction his life was about to take.

PRESS CONFERENCE

Stephen Edward James @stephenjames . Aug 1
It is a privilege and honor to announce my candidacy for the US
Senate from the great Commonwealth of Massachusetts.

Katherine Collins @kathycollins . Aug 1
Mr. James is a worthy opponent, but, what about experience?
Check out his resume...

"Stephen, make sure you smile," Doug said for the hundredth time.

Stephen forced himself to look away from the window, from the beautiful blue heron that was posing majestically on a piece of driftwood. He nodded at Doug. The campaign team had been prepping Stephen all morning, and now the press conference was only minutes away.

Wasim had meticulously set the stage in the central atrium of the Edward W. James Memorial Library, named in honor of Stephen's grandfather. The large, airy space, bathed in mellow sunlight, was the perfect spot for announcing Stephen's candidacy. Wasim had choreographed the event down to the smallest detail, including the amount of light and how it would hit the podium flanked by American flags.

Right now, they were all stuffed into a waiting room just off the atrium. Stephen sat in an armchair in the tiny room. He stared out of the window while a chaotic stream of people swirled around him. Volunteers scurried in and out with signs, placards, buttons, and flyers. Their coordinator yelled at his troops, pausing only for the occasional obscenity.

"He needs to show some energy," Doug grumbled to Wasim. But Wasim was on the phone, hectoring TV and news crews to show up on time. He gestured with his hands, as graceful as the heron's wings—*there's nothing we can do.*

"Where's Nina?" Stephen finally stood up. He tried to find her in the crush of people around him.

"I'm here," she called from where she was sorting brochures and handouts. She came around the table and stood in front of him.

"This is it," he said. He had the familiar disembodied feeling, one that descended on him during times of extreme danger.

"Don't worry. It'll be fine." She took his hand in hers. Her hair was tied in a severe ponytail, a style she had adopted recently in view of his candidacy. He didn't like it and wanted to reach out and release the silky mass from its confinement and let it flow free, like the day they'd met.

It had been a summer day, just like today. He had spent a sleepless night fighting his recurring mental battles. He'd gotten out of bed and walked out onto the balcony and looked out with tired, burning eyes. Normally the sight of the Bay and the beautiful garden, his one personal passion, were a soothing balm. But not on that dewy morning. He had gone on an early morning boat ride to calm his temper. On his return, he'd spied an interloper sitting on *his* stone bench, in *his* garden, sketching *his* home without his permission. The fact that she wore sneakers, long blue jeans, and a full-sleeved cotton blouse on a hot, muggy day, combined with her South Asian looks, had raised red flags in his head. He'd watched her from behind the trees for a while and then stepped out aggressively. She'd turned around at the sound of his footsteps. A sudden gust of wind had whipped her hair free, and it had bloomed around her in long, lovely tendrils.

"Show time, let's go." Wasim's voice cut into his reverie. "Stephen, Nina, Doug, come on, guys. We need to move!"

They walked as a group toward the atrium. As soon as they entered, there was a wave of energetic applause and the flash-flash of cameras. It was louder than Stephen had expected. He flinched for a split second before stepping up to the podium. Doug had suggested that Nina or some local luminary should introduce Stephen, but he'd felt it was unnecessary.

Wasim couldn't have chosen a better day. The audience glowed golden in the filtered sunshine. To Stephen's left, a huge picture window framed tall oak trees outlined against the shimmering silvery ocean beyond. On Stephen's right, a few feet away, his campaign team was lined up in front of the imposing fireplace beneath the portrait of his grandfather.

As Stephen stood and waited for the room to quiet down, a soothing, woodsy scent of leaves and grass and bark floated up. Wasim must have had the room sprayed with the fragrance that morning. "Don't underestimate the effect of stagecraft," he had told Stephen, "and smells. They evoke all kinds of associations in people."

The team watched Stephen anxiously. Wasim signed to Nina to move closer to Stephen. She was standing off by herself, which would make for a terrible visual. He had even picked the couple's outfits for best effect on TV and camera.

"Thank you for being here on this beautiful Sunday afternoon," Stephen began.

"Soften your enunciation, it's too elitist," Wasim had said. So Stephen tried, much to Nina's delight, and relapsed into the rhythm that came to him naturally when he talked to her about his childhood and his grandfather, the man who had raised him from day one.

"I am here to announce my run for the Senate seat that has become vacant due to the untimely death of Senator Kirk. He was a true patriot who served his country with honor and dedication. His shoes will be hard to fill, but I hope to try."

His in-laws beamed at him from the front row, so proud, so conspicuous in the sea of white faces around them. Behind them sat a sizeable crowd. The townsfolk had turned up in strength, some out of curiosity, others in genuine support of their eccentric, native son. Doug was relieved at the attendance, even though he had taken the precaution of stuffing the room with volunteers. Wasim had demanded a full room for his publicity shots.

Stephen presented his case, point by point.

"People are falling asleep," Doug muttered to Wasim. "Perhaps we should get his wife involved when we go on the road; she's more dynamic."

Wasim rolled his eyes. "Don't even try."

"My family has been here for centuries. I know no other home," Stephen said. "I understand the people, culture, and history of the Commonwealth of Massachusetts. I am one of you. I have no conflicting interests outside our great state."

That was an allusion to the outsider status of his opponent, Congresswoman Collins, who had moved from Philadelphia fifteen years ago. Her husband still owned businesses there.

Nina watched Stephen intently. She noticed every twitch of irritation and impatience and hoped that only she could see them. He was uncharacteristically tentative because he was being forced to say things that he didn't believe in. She sneaked a look at the audience. They were taking it quite well, listening respectfully if not exactly mesmerized. She turned back to Stephen. He gripped the podium tightly and, behind its protective cover, flexed his left ankle the way he did when his wounded leg cramped during times of stress.

"Please give me the opportunity. I will work with members of both parties to forge solutions that serve the interests of every citizen of this great state, not a particular class, lobby, or special-interest group."

He'd told his advisors that the speech was too heavy-handed. "Why can't we make it subtle?" he'd asked. But both Doug and Wasim had assured him that subtlety and finesse were a politician's worst enemies. "The more sensational and in-your-face we can get, the better," they'd said.

"Thank you, and God bless America." Stephen mumbled the last part of the phrase and rushed through it. Wasim and Doug had laughed when he'd said he wanted to keep God out of it. "You might as well not run," Doug had suggested caustically.

This is how it begins, Stephen thought and bowed to the crowd. A compromise here, glossing over inconvenient facts, a few deals to smooth things over, and before you know it, you are someone else.

Nina had laughed at him when he'd said that. "Being someone else should be right up your alley!" She'd never fully forgiven him for hiding his profession from her until after they were married. Deception and obfuscation weren't new to him, but in his earlier adventures, there had been a well-defined enemy and a higher goal that justified the means. But, now?

"All for the greater good," Nina had advised, "same principle here, different means."

People clapped and shouted all around him. He waved to the audience and stepped back.

"That was great," Nina whispered and squeezed his hand. Before he could answer, people surged around him—supporters, acquaintances, reporters, and his own team. He had that disembodied feeling once more, unmoored, as he watched Nina walk toward her parents.

One by one, people stepped up to him and shook his hand and said kind things: "Glad you are running"; "Your grandfather would've been so proud"; "How's your old boat doing? I saw you take it out the other day."

Wasim was taken aback at the difference between Stephen the public speaker and Stephen the glad-hander. Onstage, Stephen was stilted and strangely passive. But one-on-one, he had an old-fashioned courtesy and decency that immediately inspired trust.

He bent down to listen to people and answered questions patiently, with composure and gentleness.

"This is his best format," Wasim whispered to Doug. "We need to arrange small Q and A sessions as much as possible. He's not an exciting public speaker."

There was a brief pause when the first rush of people dissolved and the second wave was just gathering. Stephen made a quick dash to greet his in-laws.

"Congratulations, Stephen." His father-in-law, a trim man with a military moustache, shook his hand and patted him on the back.

"You were terrific!" his mother-in-law said. "Congratulations!" She was an older version of Nina, with the same dancing eyes and quick smile. She gave him a little box.

He took it from her with a grin, put it in his pocket, and hugged her. "Thanks, Ma."

Wasim stared in amazement. The candidate had smiled spontaneously! For the first time! And he had addressed his mother-in-law as *Ma*, the Hindi word for mother. What was going on?

Wasim hadn't bothered to ask Stephen to pose for publicity photos with his in-laws. He had assumed that Stephen would barely be on nodding terms with them. After all, here was a man who had severed ties with his own mother and siblings…what were the chances that he would be close to his Indian in-laws? But that clearly wasn't the case.

Wasim spotted Nina in the distance, being quizzed by an elderly couple. He strode over.

"Excuse me, folks. May I steal Mrs. James for a minute? Thank you." He took Nina's elbow and steered her to one side of the room.

"You didn't tell me!"

"Tell you what?" she asked, waving to the abandoned couple over his shoulder.

"That your mom and Stephen were close."

"Oh, that. He's her pet. He can do no wrong." She sighed melodramatically.

"Really? How did *that* happen?"

"He was in rehab for a serious injury, and my parents helped me take care of him. They became close then. My mother played chess with him."

She looked over at the trio. Stephen talking to her parents—that was a sight she never tired of. Having spent so much time in South Asia, he was familiar with the family dynamic and meticulously observed the intricate protocol of hierarchy and traditions that went with it.

"How come?" she had asked one day.

"Because that's what keeps families together," Stephen had replied, "respect."

She watched Doug swoop down and pull Stephen away from her parents and hustle him off to meet a new set of people.

She turned to Wasim. "Stephen's a really sweet guy. My parents love him."

"Oh, really? I find him intimidating."

"Why?"

"He's so intense! I'm afraid that he'll beat the shit out of me if I say something he doesn't like."

She laughed but didn't contradict him.

"Does he have a temper?"

"Only when he's hungry," she replied with a straight face, "and don't ever call him Steve."

"Good to know!" His phone beeped, but he ignored it.

"What did your mom give him? I'm curious."

"A talisman. She had promised him her father's lucky cuff links."

This is so odd, Wasim thought. The man hadn't reconciled with his own flesh and blood in twenty years, a man so aloof that people were shocked when he married, yet he had eagerly embraced his wife's family and culture. Weird.

"I'd like to show the public what *you* see when you see him. You know, try and soften his stiff image. What would you say are his best qualities?"

In the distance, Stephen shook hands and smiled, the center of a large crowd herded toward him by Doug. She watched him for a while and then answered. "I really meant it when I said he is a sweet guy. He genuinely wants to help people, and that's what drives almost all his actions, however extreme they might seem to the rest of us. Do you know that he has given away every penny of his inheritance, most of it anonymously? Even the house we live in will go to the state conservancy after us, to serve as a maritime museum. But don't mention it to him. He doesn't like talking about it."

"That's impressive!" Wasim moved closer, because he couldn't hear her in the noise. "And his dark side?" He bit his tongue immediately, worried she might think he was taking a cheap shot at Stephen's secret past. He hurriedly clarified, "You know, any scandals and such?"

"What do you mean?"

"Tax irregularities? Sexual shenanigans?" he wisecracked, even though he was serious.

For some reason she found that really funny and burst out laughing. "You guys didn't do your homework, or what?"

Stephen looked up at the sound. He saw Wasim and Nina off by themselves in one corner of the room, standing very close together. Wasim was leaning forward, whispering in her ear. She was shaking with laughter. That's not like her at all, he thought.

Only two people in the room noticed the shadow that crossed Stephen's face.

One was Doug.

WTF, he texted to Wasim, *stop flirting with the candidate's wife. Get your ass over here and schmooze.*

Wasim looked at the message and was visibly startled. He excused himself and hurriedly left Nina's side.

The other person who noticed Stephen's annoyance was Tyler. He had been sitting quietly in the back row all along.

After that morning's encounter with Stephen on the marina and the subsequent epiphany, Tyler had checked into a local motel, showered, and slept. He had woken feeling light and happy and sat down to plan.

It was great to be back at work, with a goal, with to-do lists and deadlines. Work was his identity, his panacea, his indulgence, and without it he had been adrift, a man trying to find his moorings, glumly watching hours turn to days and days to barren months. But he was finally done with all that. He had found his mission.

Tyler studied Stephen and Nina with great interest. He was surprised that Mrs. James was a very young-looking woman, greeting people with brisk confidence and a cheerful smile. During the entire duration of Stephen's speech, her eyes had never left his face, her lips moving to his words. She worshiped him, obviously.

Why not, Tyler thought bitterly, the man was loaded. What woman wouldn't worship *that*? But how did *Stephen* feel about her? What brought this unlikely pair together?

Tyler had been pondering that very question when he'd seen the look on Stephen's face at the sight of Nina and Wasim together. Tyler knew that look and the maddening, senseless rage that accompanied it. He snapped his laptop shut and stood up.

Nina was on her way to the conference room to join her parents. Tyler quickened his step and intercepted her.

"Hello!"

She stopped and smiled. "Hello, I am Nina Sharma, wife of Mr. James." Oops, she'd forgotten Wasim's advice that she should introduce herself as Nina Sharma James.

She extended her hand. Tyler shook her hand and, without releasing it, said, "I am Dave Tyler, a political reporter. I'd like to ask a couple of questions, Mrs. James."

She pulled back her hand. She had overheard Stephen and Wasim discussing a tracker named Tyler. "I need to check with the campaign manager."

"Just a few simple questions," he persisted. "How did you two meet?"

"Good-bye." She turned her back on him and walked away.

"Mrs. James!" Tyler called after her.

She made a beeline for Stephen. When she got to him, she took his arm and stood close.

"What's wrong?" Stephen asked at once. It was her familiar distress signal.

"Nothing."

But she was discomposed and gripped his arm tightly. He looked up and saw Tyler staring at them.

"Has he been asking questions?" He released his arm from Nina's grasp and put it around her.

"Yes, but that's OK. Don't bother, Stephen." She was afraid that he'd launch into Tyler.

The two men stared at each other.

"You had a question, Mr. Tyler?"

"No, Stephen, please don't talk to him," Nina whispered, but he ignored her.

"Yes, I was asking your wife how you met."

"At a party." He paused for a second and added, "Anything else?"

Something in his dismissive tone touched a sore spot in Tyler.

"What about the rest of your family? Are they here today? Your mother? Siblings?"

Doug, who had emerged from a cluster of people to look for Stephen, was alarmed to see Stephen talking to Tyler.

He rushed over and said, "That'll be all. Mr. James has another appointment. All interviews are to be scheduled with our Communications office."

Stephen wanted to reply, but Doug shook his head.

With a theatrical bow, Tyler walked away.

CAMPAIGN FEVER

The campaign went into high gear immediately after the press conference. There were meetings with donors and sponsors, meet-and-greet gatherings for supporters, town halls, "spontaneous" visits to hospitals and schools, and, of course, interviews and media events. Stephen's days started around five in the morning and often went on way past midnight. Doug and Wasim kept a complex matrix of public and private events and a map of the day's stops. A volunteer would hand Stephen crib notes if he hadn't already downloaded them to his tablet.

Stephen tried to call or text Nina whenever he could. He felt guilty that he couldn't go with her to the doctor's appointments. His mother-in-law was a more than happy stand-in. "Don't worry, Stephen," she'd said. "I'll take good care of your Nina."

They hadn't yet told the political handlers about the pregnancy, not even Doug and Wasim. Those two would definitely need to be told soon, but it was best to wait for another few weeks before they made it public. If Stephen didn't succeed in his bid, they might never really need to let the whole world know. Nina would be six months pregnant at the time of the election, and they might just manage to keep it quiet until then, with suitable camouflage. Movie actresses and other public figures did it all the time, according to Nina.

Stephen crossed out another forfeited prenatal appointment on his calendar, this time for an ultrasound, and felt a little stab of regret at losing control of his day. His time was almost entirely claimed by Doug and Wasim now. They never left his side, except to land a big endorsement or donor or to wangle the party big shots. And they never left together; one of them was always with him, being his body man. Stephen had refused to let anyone else near him. It made him even more enigmatic and fan-worthy to his young campaign staff, which was already in thrall of his family name and brooding ways.

Doug and Wasim realized early on that Stephen could be surprisingly difficult in a polite, standoffish way, even when he was not having an all-out temper tantrum. Stephen, despite his battle-hardened sensibility, was shocked by their strategies and would sometimes become stubborn.

"There is no proof!" he objected one day. "We can't say that!"

"We are not saying it. Some blogger somewhere is going to write that Congresswoman Collins took money from an Italian company to hand out lucrative contracts. The rest of the Internet will be all atwitter in no time at all." Wasim was matter-of-fact, and Doug nodded in agreement.

"No!"

"They are going to do that to you," Doug said.

"We'll worry about that when it happens."

Doug and Wasim looked at each other but wisely moved on to the next topic on the agenda.

Occasionally Stephen's former professor, mentor, and ex-boss, George Applegate, would drop in. He was a lanky, scholarly looking man, with Henry Kissinger's features, never seen without his cigarette, a habit that was quite anachronistic in this day and age. He and Stephen would immediately step out into the Public Garden next door and take a walk.

George had been Stephen's undergraduate advisor at MIT and his mentor when Stephen had turned to him for advice in navigating his contentious inheritance. As their opinions and ideals melded in the wake of 9/11, George had asked Stephen to join the CIA. Later, as Stephen's boss, George had championed his protégé up the Agency's hierarchy at a rapid clip and named him his successor to the post of head of South Asia, one of the most demanding and critical functions at the CIA. Until Stephen met Nina, George had been the only person that he trusted and sought advice from.

"Ginnie says hello and congratulations," George said. Ginnie was George's wife and Nina's surrogate mother in all matters CIA. She had helped Nina get through Stephen's shooting, news that couldn't be immediately shared with Nina's parents, not until George had the armed robbery cover story in place. Ginnie had spent every minute of those twenty-four hours with Nina, holding her hand, sharing her own experience as a CIA spouse during George's undercover stint in a very turbulent South America.

"Thank you, and please give her our regards. Nina said she'd drop by next week to see her."

In the past, Stephen's romantic life had always been out of bounds to George. During the freshman years, George had worried that Stephen might be gay, but subsequent girlfriend sightings had put that fear to rest. So, when Stephen had called him five years ago and announced that he'd married the girl he was supposed to recruit, George had been mad but not shocked. With his usual prudence and foresight, he'd swallowed his anger, frustration, and resentment and welcomed the newlyweds to his home.

George had no doubt that Stephen, whose connections, wealth, and lineage were as impressive as his intellect and frightening competence, could, with the right tutelage, become an extremely influential man. George's murky past as a Louisiana plutocrat had stood in the way of his ambitions, and so he had to pin all his hopes for political power on Stephen. He had cultivated him carefully, and until Nina's arrival, had been his sole friend and advisor. It hadn't been easy, because Stephen was naturally arrogant and did not seek any external validation or approval. It was only through his own accomplishments and scholarship that George had earned and held Stephen's respect.

Nevertheless, George and Stephen frequently ended up arguing, like they were now.

"George, I am not going to use Nina's pregnancy to push up my poll rankings."

"Why not? It's not like you're making it up."

"No...not happening."

George shrugged and kept his temper. He had convinced his friends in the GOP to back Stephen, but his protégé wasn't making it easy now. Perhaps he should go talk to Nina. She might be able to convince him. Anyway, it was time for George to get back to MIT in time to teach his class.

"OK, Stephen, I will see you soon. Give my love to Nina." George shook hands and left.

Stephen stood and watched George's car disappear around the corner. It was a tough balance, to keep his former boss in check without alienating him. George had stood by him through many crises and mishaps. Such loyalty was a rare commodity, not to be thrown away over petty disagreements. He'd have to learn to negotiate boundaries with George in this new venture and say: "You can push me this far but no farther". He turned around and walked back to his office, his temper already on the rise.

To add to Stephen's irritation, Tyler was constantly on his trail, all across Massachusetts. The tracker followed the campaign convoy, hunched in his little Miata. He posted Stephen sightings on his brand-new blog, *The Daily Howl*, with snarky commentary. The website had begun to develop quite a fan following. Stephen, with his instantly recognizable family name and its spectacularly gossip-worthy past, was Tyler's ticket to the winners' circle. *And*, Stephen had an interesting wife. How did the dour Mr. Stephen James, whose forbears wiped off the grime of the *Mayflower* from their buckled boots, meet his Bollywood bride? In Tyler world, it was all about Stephen's mysterious wife.

"Why is Mr. James hiding his wife from public view?" Tyler's website posed rhetorically. Reason thirty-three was "She can't be seen in public. Her faith won't permit it." Reason forty-eight claimed, "She is a registered Democrat. It's true." Reason sixty-five stated, "Mr. James had her classified." That was an allusion to Stephen's cryptic career as a "military consultant." Tyler's fingers flew over his laptop's keyboard all day long, tweeting, Facebooking, and Instagramming.

"Is it true that your wife's a registered Democrat, Mr. James?" he yelled out at one town hall. They were outside a popular diner where Stephen had come to meet his prospective constituents. Everyone stood around in a polite circle while the pugnacious Tyler held the floor.

"Yes, she is a registered Democrat. You knew that. What of it?" Stephen countered from the wooden crate he was standing on. He ignored Doug's warning not to engage Tyler.

"Does she support your decision to run for the Senate, Mr. James?" Tyler asked.

"Of course she does."

Tyler's goal was simple: to demolish the oh-so-proper, upstanding man-of-principles image that was part of Stephen's campaign narrative. Tyler had publicly canvassed his readers for texts, letters, voice messages, and e-mails from Stephen James, anything. He'd gotten hardly any response. How could it be that there was no trail at all? This made him suspect that his friend Jimmy's warning might have had some basis in reality. Perhaps the man was still a spook and the CIA was busy scrubbing traces of his past. That didn't bother Tyler. He was determined to find his big story.

He raised his hand once more. "Then why is she not by your side, Mr. James?"

"Because, Mr. Tyler," Stephen replied with exaggerated patience, "*she* is not running for office."

"Will she vote for you, Mr. James?"

"That's her business. Frankly, Mr. Tyler, I find your interest in my wife quite unseemly. I suggest you focus on yours."

Tyler was taken aback for a second. Was it possible that Stephen knew of Tyler's rancorous divorce? It was irrational and inexplicable, the intensity of the dislike that he felt for Stephen. He hated everything about the man—the way he walked into a room as if he owned it, the insolent grace inherited from generations of privilege, and the general smugness and air of superiority. Whether it was envy-induced resentment or the echoes of his ex's accent in Stephen's diction, Tyler's antipathy toward Stephen was getting increasingly personal.

The small crowd laughed. Doug stepped up to Stephen's side and whispered, "We need to leave." Stephen waved, shook a few hands, and turned away to get back to his campaign bus.

Tyler recovered and shouted over the crowd, "Is there a reason why she isn't seen in public? Is it her faith? Is she ill? Is she pregnant?" He had to raise himself on his toes to be heard. "Stephen! Where's Nina?"

Stephen turned around sharply. Was it just a random guess on Tyler's part, or was he doing some spying of his own? Did he have a secret master, someone much more sinister than a mere political opponent? Stephen was tempted to slap an answer out of Tyler's smirking face, but Doug muttered a warning. Stephen got in and slammed the door of the bus.

It was true that he had refused to let Nina accompany him on the road. But it's not like he had a choice. Any indecision he felt on that matter had been obviated by the pregnancy. Things were always complicated for him. Even something as purely joyful as the arrival of a new baby was fraught with unease.

He took a deep breath and looked out of the window at the traffic whizzing past. This was how it had always been between him and Nina. Theirs was a melancholy love, tinged with guilt and helplessness on his part and with sadness and resignation on hers, a love grown all the more deep-rooted for the blows they had absorbed together. It had even begun that way, in the shadow of his contrition.

It was during their first encounter, when he had found her sketching his home. In his irritable, paranoid state, he had immediately pegged her as working for the enemy.

"You are trespassing," he'd said curtly.

She'd stood up and smiled. "Oh, I thought it was a public path."

"No, it's private property."

She looked at him, taken aback at his hostility. "Sorry. I didn't know. I'm just visiting." She picked up her easel and walked away, without anger, without reproach.

He'd stood arrested, looking after her, ashamed at his behavior. That same evening he had spied her walking toward the dock by herself and joined her on his neighbor Sid Ali's property.

"You're trespassing," she'd said with a smile made brighter by the full moon.

"I'm sure Sid doesn't mind." He'd sat next to her on the dock and watched the sparkling ocean and the marina lights in the distance, the silence broken only by lapping water and the awkward squawk of an over-head gull. After a long, long time, he'd said, "Let me show you around the garden tomorrow." His garden was his love, into which he'd poured all his time, emotion, and frustration, his baby that he trusted only to his Harvard-trained horticulturist with two PhDs.

"Are you sure? You seem very possessive of it." She'd given him a sidelong glance.

And that was the look that had started it all. Stephen smiled, forgetting for a moment that he was on the campaign bus, surrounded by people.

Doug, who was sitting across from him, looked up from his laptop in surprise. He was about to ask a question but decided to leave Stephen to enjoy whatever it was that'd made him smile. It was such a rarity.

Stephen saw Doug's expression but didn't feel like explaining. It would take too long and invite more questions. It was hard to explain anyway. Philosophers and poets had tried for centuries to put that feeling into words. At first he'd been cynical. Love? What nonsense, he'd told himself. Yet, he hadn't been able to get over how happy he'd felt on the couple of occasions he had been with her—that day on the secluded beach overgrown with wild flowers, watching the beautiful Bay from the lighthouse, or that stunning sunset out in the open ocean. He had enjoyed watching her face as much as he had the breathtaking view.

A few weeks later, after a particularly brutal week at work, he'd driven to where she'd lived in Jersey City to recapture that feeling of peace. All he'd wanted was a pleasant dinner and to hear her excited account of her company's latest project funding girls' education. Instead, with an impulsive kiss, he had plunged them both into a dangerous future.

Even now, sitting inside the bus with the campaign staff chattering all around, Stephen's blood quickened at the memory of that kiss, the instant when he had decided that he was entitled to his share of happiness, screw the consequences.

He looked out of the window and saw Tyler pull up alongside in his Miata and point his camera at the bus. Stephen resisted the urge to flip him off, and turned his attention to Doug, who seemed to be asking, "Stephen, are you all right?"

"Never better," he replied.

STEPHEN ON THE STUMP

Stephen for Senator

Stephen Edward James @stephenjames . Sep 6
Met with the Springfield Small Business Owners Association.
Thank you for your support and endorsement!

Wasim and Doug had Stephen on a breathless schedule. It was the fifth week of the campaign. Any and every opportunity to get him out in the public, on TV, or in the media, they were on it. You have to be everywhere, all the time, they repeated like his personal Greek chorus. They were even negotiating a debate with his opponent, Ms. Katherine Collins. At any given moment, the two young men could be seen juggling multiple phones and laptops and yelling instructions to the team all at once.

When Stephen wasn't out campaigning, he was on the phone, calling for support and asking for money. Occasionally, he sat back between calls and observed Doug and Wasim and their frenetic activity. He felt exhausted just watching them. He'd never seen them eat; they'd just swig can after can of Red Bull, which was stacked in crates all over the place. The guesthouse had been converted to a full-fledged campaign headquarters, and the entire campaign team had moved in, with sleeping bags, to occupy every inch of space. People slept three, four to a room.

What had he gotten himself into? This was the opposite of what he'd hoped for when he had decided to retire. He had wanted an uneventful life, with happy golden children, his and Nina's, a life full of tedious PTA meetings and the monotony of domestic chores. Boring, boring, boring, that's what he'd wanted.

But Nina had been prescient. He wouldn't survive boring, she'd said. He would wilt and fade away, his vitality ebbing out with each numbing moment. In fact, barely a month into retirement, he had heard the sirens' call when he picked up the newspaper and read about yet another American post in Afghanistan being blown up. His mind had analyzed it in excruciating detail, even as he'd sat across from his lawyer, discussing the endowment for the foundation. He needed more, much more, or he would go mad. He needed a fight, and this special election had come along just at the right moment in time.

The funny thing was the process was not what he'd thought it would be. He had visions of delivering rousing speeches at street corners, rallying the troops, and so on. But most of his time was spent asking people for money. The only reason he soldiered on was he hated admitting defeat. Besides, what would happen to all these young people if he lost? Look at them, so energetic and enthusiastic, so full of idealism, slaving away for his campaign. He pushed the thought of failure out of his mind and went back to the grim demands of the call list that Wasim and Doug handed him every morning.

That morning, exactly at nine thirty, Wasim knocked on the door. "We are ready to leave."

Stephen caught sight of Doug just behind, talking on his phone, as usual. He got up, grabbed his jacket, and followed them out. He dreaded that morning's meetings with prospective donors. And when that was done, he had to return and prepare for an interview in the evening, another painful chore.

The first two meetings went smoothly, but by the time it was time to meet the third donor, Stephen was in a temper. It was almost noon.

"We snagged a piece in the *New Yorker*," Wasim said when they were back in the car. "They want Nina to join you so that they can talk to both of you together. Could she?"

"No, she couldn't."

"It might help. They thought it would be a nice angle to interview the two of you together."

"No!"

Wasim scowled and muttered something. Doug looked around to the back, where the other two sat. Stephen was pointedly reading his tablet.

Help, Wasim texted to Doug.

Call N, Doug texted back. *Find out what's going on with him.*

At the next stop, Stephen and Doug stepped out to meet the head of the Springfield Small Business Owners Association. Wasim stayed back in the car and called Nina.

She answered immediately. "Is he OK?"

"Yes, why do you ask?" He was surprised by the question.

"No reason." She sounded relieved. "What's up?"

"Stephen seems really cranky. He has an important interview this evening, and he needs to be in good form. Is there something going on with him that we should know of?"

"What do you mean?"

"Is he not well? Sleeping poorly? Problems at home..."

"No." Should she tell him about the pregnancy? No, she couldn't, not without checking with Stephen. "But I think I know what's going on. When are you guys getting back to the guesthouse?"

"Around one thirty?"

"Will he have time to come home for lunch?"

"I doubt it."

Why do women think that food is the solution to all problems? His mother was the same way: "Eat, my *beta*, eat, never mind your father."

"That's fine. I'll meet him at the office at one thirty. Don't tell him though."

"OK."

"Bye."

Wasim returned to his to-do list: call College Republicans at UMass. Both Doug and he had been surprised at how well Stephen was doing with young Republicans. The fact that he was an MIT engineer, young, and married to a woman of South Asian origin seemed to appeal to them. And the fact that he was an outsider and clearly a man of principles and courage (the campaign had dropped coy hints about the armed-robbery story) had resulted in a mini youth movement for Stephen. And, of course, with the gold fever gripping all the starry-eyed start-up-billionaire wannabes, Stephen's entrepreneurial success and impressive list of patents had made him even more of a hero. His campaign staff and volunteers simply adored him, albeit from a distance.

But Wasim didn't feel like talking to the UMass Republicans. His mind still lingered on the phone call. Nina had known immediately what was bothering Stephen and how to fix it. Wasim had never had that kind of connection with any of his girlfriends. They were nice girls, educated, cultured women, attracted by his good looks and pleasant manner. They went out with him, and some even made it to his bed. But he always felt a distance, as if it were someone else in the embrace, not him.

Stephen and Doug emerged from the building earlier than expected. Stephen looked pissed, and Doug had a wild-eyed, ruffled-bird air. "Disaster," he whispered to Wasim out of Stephen's earshot, "he was positively rude."

Wasim consoled him in an undertone. "Don't worry. We'll fix it."

By the time they got to the guesthouse, it was almost one thirty.

"I need to make some calls," Stephen said and went inside his small, private office and slammed the door.

Wasim went to his corner table in the living room. The large space was crammed with people working in a frenzy, all squeezed together in involuntary intimacy at long benches, elbow to elbow. Some didn't have a seat; they sat on the floor, stood around, or leaned against walls and did their work. The noise level was impossible, and some used headphones to block it out. He picked out an intern and sent him on a lunch run.

From the corner of his eye, he saw Nina's black Jeep pull in. She had abandoned her Volkswagen in deference to the moratorium on foreign cars. He opened the front door for her and waited.

She walked in with a backpack and two grocery bags in each hand. She set them down and removed her sunglasses. "Hi, Wasim! Hey, everybody!"

Everyone in the room looked up and sang out, "Hello, Nina!"

She was wildly popular because she always came armed with treats: spicy Indian snacks, cookies, and her specialty, chilled fruit *chaat*, a uniquely Indian variation on fruit salad that turned it into a highly addictive five-alarm fury. It was a big hit in the sweltering summer heat. She was only a few years older than most of the campaign team and volunteers and was up on all the latest pop culture. She gossiped enthusiastically with them whenever she visited.

One of the volunteers arranged the goodies on the central table. Soon a throng formed, eager hands reaching out and picking up food-laden plates.

What *is* it about food that gets us so excited, what kind of primeval knee-jerk reaction, Wasim wondered, looking at his colleagues crowding around, laughing and eating. Where'd Doug go? He searched the room and located Doug in the opposite corner, speaking earnestly to the phone.

Stephen's office door flew open. Everyone quieted down instantly.

"Nina!" He looked at her in surprise, his hand on the doorknob.

"Hi!" She waved good-bye to the others and squeezed past him into his office. He followed her inside and closed the door behind them.

"What are you doing here?" He frowned at her.

"I brought you lunch. That's all."

The room was small, but there was a love seat wedged under the window, with a coffee table in front of it. She cleared the table and started to fish out things from her backpack and put them down.

"Not now, Nina. I really don't have time. I have too many calls to get through."

"You do your thing. I'll just set this up. I promise I won't say a word."

He stood over her and bit his lip.

"Go on. Make your calls. I'll be done in a second."

He threw himself down next to her on the love seat. "I hate it," he said. "I hate asking people for money, and that's all I do, all day."

She didn't say anything, just continued to set things out—two napkins; a fork and a spoon for each; two bowls with lids; two rectangular boxes, also with lids; two mugs. Then she pulled out two bottles of water and a flask. As soon as she removed the lids off the bowls, a rich aroma of spicy tomato soup filled the room. She removed another box from the recesses of her capacious bag and unwrapped a still-steaming loaf of bread.

"What's all this?"

"Eat." She handed him a hunk of bread, a pat of butter melting down its warm crevices, and then a bowl of soup with a spoon.

He ate, reluctantly at first, and then as the sensory invasion of the food charged from his mouth to warm his insides, he slowed down to enjoy the meal.

"I know what you are doing." He finished his soup and set the empty bowl on the table.

"Fattening you up for sacrifice?"

He laughed. "The kids called you for help, didn't they? I've been a real bear the last few days."

"So I heard."

"I absolutely detest this constant money grubbing. It's the worst form of torture."

"Really?" She reached behind him and traced the welt that ran from his left shoulder blade, across his back, to just below the rib cage on the right side, inflicted by the warden at Khairpur's prison in Pakistan. It was prominent even under two layers of clothing.

"Physical pain I can deal with, but this constant subjugation of my ego is driving me up the wall. And some of these people are complete idiots."

"You wanted a challenge..." She removed the lids of the rectangular boxes and gave one to him. It was his favorite comfort food—spinach, potatoes, black beans, and rice. His mother-in-law had gotten him hooked on it during his long recovery period after the shooting. He couldn't resist the fragrance of basmati rice and started eating even though he didn't fancy such a big meal in the afternoon.

"Besides," Nina continued, "people are falling over themselves to give you money."

"That makes it worse. These are people I know... people who owe my family favors. They are not in a position to say no. I feel really cheap about it."

"Well, get used to it, my love. That's what politics is all about. You don't get to change the world without wading through some crap first."

Stephen was by nature solemn, but now he looked uncharacteristically dejected. "I know." He relinquished the empty box and napkin.

She put the boxes away in a grocery bag. "I'll let you get back to your calls now." She smiled at him and stood up to leave. He didn't reply, just looked at her with those melancholy gray eyes that could turn to ice in an instant.

She sat down and patted her lap: *here, lie down for a few minutes.*

About thirty minutes later there was a knock and the door opened to reveal Wasim and Doug in the doorway. The unscheduled break had already wrecked their tight schedule. The two men looked in but hesitated to enter. Stephen seemed to be asleep, his head on Nina's lap, legs stretched out on the love seat's arm. But at the sound of their footsteps, he opened his eyes and sat up.

"Excuse me," he said and disappeared into the bathroom that was attached to his office.

Nina looked at the campaign pros. "You guys need to schedule a little downtime for him," she scolded. "He is not a people-person. This stuff is rough on him."

They nodded politely, knowing perfectly well that alone time was next to impossible, given the compressed time scale of the special election.

By the time Stephen came out of the bathroom, Nina was ready to go. "I'll see you at home." She kissed him self-consciously in front of the other two men and left.

That evening, there was a huge commotion. The Speaker of the House had come to Martha's Vineyard. He was a Massachusetts native and, like Stephen, a sailing enthusiast. He wanted to meet Stephen.

Doug and Wasim scrambled like mad and re-arranged Stephen's schedule. They alienated some local leaders in the process, but, "Come on; it's the Speaker," they reassured each other. They sent a team of advance men to set the stage for a couple of meet-and-greet fund-raisers in Martha's Vineyard. It was lunacy, trying to make things happen at four hours' notice, but the Speaker lent his resources, and they ended up with not two but four events. It was going to be a long night.

Doug was to travel with Stephen. He ran upstairs to get his things. Wasim decided to stay back and move the debate negotiations forward with the Collins team and finish some of Doug's calls for him. He was about to make a call when Stephen popped his head out of his office and waved to him: *Could you please come here?*

Wasim went inside the office and closed the door. It was a standing rule—always close the door behind you as soon as you enter.

Stephen's gym bag was on the desk, a sinister-looking oversized thing that went with him everywhere. Doug and Wasim frequently speculated about its contents.

"A decapitated head, an AK-47 rifle, classified documents," Wasim had said on one occasion.

"No, no, pink tights, blond wig," Doug had countered.

"Wasim, could you do me a favor?" Stephen opened the bag.

"Of course." Wasim was surprised.

"I meant to do this later this afternoon." Stephen gave Wasim a thick white envelope. "These are urgent papers that Nina gave me to sign, for the foundation. She needs them by tomorrow. Could you please drop them off with her?"

"No problem."

"Please give them to her in person. I don't want anyone else handling the papers."

Wasim took the packet. Stephen took out another item from inside the bag, a large box of chocolates. "Give this to her too."

"Special occasion?"

"No, she likes them."

Wasim took it with a smile. "I'll give them to her."

"Thanks."

It was quite late by the time Wasim got done with the press release recounting the meeting with the Speaker (he endorsed Stephen) and the day's campaign events. He passed it on to the guy who pushed out the press releases each night.

Wasim sat back in his chair and stretched. His eyes fell on the immaculately wrapped chocolate box. Oh crap, he panicked. She might have gone to bed. He dialed her cell phone, cursing his stupidity.

"What's up?" Nina answered immediately. There was always a tinge of anxiety in her voice, as if bracing for bad news.

"Sorry to bother you so late, but I need to drop off some papers."

"That's right. Stephen mentioned that you would."

"Is it too late for me to stop by?"

"Hmmm…it's easier for me to come to the guest-house. The security program won't let you in, and it's too much of a pain to change it."

"Sure, but is it safe for you?"

"It's just a five-minute drive down the road. Anyway, I have protection. See you in a bit."

Protection? He wondered if she had a gun. Or dogs. No, a gun, he decided. Stephen would have definitely bought her a gun.

He cleaned up his desk. Then, suddenly hungry, he wolfed down a protein bar and emptied a can of Red Bull after it.

He heard a car door slam outside and the sound of voices. Who is she talking to? He looked out of the window but couldn't see anyone. She knocked softly and pushed the door in.

"Hi!" she said. "I brought you Stephen's dinner."

"Nice!"

It was so rare to get a home-cooked meal, particularly one made up of Indian food. His mouth watered, and his stomach growled, a Pavlovian response to the familiar childhood aroma coming out of the box.

"Please, go ahead, eat." She sat down across from him and waved to a lone staffer toiling away in a far corner.

Wasim didn't need to be asked twice. He attacked the food.

"This is delicious. Thank you," he said between mouthfuls.

"You are welcome." She started to examine the papers that Stephen had signed.

"Were you talking to someone outside?"

"My kid brother. He came over to keep me company."

Ah, that's the protection, he thought. Nina's younger brother, Neel Sharma, was Stephen's partner in the engineering consultancy. Stephen had asked him to run it while he was busy with the campaign.

"He should come in. I'd love to meet him."

"Some other time. He's in his pajamas and watching some game in the car."

He was about to ask what game when he saw the chocolate box buried under papers that he had pushed aside while cleaning up.

"Oh, I forgot. Here's another packet I was supposed to give you."

She gave a happy, pealing ripple of a laugh and opened the box. She knew exactly where to look for the little note inside. This was a regular feature, clearly.

She reached for her phone and started texting vigorously, glowing and beaming.

Wasim was uncharacteristically moved. There was so much cynicism and negativity in his profession. It was a pleasure to see such unadulterated joy.

"You two seem to really get each other. How long have you been married?" He opened the last box of food and was delighted to see it was *kheer*, his mother's specialty.

She put down the phone and looked at him. "Five years next month."

"How long had you known each other before that?" He wiped his hands and mouth on a napkin and threw the empty containers in the garbage bin beneath his desk.

"Two months, give or take a week."

"Wow. Really?"

Nina's eyes were her best feature, expressive and changeable as her moods. But now they became opaque, and Wasim couldn't read her anymore.

"Yes." She folded her hands in her lap and sat up straight. He seemed to be circling some topic that he didn't have the nerve to broach.

"That's pretty impulsive. Who proposed?" Immediately, he worried that he might have gone too far. "I'm sorry, none of my business."

"That's OK." She opened her mouth to say something but stopped and stared down at her hands and at the wedding ring on her finger.

Of course, Stephen had done the proposing, in his clinical but determined way. He had knocked on her door at two thirty in the morning. And with his characteristic directness, he'd announced, "Let's get married." Before she could answer, he had reached for her hand and slipped an old silver, rolling ring on her finger. To this day, she couldn't figure out why she had agreed at that particular point in time, when she had not yet known of his reckless courage, his principles, or how deeply he loved her. Because he had given no sign of it, no word, no endearment, no magical proposal, just a prosaic statement that they should get married, with a sly hint that she'd be bored by any other man. She had looked into his eyes, mesmerized, and nodded.

Nina became aware of Wasim's eyes on her. She shook her head and smiled. "I'll tell you another day. It's a long story. But the reason we *get* each other is that we were tested really early by the most horrific circumstances. We skipped the petty squabbles and bickering that people have to get through before they find understanding and compassion. We got there in six months."

She stood up. "The amazing thing is it's in times of crises that you know how you truly feel about a person."

She picked up the papers and chocolates and put them in her backpack. "He takes insane risks and drives me crazy. But he *is* amazing, and he *will* change the world for better."

"That's quite an endorsement! He's lucky to have you in his corner."

"Believe me, I tell him that every day." She laughed and picked up her backpack.

"How did you two meet?"

"It depends on whom you ask."

"Did your parents object?"

"They did at first. They worried that race might be an issue and that he looked too old and was too serious, that he came from a broken family riven by property disputes, you know, plus alcoholism, infidelity, dysfunctional family—all the things that Asian parents are terrified of." She looked at Wasim and shrugged. "But they knew how stubborn and determined I was. And now, he's my mother's favorite!"

"What about his family?"

"Well, you know his story. His grandfather brought him up from the day he was born, and after the deaths of his father and grandfather, he broke all ties with his mother and siblings. There were some distant relatives, but he was not close to them. Ultimately, there was nobody whose opinion he asked for or cared about."

After a minute of silence, he asked on an impulse, "May I ask you for some advice?"

"Sure." She sat down.

His words came pouring out in a rush. "You know that my parents are from Pakistan. My father is very conservative, but my mother just wants us kids to be happy. My sister defied my father on almost everything—dating, education, marriage. They don't talk much, my father and my sister."

He tapped his phone on the table. "My father thinks I am weird. I like to read, I am not much of a mosque goer, and my friends are mostly non-Pakistanis. I dress too stylishly, I study 'girl' subjects, like political science. I don't have a 'real' job, just running around the country, helping people get elected."

He looked at her. "My father is terrified that I might be gay. That's his worst nightmare."

She knew what was coming next.

"I am afraid he is right."

He watched for her reaction.

"When did you know?" she asked without any emotion.

"A few minutes ago, while you were talking about the two of you."

"You're kidding!"

"A little."

He had suspected it for a while. There was no mistaking the excitement he'd felt around some of his male friends in the past. But he had succeeded in pushing it deep down, or turned it, with some effort, toward the other sex. Not anymore. These days it was hard to stop his hands from trembling when Doug stood close or leaned over him to reach for something.

He turned to Nina. "I realized that the two occasions on which I felt the way *you* feel about Stephen were both in relation to other men."

She waited for him to continue.

"The first time it happened, I was in high school. He was my best friend, and he was straight. I told myself that it was just strong loyalty that I felt."

He looked up at the ceiling. "But I thought about him whenever I wasn't with him. I thought about him a lot. But he had no clue. I was a very good basketball player, and no one suspects a jock."

"I was convinced that it was just teenage confusion. I dated as many girls as I could and made my father happy in a perverse way."

He sighed and sat up. "Then recently, I met this guy. He's smart, well-read, good-natured, and we get along like mad."

"Doug?"

"How did you know?"

"Lucky guess." She was amused that he was surprised.

"You are the first person that I have mentioned this to, not even my sister. I still need to get my head around it."

"Of course. But you should let Doug know how you feel about him."

"I will."

Nina stood up. "I have to go now. Neel will start honking any minute. Good luck, Wasim. Don't worry. Things have a way of working out."

PROS TAKE A BREAK

 Stephen Edward James @stephenjames . Sep 15
We are at the Fog Shore Diner in Barnstable. Best Apple Danish
ever!

Wasim was really glad when the James Bond gate, their nickname for the entrance to Stephen's home, closed shut behind him. It had been a manic day. They had done three TV appearances and four meet-and-greet events. He pulled into the parking lot outside the guesthouse and leaned back in the seat, drained of all energy. He hadn't eaten since breakfast, and Red Bull fumes weren't cutting it anymore.

The front door to the guesthouse opened, and Doug came out, pulling on his jacket. He spotted

Wasim's car and came over and looked in the window. "Hi, there!"

"Hi." Wasim turned his head and looked at Doug, faint with hunger and exhaustion.

"Want to get some dinner?" Doug asked.

"Yes. But you drive. I'm tired."

"Sure. Move over."

Wasim slid into the passenger seat. Doug got in and methodically adjusted the mirrors.

"Where do you want to go?"

"I don't care, anywhere that's calm and quiet."

The car shot out of the compound and sped into the darkness outside. Wasim pushed back his seat and closed his eyes. "Mind if I take a little nap?"

"Not at all." Doug looked over at Wasim, but he was already out.

When Wasim opened his eyes, the car was stationary. Doug was in the driver's seat, with his face lit by the ghostly glow of his iPad balanced on the steering wheel. He had his headphones on.

Wasim sat up. "Where are we?" His mouth and lips were parched.

"Outside the restaurant."

"What!" He rubbed his eyes and straightened his seat. "Why didn't you wake me? How long have I been sleeping?"

Doug looked at his watch. "I'd say an hour and a half."

"Oh man, I'm so sorry! You should have woken me!"

"You were fast asleep. I didn't feel like disturbing you. I thought I'd give you another fifteen minutes. It was nice for me too. I caught up on my music news."

Doug had a geeky, boyish face, like a young Bill Gates. It hid a shrewd political mind behind a sweet, disarming smile. Music was a necessity for him, along with Red Bull. Whenever he could, he tried to stay abreast of his hometown's prodigious talent.

They went inside the diner, the only one close by, open twenty-four hours a day and thriving, thanks to the young campaign team's unstinting patronage.

The booths were spacious and spotless. A waitress seated them and handed out menus that were almost an inch thick. It took them five minutes just to skim them. In their famished state, they ordered half the restaurant's offerings.

She made multiple trips and soon covered their table with dishes. She surveyed it one final time and left them with an indulgent, "There you go, boys. Enjoy!"

They ate with intense concentration. Creamy, salty mac and cheese slid off their tongues pleasurably, and the French fries snapped with a crunch and let out wisps of steam. They paused only to take quick gulps of water.

"Am I really hungry, or is the chef super talented?" Doug asked.

"You're hungry."

The waitress came to check on them fifteen minutes later. "That's the fastest I've seen food disappear!" She laughed and began to clear the dishes. "Can I get you anything else?"

"I'll have a chocolate sundae, please," Wasim said.

"I'll have a coffee," Doug added, "with skim milk, please."

The waitress left, skillfully balancing a stack of dishes on her forearm and hands.

"That was just what I needed," Wasim said contentedly, "a nap and a nice meal."

The diner was nearly empty at that late hour. A young couple sat in one corner, a man in another, and Wasim and Doug had their own corner. Whitney Houston caressed them in mellow tones from overhead speakers: "I will always love you."

Doug stretched out his legs along the seat of the booth and leaned back against the wall, his left hand resting flat on the table, fingers tapping to the music. Nobody on the campaign knew it, but he was a talented clarinet player, saxophonist, and a half-decent pianist, and he missed playing with his friends back in New Orleans. Some of them were truly talented, descendants of music royalty. One of his childhood friends had just played at the nearby Newport Jazz Festival, but Doug hadn't been able to go watch him.

"You know, I think this Tyler guy is getting to Stephen," Wasim said.

"Tyler's an asshole. He's just trying to grab eyeballs."

"I'm afraid that Stephen will snap one day and say or do something that'll be caught on video. That will be the end."

"That's not going to happen. Stephen is very much in control of his emotions. He's irritable because he allows himself to be."

"I hope you are right."

Doug changed the topic to distract him. "Do you think Stephen has a shot, Wasim? I worry that he's just too disinterested."

"You know, I can't figure him out. He is definitely very competitive and motivated, and he's clearly working very hard. But I think this whole courting the public goes against his grain and training. He's just too reserved and deliberate."

"I wonder what it'll take to get him going?"

"I don't know. But whatever it is, it'd better happen soon."

The waitress brought their sundae and coffee. "Can I get you boys anything else?"

They declined. She slapped down the check on the table and left after a perky "Enjoy!" It was hard to guess her age, forties perhaps, with her bleached, blondish look and a smile that glowed with neon brightness against her chemically tanned skin. But she was nice to them, and they put in a large tip.

"Want some?" Wasim offered his ice cream. Doug took one spoonful and then another and another and another.

"See," he complained, "this is the problem. I can't stop once I start."

It was nice to be away from the office and the campaign frenzy, to relax and eat ice cream.

"Did you always know you were gay?" Wasim asked.

Doug stopped, his spoon balanced in midair, about to scoop out ice cream. He put it down and looked Wasim in the eye and said clearly and succinctly, "Yes."

There were times when Doug had been certain that Wasim was gay, especially when alone with him late at night, planning the next day's schedule. Wasim would shed his supercompetent daytime persona and turn into a stand-up comic, cracking joke after joke and doing wicked impressions of various people, including Nina and Stephen, keeping Doug in splits for hours. The way Wasim looked at Doug at such times had led him to suspect deeper feelings. But on one occasion, when he'd rested his hand lightly on Wasim's, just casually, Wasim had pulled it away immediately. Doug had never tried it again, nor broached the topic of being gay, but now Wasim was bringing it up on his own.

"When did you come out? How did you tell your parents?" Wasim asked.

Doug waited for an instant before answering.

"It was during my senior year in high school. I came home from a date. My mother always waited up for me because I was a new driver. It was very late, but that night she was playing the piano when I got home.

She does that to calm herself when she is worried or under stress."

He looked past his crossed ankles, at the tips of his shoes glinting under the overhead light. "She asked me if I had a nice evening. I said I did. She got up, kissed me on the cheek, and said good night. I don't know what got into me, but I asked her, 'How come you never ask me about my date?'"

He swung his legs down off the seat and faced Wasim. "'Who's your date,' she asked. Of course, she knew. I said, 'Kevin.'"

Doug moved the salt and pepper shakers around. "She sat down. I felt terrible. I could see her struggling and trying to cope with the shock of certainty but at the same time trying to hide it from me, so as not to hurt me. I think she was more worried about my safety and how I'd be treated, rather than shame or anger."

He looked up at Wasim. "I sat next to her and hugged her. 'It's going to be OK. I'll be fine,' I said. After a few minutes, she hugged me back. 'I want you to be happy. That's all I want,' she said."

He laughed. "That was it. I am sure she must have been horrified, but she didn't show it. I told her that I'd tell Dad the next day but if she felt that she didn't want to keep it from him until I had a chance to talk to him, she should tell him."

Wasim had an eerily rapt expression. "What did he say?" he asked. His voice was hoarse.

"He used to leave for work really early. When I woke up the next morning, there was a note on my dresser."

"What did it say?"

Doug took out his wallet and carefully removed a folded piece of paper. He gave it to Wasim.

Wasim opened it. His hands trembled. Doug watched him.

Everything's fine. I'll talk to you tonight. Love, Dad.

"That's wonderful!" Wasim returned the paper without looking at Doug.

"Yes, I was very lucky."

Doug felt sorry for Wasim. He had seen the struggle of denial before, so painful, so terrible, so unnecessary. Nothing would change the outcome, no amount of lying or self-deception, but so many wasted their lives trying to pull it off. Doug realized how fortunate he was to have supportive family and friends. Most of his gay friends had much tougher paths to acceptance, but the ones that tried to hide it were the most miserable of all.

"It was difficult in the beginning, but then I realized that I am who I am and that I could either spend my entire life living a lie and making some unfortunate woman unhappy or face the prejudice and hate but live a full life, pursuing love and happiness on *my* terms."

Wasim sat still, without saying a word.

"My parents made it easier and fought many of my battles for me. I am happy to do that for any friend

86

who needs my help." He desperately wanted to comfort Wasim, but any physical demonstration would make matters worse.

"I have that strength and experience now—to help, that is. I wish I'd had it when I was younger. I lost a good friend because I was too much of a coward. I hadn't come out at that point."

Wasim leaned forward and waited to hear more.

"My friend Jerry was a talented violinist. We used to talk about being gay, even though neither of us quite admitted to it. Then we went away to college in different directions. He used to write that he had been looking around and that he had found an Internet dating site that was anonymous and untraceable."

It was difficult for Doug to talk about it, even though it was getting to be almost a decade since the incident. "I told him to be careful. He was in an ultraconservative part of the country. I was lucky to be attending school in DC."

Doug paused for a long time and tried to collect his thoughts. "One night, he went out with a guy on a date. Somebody followed them, taped the sexual encounter, and posted it on a popular student site. It was taken down within ten minutes, but by then everybody had seen it."

Wasim sat back in his chair. He remembered reading that story. It had been a national sensation. But he had quickly pushed it aside from his consciousness at that time and refused to acknowledge its relevance to him.

Doug looked down at his fingers and wiped off a bit of ketchup. "Jerry jumped off a bridge the next day, two days after his nineteenth birthday. He was done with life."

They sat like that for a long time. Wasim avoided eye contact while Doug tried to get back his composure.

It was getting late, and they had another crazy day coming up.

"We should leave," Doug said finally.

They walked back in silence to the car. Doug drove. Wasim sat slouched in the seat, looking out into the darkness. They exchanged cursory good-nights and returned to their respective rooms in the guesthouse, rooms that they shared with others, rooms that offered no privacy or space for introspection.

STRATEGY

A black-and-white video cuts back and forth between two shots. In one, Stephen sits behind a desk while Wasim bends down to whisper in his ear. In the other, Nina stands under a banner that says "Education for every child!" and gesticulates vehemently. A grim, male voice intones, "Stephen Edward James, who has his ear? Can we trust his conservatism? Or, is he a liberal who plays a Republican on TV?"
—*TV ad, "RINO", The Conservative Coalition*

The guesthouse was very quiet. Most people had gone to bed. Wasim had the living room to himself while he tried to wade through the draft of the daily campaign bulletin. It had to go out in the next hour. He closed his eyes, exhausted to a point where he couldn't feel anything anymore.

It had been a tough week. The campaign wasn't getting any noticeable traction. Stephen was either irritable or sluggish and disinterested. It was as if he were in two minds about running for office and couldn't even convince himself, let alone the electorate. At this rate, the campaign would implode in a matter of days. Doug talked of a radical shake-up: "Perhaps we should get his wife to run instead," he'd half-joked.

Wasim forced himself to finish reading the bulletin and e-mailed the approved draft to the media guy. Soon it would zip through fat digital pipes to news outlets, social networks, and mailing lists.

He slumped back in his chair and stretched. He knew he should really go to bed, but his brain was all abuzz. Let's see what new shit *The Daily Howl* is dishing out, he thought and clicked on the bookmark. The page took a long time to reload and then lit up in a lurid font:

Republican candidate's communications director, Wasim Raja, linked to charity that fronts for a terror group.

Wasim's heart stopped beating for a second and then took off like a racehorse. He got up from his chair in a daze. His legs automatically carried him up the stairs to Doug's room.

Doug came out as soon as he heard the knock. Wasim's face looked oddly out of kilter.

"What's wrong, Wasim?" He stepped out of the room and shut the door behind him, so they wouldn't be heard. Maybe something had happened to Wasim's family. Perhaps he had been outed!

Wasim signaled for Doug to go with him.

They left the guesthouse and went into the adjoining Public Garden. It was chilly. The sky was beginning to fill with a murky, predawn light.

Doug shivered and pulled his robe tight around him. "What's the matter?" he asked again, but Wasim didn't answer.

As soon as they were out of sight of the guesthouse, Wasim gave his iPad to Doug and collapsed on a concrete bench, his legs trembling. He closed his eyes and listened to Doug's breathing as it paused and then resumed, ending in an expletive.

"Crap!" Doug repeated. He sat down next to Wasim. The bench was hard and cold. He wanted to reach out and take Wasim's hand. After their conversation at the diner, Wasim had been more open when they were alone, almost affectionate. But Doug didn't want to be the one to make the first move, and now was definitely not the time.

"It's not true, you know," Wasim blurted out.

"Of course not, Wasim! I was just trying to figure out how best to handle it. Don't worry…we'll fix it. But we need to talk to Stephen immediately."

Doug called Stephen and briefly explained the situation.

"I'll meet you there," Stephen said and hung up.

The night was cool, but the garden was still fragrant from summer's memories. Doug and Wasim sat on the unforgiving bench and anxiously waited for Stephen.

"I knew it was only a matter of time before somebody did this," Wasim said. "All they think when they see my face and hear my name is TERRORIST! No evidence needed."

Doug turned to him. "We'll figure it out," he repeated, gently.

They tried to stay calm, even though this could very well be the undoing of the campaign, their careers, and any possibility of a relationship.

In a few minutes, Stephen came striding down the path from the guesthouse. He was uncharacteristically dressed in gym shorts and a sweat shirt. He'd been about to get on the treadmill for his early morning workout when he'd received Doug's call. His flashlight swayed from left to right, lighting up his sneakers and the path in front.

They stood up and watched Stephen run the last hundred yards toward them.

By this time, Wasim had worked himself into a choking, gulping anger—at Tyler's maliciousness and at the unfairness of the accusations leveled at him based solely on his parents' nationality.

"I am sorry," he sputtered to Stephen and then thought, why the fuck am *I* apologizing? "I just saw this stupid article on Tyler's website. It's a disaster." He passed his hands through his hair and then folded his arms across his chest. "I'll resign. But just so you know, it's total crap. The whole article." He was so angry he couldn't get the words out without clenching his teeth.

Stephen had read the article on his way over. He had already decided what to do.

"I don't understand. Why should you resign?" he said. He rested the flashlight on the bench. Its beam cast sinister shadows on their faces.

Stephen had a big dossier on Wasim and Doug and on most of the campaign team—an occupational curiosity. From what he had read, it was unlikely that Wasim's past contained anything to support Tyler's claims. Of course, one could never be sure.

Wasim had expected an explosive reaction from their temperamental boss, not this avuncular concern. "Because you will be spending all your days explaining this away for the next week. And your opponent will chew you out at every opportunity. Your chances of winning will be zero," he said impatiently. He was in no mood to stand around giving explanations. He just wanted to pack his bags and get the hell out.

"Are you going to give up so easily?"

Wasim stared at him. He could swear that Stephen was actually smiling. "What do you mean?"

"Where's the fight? This guy has called you and your parents terrorists. Are you going to just walk off and let him get away with it?"

"What do you expect me to do?" Wasim's voice sounded high-pitched to his own ears, but he couldn't stop. "My world is very different from yours. I get searched at airports each and every time. Cops find reasons to stop me on the road. My car gets towed for offences that others get off with warnings."

"All the more reason that you should stand up to this kind of blackmail."

Wasim didn't answer. He sat down on the bench and buried his face in his hands. The sky had brightened, and the guesthouse was beginning to show signs of life.

"We need to teach this Tyler guy a lesson," Stephen said. He stared at the top of Wasim's bowed head.

Tyler had been nibbling at Stephen's ankles with annoying little anecdotes and gossipy pictures, usually of Stephen looking pissed or of Nina at some rally against domestic violence, all with misleading headings but nothing that would justify a serious rebuke. This was the chance that Stephen had been looking for, to swat Tyler once and for all. He was fed up with the vulgar garbage that was posted on *The Daily Howl*. It was likely that the Collins camp had fed Tyler this tidbit about Wasim's visits to Pakistan, and Tyler had run with it, not bothering to check the facts.

"What did you have in mind?" Doug asked.

"I think the Collins people are behind this. I'd like to hang it on them."

"I like it!" Doug said. It was high time they went on the offensive. They had been running a tentative and feeble campaign with no bite. He turned to Wasim. "What's the best way to go about this?"

"We should get on Fox News." Wasim looked up. "And neutralize the story before it gets into the news cycle."

"All right, let's do it then." Stephen patted Wasim's shoulder. "Hang in there. We'll take care of this."

As soon as he returned home, Stephen called his brother-in-law, Neel.

"Hey, boss! What's up?" Neel's voice sounded sleepy.

"I need your help." Stephen could imagine Neel wincing as he struggled to wake up and pay attention.

"You awake, Neel?"

"Yes, yes, I am listening," Neel's voice came feebly over the phone.

"You remember that tracker, Tyler, who's been hounding us? He has published a report. He claims that Wasim visited Pakistan multiple times in one year, and that his grandfather was a close friend of Al Hakim, a well-known funder of terror networks. Could you check that out?"

"Sure."

"While you're at it, could you please look into what this Tyler character has been up to?"

"Will do. What are you concerned about?"

"Not sure yet. He keeps harping on Nina."

"Just gossip, I guess."

"I think it's more than that."

"Like?"

"What if he is acting on someone else's orders? What if they are spying on us? Looking for opportunities to hurt Nina."

"Who? The Collins campaign?" Neel tried to joke.

"No, the old network."

"You are being paranoid! Akhtar's dead and gone. His network has collapsed."

Zia Akhtar had been Stephen's nemesis.

"Neel, you know better. They always come back, stronger and more vicious."

"I wouldn't worry, Stephen. Anyway, I will keep an eye on Tyler."

"Alright, thanks. I'll talk to you later. Bye."

Stephen looked at his watch to see if he'd have time to exercise. No, he was already running late. He rushed to the bathroom to shower.

Nina was still asleep when he emerged wrapped in his bathrobe. He looked at her face, so peaceful and content, smiling even in repose. Her figure was just a little bit fuller under her nightgown. He put his hand lightly on her stomach. It was too early in the pregnancy for the baby to kick or move. He wanted a daughter with Nina's eyes and infectious smile, but with his toughness and physical abilities. Nina was hopeless in that respect—she wilted in the sun like a hothouse flower, and couldn't hit a ball to save her life.

His phone beeped a reminder. He should really get dressed and leave but he wanted to linger a little longer near Nina, to absorb her peace and calm before facing the shitstorm that Tyler's story would've unleashed. He sat down in an armchair next to the bed, still in his damp bathrobe.

Nina felt his gaze upon her. She could smell his aftershave even before she opened her eyes. When she did, his face was just a few inches from hers. He had leaned forward and was just about to kiss her. His hair was unruly from the vigorous toweling and had not been combed into submission yet. She loved it like that, bereft of its armor of formality.

"Hey!" She smiled.

"How are you feeling?" He kissed her and straightened up.

"Good! I slept really well."

"Can I get you anything? Milk? Juice?"

"No. I will start with these crackers here."

She sat up slowly and took a sip of water to prevent morning sickness.

"Aren't you supposed to be at work? How's your schedule?" she said.

"Brutal," he replied. He did not mention Tyler's story.

"I have to go for a blood test today." She put down her water bottle and bit into a cracker.

"Ma's going with you?"

"No, it's just routine. I didn't want to bother her."

He felt guilty. What kind of a man missed his un-born child's appointments? Especially given how trau-matic the loss of their earlier pregnancy had been. Perhaps he had the same indifferent genes as his mother. Or, the utterly selfish and cowardly DNA of his father—a man, who, caught between father and wife, chose to kill himself rather than face his responsibili-ties, with no consideration for his three children.

Nina saw the familiar cloud come over his face. "Stephen, look at me." She climbed out of bed and came over to where he sat.

He took her hand in his. Her hair, always beautiful, had grown more lush now, tumbling down her shoul-ders in luxuriant waves all the way down to her waist.

"Stephen, it's not a big deal. It's just a silly old blood test."

He nodded. Without a word, he got up from the chair, gave her a big bear hug, and left to get ready for work.

When he arrived at the campaign office, it was ut-ter chaos and panic. Wasim was on three phones at once. A continuous beeping of email and text messag-es arriving in an unstaunchable torrent filled the air.

Doug jumped up as soon as he saw Stephen.

"Stephen, Tyler's story is spreading! We are trying to get on Fox News. But that might take a day or two."

"Don't worry. We'll handle it."

Stephen brushed him off and tried to enter his office and close the door.

"How?" Doug insisted without budging. "I heard that TV crews are setting up outside."

"Let them. Make sure no one talks to them. Absolutely nobody."

Stephen waited for Doug to leave. But he just stood there.

"I need to get on with these calls, Doug."

"Stephen, this could become huge. We should cancel today's schedule, perhaps. Put out a statement?"

"No and no."

"Well, we need to do *something*. Otherwise, people will assume it's true."

"Let's give it a day and see what happens."

"Both Wasim and I think that's not a good idea. We should put out a rebuttal."

"What purpose would that serve? It would only add legitimacy and give the story more traction." Stephen rattled the door handle.

"How would waiting a day be useful?"

"We might hear from Fox News. That's the proper platform for us."

"Are you sure?" Doug gave in despite his better judgment.

"Yes. Absolutely."

Doug left. Stephen closed the door and walked back to his chair. He'd faked a confidence he hadn't felt. Stephen's dossier on Wasim was at least a year old.

What if there had been changes in Wasim's life? What if he had been radicalized?

Stephen shook his head and dialed the first number on his list, steeling himself to be pleasant and polite when all he wanted to do was slam down the phone receiver. He'd rather be holed up in a Pakistani prison cell, plotting his escape.

By that afternoon, TV camera crews and photographers had surrounded the compound. Wherever Stephen's campaign bus went, a long convoy of cars, vans, and motorcycles followed with microphones and cameras, clicking and filming in a maddening chorus. Each new intrusion made Stephen more furious and intractable.

"We are not saying a word!" That was his response each time Doug or Wasim made a renewed plea for a statement. "I hope everyone on the staff knows that. Not a word!"

Stephen constantly worried about Nina now. If the campaign got into a shouting match with Tyler, Nina *could* become an object of pursuit—either by the press looking for a response, or by some crazed gunman. There were lunatics of all persuasions. With her South Asian looks, she could easily be tarred with the same brush as Wasim had been. Or, an enemy from Stephen's past could use Wasim's trial by the media as an excuse to avenge perceived injustices and harm Nina to get to Stephen. If only Neel would come back with some information!

"We got the interview!" Wasim announced around four in the afternoon. He had dark circles under his eyes, and his voice was hoarse from being on the phone without a break. "The taping is scheduled for tomorrow evening at Fox studios in New York City."

Immediately the campaign swamped social media with announcements of the upcoming interview. The young volunteers tweeted and retweeted until their fingers became numb.

Fox was only too happy to give airtime to a young Republican hopeful, especially since it played so well into their narrative of liberal dirty tricks engineered to take down a good, principled man.

Just prior to the taping, the team gathered for a final huddle while they waited for Stephen to be called onto the set. Wasim sat hunched in a chair. He had been on the phone for the last thirty-six hours, lining up TV interviews, radio shows, and calls. It was a confusing time for him. He was angry yet hugely appreciative of the opportunity to clear his name and grateful for the support being extended to him by almost everyone around. More than anything, he was totally exhausted. He hadn't slept in almost forty-eight hours.

Doug stood behind Wasim's chair, busy on his iPad. Nina sat in the only other chair in the small, windowless room. A basket of muffins and a few bottles of water sat on a tiny table between the two chairs.

Stephen was more animated than they'd ever seen him. He trusted his instincts about Wasim even though he hadn't heard anything from Neel other than: *Fricking George is at an undisclosed location…can't find him. Trying other avenues.* What if his instincts were wrong? *Wasim could turn out to be a terrorist,* a voice in his head said, but Stephen ignored it, and prowled the room with the light of battle in his eyes.

Doug was baffled. Stephen had frustrated them for almost two months. They had wondered daily why he had entered the race at all. But ever since the story broke, Stephen seemed more energized and determined than they had ever seen him.

When Nina heard of the incident, she had insisted on coming with them to New York. She knew Stephen too well and the kind of risks he took when provoked. She watched him now through narrowed eyes, while he circled the periphery of the tiny room. On his next perambulation he paused next to her and tugged her ponytail. "Lighten up," he said.

"Stephen, what are you up to?" She freed her hair from his fingers.

"Nothing," he said with a big smile.

"Why? What?" Doug looked from one to the other.

"He's plotting something," she said.

"Who? *Me?* No!" Stephen protested.

An usher knocked on the door. "We're ready for you, Mr. James." Doug and Wasim went out with Stephen, while Nina stayed behind and watched the show on the TV monitor in the room.

Stephen walked onto the set.

"Welcome to our program, Mr. James. Thank you for joining us," said Sean, the popular TV-show host.

"Thank you for having me, Sean."

The famous newsman leaned forward in his director's chair and looked earnestly at Stephen, who was seated in a similar chair a few feet across from him. An assistant came and fussed with Stephen's hair and dabbed him with powder. Another assistant fixed a microphone on him. The producer shouted, "Ready...and roll."

Sean began, "Congratulations, Mr. James. We hear that you are doing really well in the liberal state of Massachusetts, giving Congresswoman Collins a run for her money."

"Thank you, Sean. We have a fantastic team. We are knocking on doors, meeting people, doing whatever it takes. The people of my home state of Massachusetts have been incredibly supportive."

Stephen was relaxed and easy and spoke with a broad New England accent, punctuating every other sentence with a smile. He was quite charming, the picture of gentility in a starched, white button-down shirt and immaculately creased pants.

Wasim noticed the diamond cuff links—Nina's grandfather's, the lucky charm given to Stephen by his mother-in-law. He pointed them out to Doug: *cuff links*!

Doug had suggested preparing for the interview, but Stephen had waved him off, *no, not necessary.* "Whatever you do, don't take on the press," Doug had advised. "Look what happened to Gary Hart."

Sean stabbed the air with his pen for dramatic effect. "Mr. James, I heard that the Democrats are playing real dirty. Innuendoes. Aspersions. Whisper campaigns. Sleazy websites." He counted them off on his fingers. "They are throwing everything *and* the kitchen sink at you!" He threw up his hands in outrage.

The race was attracting a ton of national attention, and Tyler's tabloid coverage had contributed greatly to the buzz around it. In one public confrontation, Tyler had pressed Stephen as to why his mother and siblings weren't around. "Can we trust a man who doesn't talk to his own mother?" *The Daily Howl* demanded.

Stephen had defused it by being candid. "My mother handed me to my grandfather as soon as I was born. He brought me up. It has been written about in great detail over the last two decades; everyone in Massachusetts knows about it, Mr. Tyler. I think there was even an HBO miniseries, I am told." It was a surprisingly effective strategy on Stephen's part and had killed that line of inquiry immediately.

Yesterday's sensational headlines about Wasim had placed the Senate race at the very top of the news brew. The story was being picked up rapidly all across the Internet, despite Stephen's campaign's best efforts. But there was a silver lining: it was likely that millions would watch Stephen's interview now.

"That's true, Sean." Stephen shook his head. "We have run a clean campaign. We focus on issues and highlight how we differ from our opponent. Take national security. We are determined to keep our country safe, while Congresswoman Collins shies away from making hard choices. Look at her voting record! Unfortunately, as the race began to tighten, my opponent has waged a proxy campaign through salacious blogs to make baseless accusations."

Sean leaned forward earnestly. "What kind of accusations, Mr. James?" he asked, oozing sympathy from every pore.

"They have accused my communications director, Wasim Raja, a remarkable young American, of links to terrorist groups. Do you know why?"

"Why?" Sean asked in a hushed voice.

"Because somebody, somewhere, said so, without a shred of proof or evidence. Solely on the basis of that."

"That's ridiculous!" Sean was shocked, so shocked.

"You bet! It's a travesty. Wasim is a role model for young people. Highly educated, hardworking—at the age of twenty, he turned the world of political campaigning upside down. We should be celebrating him, his talent and drive, not trying to smear him!"

Wasim and Doug looked at each other.

Sean exploded at the camera. "This is what they do! Smoke and mirrors, half-truths, and outright lies! Is there nothing they won't stoop to?"

"The irony is," Stephen said to the camera, "that the congresswoman is such a champion of civil liberties, such a vocal advocate for the rights of minorities. But when it comes to American Muslims, she is strangely silent. Why hasn't she condemned the base-less attack on Wasim? She knows as well as I do that Wasim is being unfairly targeted because of his faith. Congresswoman Collins, do the right thing. Defend Wasim Raja against such lies."

Sean took it from there.

"They should be ashamed!"

"That's right." Stephen nodded.

"I hear that they are going after your wife now. That's unheard of! Attacking family! How low can they go?"

"Well, they are using this blog as a surrogate. My wife has been called an ivory-tower communist, accused of poverty tourism, and recently, they called her a 'real housewife of New England.' And all she does the whole day long is find ways to keep girls in school in poor countries."

"I met Mrs. James in the dressing room. She is a charming young woman, and she is doing amazing work."

"Yes, she is." Stephen turned to the camera and, with a big grin that crinkled the corners of his eyes, waved. "Hi, sweetheart!"

"The women's vote, right there, we have it!" Doug whispered to Wasim. He was beside himself with excitement that Stephen was finally showing signs of life.

In the dressing room Nina watched with a sinking feeling. Stephen was in character. During the early days after their marriage, when she had no idea what he really did for a living, she used to worry at his chameleonlike ability to change. On one trip to India, he had turned into this slaphappy, beatific hippie in blue jeans and a crumpled linen shirt, hanging out with the locals in remote villages while she worked with the rural NGOs there. It had bothered her at that time, this strange, trippy behavior. Was he on drugs, she'd asked, full of dread. He had laughed and explained it away as an amusing diversion. Now that she knew the truth, she was not surprised at whatever character he pulled out of his head.

"Mr. James, is there anything you'd like to say to our audience?"

Stephen's voice was suddenly cold and cutting, his words enunciated with precision. "I think it is reprehensible, the lies that have been flung at my communications director, Wasim Raja. They owe him an apology. Next time the publisher of this blog decides to say, write, or imply anything, in any medium or even in a whisper, he'd better back it up with evidence. If not, there will be consequences. That's a promise."

Here, Stephen paused and stared sternly at the camera, as if searching for Tyler in its electronic circuitry. Then suddenly, he smiled and looked over Sean's shoulder at where Wasim stood.

"And, Wasim, no, I do *not* accept your resignation."

Sean stood up and applauded. Stephen stood up as well.

"Thank you for having me on your show, Sean."

"Mr. James, please come back and visit us. You are always welcome here." Sean shook his hand energetically.

On the drive back, the team celebrated. Stephen's interview would reach millions of viewers, and he had performed exceptionally well.

"Thank you, Stephen," Wasim said. He twisted around in his seat to look at Nina and Stephen, sitting in the backseat of the car. He was truly touched by Stephen's unqualified and unquestioning support.

"Of course!" Stephen leaned forward and shook Wasim's hand.

Just then, Neel's message flashed on Stephen's phone: *You backed the right horse.* Apparently, Tyler's source had concealed a crucial part of the information from Tyler. Wasim was barely four years old when he had accompanied his mother to visit her father, who had been on his deathbed. She had returned to Pakistan three times in a span of four months, and one final time after her father's death to attend his funeral. So on paper, Wasim had indeed made four trips to Pakistan in as many months.

Stephen looked up from his phone. "Gentlemen, I want you to book me on as many shows as possible, as many public events as you can organize. We can't let this filth go unanswered anymore." They were already booked for a piece with the *New Yorker* later that day, and Wasim was milking all his contacts to get Stephen on *The Late Show with Stephen Colbert.*

Doug and Wasim looked astonished, much to Stephen's amusement.

"What can I say? I need a brawl to get me going," he said. "Ask Nina. She spends half our vacations dragging me away from fights."

She rolled her eyes and continued to stare out the window. She was unsettled by Stephen's newfound enthusiasm and exuberance. He had his arm around her and squeezed her closer to him in an attempt to stem her anxiety. It was getting toward the end of the first trimester, way past the point where they had lost the earlier pregnancy. But he could still see its ghosts in her eyes.

The interview hit the airwaves later that evening. Tyler watched the show on a large-screen TV in the house he rented a few blocks from Stephen's home. The rental made a big hole in his budget, but he didn't care. He now had a carefully cultivated persona, dressed all in black, expensive cameras around his neck, with long, flowing hair and a carefully groomed beard. Out with the research engineer, in with the political gossip guru! There was even a woman in his life. The fact that his ex's money paid for all these luxuries, including the woman, made them even more delicious.

"Arrogant prick," he muttered and reached for the remote to change the channel. Cooking, shopping, travel, football, more football, movie, movie, two naked women pleasuring each other…he parked it there for a while and then turned off the TV.

He picked up the phone and punched a number.

"Are you free tonight?" he demanded peevishly. "Can you come over right away?"

There was a pause while he listened to the other party. "That's fine. I don't give a fuck whether your rates are double or triple." Another pause. "OK, see you."

He mixed a drink and settled down on the couch with his laptop. Ashley would be over soon.

A minion from the Collins campaign staff had passed him a tip two days ago: Wasim Raja had made multiple trips to Pakistan in the span of four months. The minion supplied documents with much of the information redacted but essentially provided evidence that Wasim had entered and exited Pakistan at least four times in a calendar year.

Tyler's Google search had revealed that Wasim's dead grandfather and a powerful man behind a terrorist-funding charity were at the same university at the same time. The two men could potentially have known each other. Then from grandfather to Wasim was an easy leap. Tyler had not made any specific accusations. In fact, his article was noncommittal, despite the hysterical headline. All Tyler had wanted was to stir the pot and whip up some publicity for *The Daily Howl*.

Who knew that it would light a fire under the snooty ass of Mr. Stephen Edward James III! Tyler fumed at a fate that handed the likes of Stephen James everything on a platter but robbed Tyler of even the humblest of joys—a faithful wife, for one.

Twenty minutes later Ashley showed up in a blond blur. She wore her signature jeans, which seemed painted on to her shapely legs, and an equally well-fitting sweater. She threw her bag down in a corner and came and stood in front of him, her curvy red sweater right in his line of sight.

"What are you in the mood for?" she asked.

Tyler was too worked up to reply. Instead, he pushed her aside to get a better view of the TV. He had recorded the interview to show her. "Look at this! The jerk didn't mention *The Daily Howl*, or me. And he kept calling it a blog. It's not a blog, you dumbass, it's a news site." He shook his fist at the TV.

Oh good, it's one of those talky nights, Ashley thought. Tyler was an easy client. What he needed most was someone to talk *at*, rather than the high-energy demands of some of the others on her roster. He needed an attentive listener to baby his fragile ego that had been mangled by his ex's spiky heels—someone who would put the pieces back together and say, "There, there, you are an important man."

She threw her shoes in a corner, pulled off her jeans, and sent them flying after the shoes. The next minute, she was snuggled up to him on the couch, sipping his drink.

"Go on," she said.

Ashley was in her late twenties, a teacher's aide before she had stumbled into her current career and decided to pursue it full time. She was not exactly beautiful but quite attractive, radiant with the glow of good health and youth, enhanced by her miraculously long, sinewy body and the magic of a good stylist. Her profession had taught her the value of listening—stock tips, political gossip, palace intrigue, and confessions of kingmakers—you never knew what useful nugget would come your way, not to mention referrals. She was Tyler's most expensive indulgence.

He made her watch a replay of the interview and kept up a virulent commentary. With every close-up of Stephen, he got more and more agitated.

"Did that son of a bitch actually threaten me? Did he? Did he?" he demanded.

"Looks like it," Ashley replied with a smile. She was about to make a lot of money, enough to cover a couple of mortgage payments on her pricey condo.

RUMORS

Dear Readers,

Do we have news for you! Rumor has it that Republican candidate Stephen James has more serious worries on his mind than the Senate race. We hear that his lovely wife, Nina, and a certain tall, dark, and disturbingly handsome communications director are, shall we say, close? You've seen the pictures right here on our pages; you know what we're sayin'. As that old country song goes, they "laugh just a little too loud, stand just a little too close...stare just a little too long..." They definitely give us something to talk about!

—The Daily Howl, *"Something to Talk About"*

Stephen didn't think of himself as a jealous man. Jealousy implied insecurity, which, in turn, implied a lack of confidence. His confidence bordered on arrogance, which many people found off-putting. But he had to admit to himself that it was jealousy that he felt at the moment.

It was ironic, because Nina was usually the butt of his green-eyed-monster jokes. If she saw him talking to another woman for longer than what *she* thought was necessary, she'd get all huffy. Recently, his campaign had attracted a gaggle of socialites who were keen to fund-raise for him. He'd made it a point to take Nina with him to all such events, but it irked her anyway. "Man, they are all over you," she'd complain. "I bet they wonder why you married me." Even the female interns and volunteers in his campaign would occasionally get a vetting from her. And old girlfriends! Mere mention of one would have smoke coming out of her ears. She had no sense of humor when it came to this topic.

Stephen was surprised at his own irritation. Tyler's website had done an outstanding job of posting pictures of Nina and Wasim together, catching them in animated conversation while Stephen stood apart, talking to someone else or simply looking away. The two looked like a natural couple. Tyler had doubled down on the innuendo and sleaze after Stephen had taken him to task for the Wasim-terrorist story.

Stephen looked across the room at Wasim sitting at his desk, glued to the phone as usual. In addition to his own load, Wasim was filling in for Doug, who was away in Washington wrangling money out of the

Republican Party. Even in the cluttered office, leaning back in his chair and flipping a pen in one hand, Wasim had a Bollywood hero's dashing style and charismatic good looks.

Nina and Wasim shared an effortless kinship, breaking into Hindi to discuss old movie songs. Or they'd talk of childhoods spent navigating feelings of otherness, of mangled names and cruel playground taunts—a world that was totally alien to Stephen. Whenever Nina dropped by the campaign office, she'd spend at least ten minutes chatting with Wasim. They'd be laughing and talking in no time, resuming where they'd left off without missing a beat. No woman could resist the obvious admiration Wasim felt and showed for Nina.

Just two days earlier, Nina had come to the guesthouse to meet Stephen. They were to attend a wedding in Boston. She was dressed in a sari made of a diaphanous pink material that clung to every curve. Surprising, because her normal style was severe and buttoned-down, just like Stephen's. But in that sari, she was a different creature altogether. Subtle silver sequins on her blouse sparkled with the rise and fall of her breath. The same blouse left bare a smooth expanse of her golden back and drew attention to a slender waist that hadn't yet felt the pull of the pregnancy.

Every male eye in the room had taken note, at least briefly, Wasim, most of all. His eyes lit up, and he had walked up to her to compliment her lavishly. Since then, Stephen's annoyance burned like a hot blade whenever he saw the two of them together.

Recently, to add to Stephen's suspicions, Wasim and Nina had been talking on the phone quite a bit. Which was odd, because she hated being on the phone with anyone other than her mother or Stephen. E-mail me, she'd tell those who wanted to get in touch. But now, she always took Wasim's calls and spoke earnestly at length. "I am helping him with a personal matter," she'd said in the briefest attempt at explanation. Stephen was too proud to ask for details, and she didn't volunteer any.

That was the other odd thing. She was incapable of keeping anything from Stephen, consumed by guilt at the most trivial violation of her strict code of propriety, a trait he found most endearing. But in the matter of Wasim, she offered no confessions or explanations.

Not that she hid anything from him. Her phone was everywhere, a constant temptation—in the bathroom, by the bedside, on the coffee table, and occasionally in his pocket, if she didn't have her handbag with her. One day, he couldn't stand it anymore and scrolled through her phone. Several calls to Wasim each day but no text messages. What the fuck did they talk about? He was so irritated he became snippy with Nina all morning, the whole distant, stiff-upper-lip deal.

She doesn't deserve it, he thought now, suddenly full of remorse. She is the gentlest and kindest of all people. His eyes fell on the clock on the wall. It was getting late, but if he hurried, he could get home before Nina went to bed. He rushed through his last three calls, grabbed his jacket, and went into the common area where Wasim sat.

"Good night, Wasim. I'll see you tomorrow."

"Good night, Stephen." Wasim looked up in surprise. The boss had been moody the last two days, just short of growling at him. Every morning, Doug and Wasim would wager on which Stephen would show up, Jekyll or Hyde. Stephen had been exceedingly supportive during the whole terrorist-accusation period, but once that crisis was over, he had relapsed into his old moods.

Stephen drove into the night, trying to think of a florist who'd be open this late. He remembered his friend, the horticulturist, whose greenhouses had stayed afloat because of Stephen's discreet infusion of funds a few years ago. A quick call to him and the flowers were ready for pickup. He collected them and, after a brief chat with the horticulturist, headed home. On the way back, he nearly ran out of gas and pulled into a pump to fill up.

Just as he was about to exit the gas station, a familiar car zipped past, with Wasim at the wheel. Without conscious thought, out of years and years of habit, Stephen slipped into traffic behind him. It seemed like the most obvious thing to do.

Through the central part of town, down the main drag, Wasim sped. By the water, over the bridge, across the plaza, beyond to where the mansions sprawled in the next town, and past the mansions, then back down to the water and on and on to a scenic walk on a cliff's edge that overlooked the crashing water below.

Wasim parked the car on the street in a metered slot. He locked it and walked with quick, long strides toward the scenic walk.

Stephen parked as well, just around the bend. He swapped his jacket for a sweat shirt and put on a baseball cap. He got out of the car and ran until he caught sight of Wasim and then trailed him at a decent distance. There was really no reason to follow Wasim, but it was an old occupational instinct to act on aberrations.

Wasim sprinted up stone steps and hurried along the narrow walk. The streetlamps shed enough light to see the path but not much more. A high tide pounded the rocks below.

Wasim maintained a brisk pace up the steep gradient, shooting glances over his shoulder. There were people milling around, even at that late hour, dog walkers and night joggers, and Wasim seemed not to notice Stephen.

Where was Wasim headed so late at night? Why was he in this strange town so far from home? Stephen was more curious than concerned.

The path soon widened into a broad ledge with tiered seating to admire the view. Wasim stopped, dusted off one of the benches, and sat down. He smoothed his hair, straightened his shirt, and adjusted his pants. Then, he sat back and stretched out his long arms along the back of the bench.

It was a love tryst! For a mad, mad instant, Stephen's mind rushed to the unthinkable—Nina. Wasim was waiting for Nina! No, no, he cursed his own twisted mind.

He pushed through the overgrown hedge on his right, which separated the path from the palatial estate behind, and squeezed into the gap between the hedge and the wrought-iron fence that guarded the property. Stephen waited there, his imagination running in a thousand different directions, all of which ended with the same conclusion: Nina in Wasim's arms. He had a good view of the young man sitting below. Wasim stared impatiently farther up the path, waiting for his lover, marking the passage of minutes with anxious jabs at his phone.

Stephen's throat tightened. He knew that it couldn't be Nina, because she was at home. On most days, she waited until ten for him before she had dinner. But maybe she had set up this tryst because Stephen had said he'd be late.

But then, Wasim had seen him leave, so he would have warned her.

Stop it, Stephen yelled at himself. Here was a woman wise enough to stop talking to her male friends because she realized that it bothered him, and she did it ungrudgingly. He never acknowledged it, but he knew that she had done it for him, to keep his insecurity in check and his ego intact. But the ghosts of the past were hard to exorcise, and his father's death had forever cast a shadow over his relationships. In Nina, he had found his perfect mate, a woman with old-fashioned notions of propriety, with an intense, childlike attachment to him, and, best of all, with the brains and intellect to keep him challenged. Don't screw it up, he warned himself now.

Wasim stood up. Stephen looked into the darkness to see who was coming. A small figure carrying a bag had just come into sight. Before Stephen could make out who it was, the person ran to Wasim with outstretched arms, to be scooped up and kissed.

"Son of a bitch," Stephen muttered in amazement when he recognized Doug. He turned around and walked slowly to his car. Once inside, he carefully shut the door, threw his cap in the backseat, and burst out laughing. His much-lauded instincts had definitely grown rusty. His campaign manager and communications director were getting it on right under his nose, and he hadn't a clue!

He drove home humming. He was a terrible singer, but the relief and sheer happiness he felt demanded release.

He parked in the secure garage at home and took the small elevator that went directly to the master suite, located on the top floor of the Victorian mansion. A sprawling bedroom spanned the side of the house that faced the ocean, opening onto a wide balcony that paralleled the porch below. It overlooked the terrace, garden, and Bay. A huge office took up the opposite half of the top floor and watched over the front of the property. It housed Stephen's workshop, where he tinkered with mysterious gizmos and electronic-surveillance toys.

The elevator was the only access to the top floor, other than a secret staircase that only he, Nina, and a handful of others knew of. When he'd renovated the mansion last year, he had gutted the insides and built the spacious, airy rooms that Nina wanted and installed his proprietary supersecure electronic gadgetry to keep her safe. The elevator dinged, and let him out on the interior, circular balcony.

"Nina!" he called on his way to the bedroom. He was glad to pull off his tie after almost sixteen hours.

"You're home!" she sang from somewhere in the living area of the master suite. She hardly got to see him these days. On most nights, he came home after midnight and fell into bed, exhausted, without the energy to even eat.

"Yes." He found her on the sofa, watching TV, and gave her the flowers, her favorite, stargazers.

"Oooh, lovely."

She took them and inhaled their heady fragrance. The flowers were their secret peacemaking weapon, with a magical ability to transport them to the night he had showed up at her apartment in Jersey City, unannounced, the night he had decided that she was the key to his happiness.

Nina followed him into the bedroom and put the flowers in a vase on her ornate side table. The huge canopy bed and its accessories had belonged to Grandpa James and were the only furniture that Stephen had kept after the renovation. Whole rooms of chairs, tables, sofas, and other flotsam and jetsam accumulated by his forbears were carted away by charities before the interior was demolished. He had given everything away without as much as a look.

"It's your heritage, your history, your connection to your childhood. You'll regret it," Nina had said.

"Screw my childhood," he had replied.

He changed into his pajamas and went back to the living room. The TV was still on. It was blaring an episode of *Chopped*, where a geoduck was being eviscerated. Nina refused to watch any other channel, because Team Collins had flooded the airwaves with anti-Stephen ads. Nina couldn't stand it. "They are lying," she'd say indignantly, like a child, and quickly change the channel. She had finally settled on Food Network as the only safe haven.

He switched to ESPN and picked up the bowl from which she had been eating dinner.

"Why the flowers?" she asked.

"Just felt like it," he replied and started to eat. "This is delicious! Ma sent it?" he asked.

"You're in a good mood! What gives?" she said.

He had been brusque the past few days. She had pleaded—"What can I do, Stephen, if Tyler posts those pictures? You know the truth, don't you? Wasim is a friend, that's all."

Normally, she'd have stopped talking to whoever was the cause of Stephen's petulance. Not because she was afraid of Stephen but because she knew the reason for that raw bruise on his heart.

He had told her his family's story with unexpected candor, a week after they were married, in perhaps the longest conversation they'd ever had. She had slipped into bed next to him that night, and he had turned to her and begun without preamble:

My mother and father gave me away to my grand-father the minute I was born. She and my father never got along. She was unfaithful to him almost as soon as they were married. I was unplanned, unwanted. I grew up with my grandfather, and I hardly knew my parents or siblings.

When I was fifteen years old, my father killed himself by jumping off his yacht, his precious golf clubs strapped to his chest. His business partner's wife had caught my mother in bed with her husband. There was no sweeping it under the rug anymore.

My grandfather was inconsolable. My father was his only child. He was furious at my moth-er, and he disinherited her and her two older children, my siblings, whom he publicly called bastards, whom he never acknowledged as his son's children. My mother and my two siblings fled the country.

My grandfather was all I had. He took me everywhere with him, anytime I was out of school. He taught me how to ride a bike, how to ride a horse; he taught me how to sail, how to shoot, how to tie my tie. He died a year after my father.

Nina had listened with her entire being, soaking up his feelings like a sponge. He had seemed so young and vulnerable, lying on his grandfather's extravagant, plush bed, like a shipwrecked child adrift in the vast ocean.

"You must be bored," he'd said when he was finally done with his long recounting of family history. She wasn't bored at all; she'd wanted to familiarize herself with every nook of his lonely life, because she had sensed the depth of his sadness during their very first meeting.

He had smiled at her. "I am in your hands now. Do what you want with me. I am tired of being in charge, being responsible, running the show, planning, doing, striving, struggling, being in control. I am tired. I need rest, and I need you to take charge of me," he'd said.

And she had taken charge of him, with an overwhelming sense of responsibility and commitment. He hadn't made it easy. In the early weeks of their marriage, his moods had been a constant challenge for her.

Anything could send him into a brooding fit—hunger, tiredness, impatience, or things not going the way he had planned. A big part of being with him had been learning to manage those moods and calm him down and realizing that they were not directed at her. She either ignored them or, when her understanding ran out, snapped at him to stop it. Then they'd both go into a sulk until one of them, usually him, decided to end it and make up.

But this Wasim-related spell had been particularly difficult. She could have gone to stay with her parents for a while, but she knew that he needed her more than he realized or admitted. She couldn't abandon him. And at the same time, she couldn't abandon Wasim, who was in deep trouble. He was like Neel, a kid brother. He had turned to her for help while he figured out how to navigate his new love and how to confess it to his parents.

She was about to tell Stephen the matter with Wasim when he interrupted her. "I know your secret," he said.

"I don't have any," she retorted.

They'd played this game before. In the beginning, she would naïvely try to list all the secrets she could think of, much to his amusement. After the first couple of times, she'd wised up.

She sat down next to him and took her bowl back. Her body was getting ready for the baby and demanded to be fed.

"I know your Wasim secret and the personal stuff you've been advising him on." He put his arm around her waist and kissed her neck. She was warm and soft and smelled of roses.

She pushed him away. "Well, now you know why I couldn't tell you."

"Why not?"

"Because it's *his* secret. You are his *boss*. It has consequences."

"I think you should have told me. There should be no secrets between us."

"Oh, really?" She laughed angrily and continued to eat, simmering at all the secrets he'd kept, more dangerous and personal ones that affected them both, important ones that he'd conveniently forgotten to mention when he'd suggested that they get married.

Thanks to *his* secrets, their marriage had almost collapsed before the six-month anniversary. When she thought back to that moment, when they had fled New Delhi an inch ahead of death and he had confessed his true vocation to her, Nina's heart still ached. In one instant, her bright, happy world had disappeared. She'd felt stranded, in bed with a stranger, in an unknown, dark, and dangerous land without a map, without a flashlight, afraid to take a step, lest she fall off the edge of a cliff into an unseen chasm.

A lot had happened since then, including many acts of fierce and reckless devotion on Stephen's part. But he could never erase the fact that he had not told her the truth when he had asked her to marry him. And she'd never forgiven him for that, and during times of stress, all that resentment made its way to the surface.

"Nina! Look at that pass!" Stephen nudged her and sat up to watch the replay. The ESPN commentator was shouting himself hoarse.

Nina looked up from her bowl and turned to him with big, accusing eyes.

"What?" he asked, taking her spoon and beginning to eat. He loved his mother-in-law's *khichdi*, fragrant with basmati rice, ghee, and cilantro, studded with vegetables in jewel tones—carrots, yellow peppers, and peas. Nina was used to this habit of his and involuntarily filled her bowl with more food than necessary, even when he wasn't around.

"Nothing." She turned away.

He continued to eat and watched a bunch of men pile on top of each other, scrabbling for the football.

After stewing for a few minutes, she got it out. "Stephen, it bugs me that you don't trust me in this Wasim matter. How—"

"I'm sorry," he interrupted.

She stopped midsentence. Apologies were rare and seldom offered at this stage in an argument. Usually, it was after a major crisis, where he'd recklessly put either one or both of them in danger and caused some harm.

"I'm sorry to have been such a pain in the ass."

She looked away, embarrassed and moved at the same time, close to tears. "No need for apologies," she mumbled.

She had been working long, demanding days, trying to get the foundation set up and functioning before the baby arrived, meeting lawyers and trustees in order to complete the legal work he had off-loaded on her when he started running for the Senate. And now he was never around, out on the road constantly, campaigning and fund-raising, rallying volunteers and whatnot.

She missed him terribly. His grouchiness the past few days had made her feel utterly lonely, all alone in that big mansion, but she was too loyal to discuss it with anyone, even her mother. All the stress and bottled-up emotion of the past few days conspired with surging hormones and pushed the tears down her cheeks. She tried desperately to quell them.

He felt awful. She was not a crier, surprisingly tough for a girl from a sheltered, coddled background—perhaps that's what gave her the inner strength. Even during their worst arguments, she'd either clam up in anger or haughtily walk out of the room.

He bent down and looked into her face. "C'mon, Nina, where's that lovely smile?"

It was an old trick of his, to pander shamelessly when she was angry, perfected during the early years of their marriage. It still worked.

INTRIGUE ON THE TRAIL

Collins
Experience Matters

Katherine Collins @kathycollins . Sep 27
Mr. James, please tell your party that climate change is for real!

The brainchild of a rock-star architect, it was an eccentric building with planes and surfaces that intersected at unexpected angles. Inside, it housed a secret research hub of the premier engineering institution in the country.

Stephen looked at the building with longing. That was where Bay State Consulting, his engineering company, was located. That was where he'd love to be, surrounded by fellow engineers, heatedly discussing the intricacies of video imaging and face recognition.

Instead, he was headed to his former professor's home for a fund-raiser. His campaign crew was with him. The team was making stops along the way to attend a few smaller events. They were almost done, except for the fund-raiser, which was still a few hours away, but Doug and Wasim claimed that there wasn't enough time for him to make a brief stop at his lab.

His phone pinged, and up popped a text from Neel: *Need to talk.*

"I've to take a break," Stephen announced firmly to forestall any debate. "Drop me off at that corner."

Doug frowned. "Not now! We are scheduled to meet the mayor before the fund-raiser. He is going to endorse us!"

"Stall. I'll be back in an hour." Despite Doug's tight-lipped sulking, Stephen stepped out of the car and closed the door behind him.

The cool, fresh air chased away the hectic monotony of the day. He took a deep, invigorating breath and walked across the quad to the lab where Neel was. The familiar smell of rotting autumn leaves mingled with the garlicky aroma of pizza from nearby food pits. It brought back memories of exams and all-nighters. The intervening decades had invested even those grief-ridden college years with a mellow glow of nostalgia.

Glass doors guarded the building's three-story-high foyer. He passed through the stylish lobby and down a long hallway to a thick steel door at the very end. Long-ingrained muscle memory sent his fingers flying on the security panel, and the door opened on smooth hinges.

The lab's bright interior came as a pleasant surprise after the opaque steel door. An undulating, candy-hued paper dragon hung from the ceiling, bobbing over the heads of the young scientists toiling beneath. It fluttered whenever the air ducts sent a blast of turbulence its way. Toys, juggling balls, bowling pins, scooters, and other techno-hipster paraphernalia lay scattered. The inhabitants themselves came in many shapes, colors, and forms, enslaved by a multitude of monitors.

Stephen looked around for Neel. Some of the old-timers recognized Stephen and nodded. His engineering company had a share in this joint venture between the Department of Defense, MIT, and smaller research outfits. His presence and visits had declined steadily ever since he'd gotten married, and now that he had handed over his company's management to Neel, he hadn't made an appearance in months.

Neel spotted Stephen and emerged from his pod, where he had been setting up a camera configuration for 3-D video. He waved to Stephen and glided down the hallway on a strange contraption, a cross between an ATV and a hovercraft.

He came to rest next to Stephen and grinned. "You should see it at night. It's amazing. Good job with the design, Stephen!"

"Thanks!" Stephen looked at it admiringly, with envy even. "It's come a long way since the last time I saw it."

Neel and his team had pushed it way beyond what Stephen had designed. He was really intrigued, but it would have to wait.

"Let's step outside," he said, with a twinge of regret for having given up his engineering pursuits.

Neel parked the curious vehicle along the wall near the end of the hallway and grabbed a sweat shirt from a stand draped with coats and jackets. The October air outside was uncharacteristically chilly. He peeped over the shoulder-high wall of a cubicle and said to the unseen occupant that he'd be back soon and was rewarded with a mumble.

Neel was a typical twentysomething, dressed in jeans, feet ablaze in trendy lime-green sneakers. With his slender runner's build, dark, piercing eyes, and thick black hair that was never allowed to grow beyond half an inch, he exuded a careless coolness.

When he first met Stephen, he'd wondered why Nina wanted to marry this uptight, humorless guy who looked so much older than her. There had been plenty of Indian American men circling Nina. He'd always expected that she would marry one of them and make their parents happy, while he, Neel, would be the one to incur their disapproval with some exotic choice.

The speed with which the two had gotten hitched had shocked Neel even more. Nina was usually very cautious and circumspect in such matters. To his relief, from what he had observed during his first visit to the home of the newlyweds, Stephen had genuine regard and affection for Nina. Subsequent visits had convinced Neel that they were truly happy. Stephen would go out of his way to make Neel feel welcome, and Neel had been thrilled to see his older sister, his hero, look so radiant. Over time, his admiration for Stephen grew—how deeply and carefully he thought about matters, how clearly and precisely he articulated them!

Stephen too had grown fond of Neel, because Neel was a lot like Nina—bright, good-natured, and happy, only sillier. He had watched Neel evolve from a carefree undergrad to a capable and surprisingly deliberate young man.

The two men shared an unorthodox relationship. Both were engineers with a rabid interest in sports. And, in a strange turn of events, Stephen was directly responsible for Neel's brief flirtation with the CIA.

The present situation was a mutually convenient arrangement. Neel enjoyed building and designing new technologies. His stint at the Agency had been quite tumultuous. It included three brief but explosive adventures in as many years. The final straw came when he'd smuggled his informant's kid sister out of Pakistan to a US base in Afghanistan. The informant was dead, and Neel had promised to take care of the girl, who had already been shot at twice by the Taliban. Neel's handler had complained to George Applegate, who had promptly grounded Neel and posted him behind a desk in Virginia. Neel was only too happy to quit when Stephen asked him to help out.

Neel had become somewhat of a philosopher and ethicist during his three years at the Agency. Stephen glanced at Neel, walking next to him, and smiled at how much he had changed. He was glad of Neel's access, skills, and sympathetic ear. It was a relief to be close to someone who had walked in his shoes. Nina would never understand.

They crossed the busy quad and headed toward the Charles River. The trees were a dazzling palette of gold and rust, with leaves ready to swoon at the first gust of wind.

"How's Nina doing?" Neel asked. Unlike their parents, he had known about Nina's earlier miscarriage and had been her rock during those months when Stephen and she had found it too difficult to talk to each other about it.

"She's well. I think we are safe now, second trimester."

They walked across the Harvard Bridge, dodging the evening dinner crowds. The two men made for an interesting sight. One was pale and formal, in a flawless suit and impeccable shoes, striding straight-backed, while the other was dressed in a sweat shirt and jeans, with the rolling gait of studied casualness favored by the hip. People turned and stared briefly, but Stephen was hard to place, safe behind the anonymity of his sunglasses.

They stopped when they reached the midway point on the bridge. Neel rested his foot on the railing and stretched. He was a runner and a soccer player. Stretching was something he did without even thinking. Stephen draped his overcoat on the beam and leaned on it to look down into the dark, rippling water below.

Stephen had stood in that exact spot so many times during his bleak college years in the wake of his grandfather's death. It was also the spot where, toward the end of Stephen's senior year, George Applegate, his professor and mentor, had broached the subject of Stephen working for the CIA.

Two rowing crews emerged abruptly from beneath the bridge. The rowboats cut through the water like twin blades. Soon the crew's calls faded as they sped away. The sight pleased Stephen immensely. It was a treat to get away from those two campaign maniacs and retreat to the peace and calm of his favorite setting, the water.

"What's up? Why did you send me that text?" Stephen's gaze, as usual, drifted to a tiny scar close to the hairline above Neel's left temple. It was almost imperceptible, but it was a magnet to Stephen's guilty eyes. He was the reason for Neel's scar, acquired while trying to drag a wounded Stephen out of an ambush.

"Remember you'd asked me to check on Tyler?"

"Yes?"

Neel grinned. "He has a new lady friend."

"Anyone we know?"

"Not really, but I can get in touch with her. She works for a swanky escort service. I'm sure she'll cooperate."

A pretty Indian girl walked by and said hello to Neel. Stephen watched with interest while they had a brief conversation. Nina kept Stephen abreast of Neel's complicated romantic life.

"New girlfriend?" he asked after the girl left, unintroduced.

"No!" Neel answered a little too quickly. "Don't believe everything Nina tells you." He frowned at the river below. "Getting back to Tyler, he's circling the CIA angle."

"Really?" Stephen gave a short laugh. "I'm impressed. I didn't think he had the balls. How do you know?"

"Because I read his e-mails." He showed his phone to Stephen. "Look."

Jimmy! You promised to check on former colleagues of BS. I need some names soon. —D

"BS?" Stephen's eyebrows rose.

"Big Shit. That's what he calls you." Neel found that very funny and broke into a burst of deep chuckles that made people around turn to look and smile in response.

People were drawn to him easily. That was why Stephen had always thought that Neel would make a great recruit, but Nina would've killed him if he had tried. Neel had excellent powers of observation and recollection. And he picked up languages without effort.

During Nina and Stephen's Indian wedding ceremony, Neel had entertained Stephen with an incessant stream of gossip and impressions of the guests in at least four different languages and accents. He had caught the eye of the big man, George Applegate, who had been in attendance with his wife, Ginnie, as Stephen's sole invitees. Despite Stephen's protests, George had lured Neel to intern at the Agency and had offered full employment after his graduation.

"By the way, did George have anything to do with leaking the report on Wasim's childhood visits to Pakistan? It seems like a coincidence that it happened just when my campaign was flatlining."

Neel smiled but didn't say anything.

"Tell him to keep his hands off my campaign. I don't need his help, and I am not going to be his fricking Manchurian candidate." Stephen knew Neel was close to George, even though their official relationship had been terminated. Not that it was bad; it was certainly a valuable connection to have.

Neel changed the subject diplomatically. "What do you want to do about Tyler? George is worried he might uncover the Sid Ali episode. If you don't do something, I am sure George will."

Just then, Neel's phone rang. It was Nina.

"Hey, Neenz! What's up?"

Stephen gave him a worried look—*Is she OK; is there a problem?*

"I am standing here with your beloved. He stopped by to say hello."

Neel listened for a while and then said, "OK, I'll tell him. Bye."

"Your minions have complained to her that you disappeared and left your phone behind on purpose. They want you back, pronto."

Neel put away his phone and hooked his thumbs in the pockets of his jeans. "How about I mess with Tyler's credit cards, hack his accounts, and listen in on his calls?"

"Not a bad idea." Stephen watched the water set aripple once more by a rowboat skimming its surface. "Just watch. Don't do anything—that should be enough for now; we don't want to make it too obvious. We'll figure out what to do with him after the election."

Neel nodded.

"Could you do it without leaving a trace?"

"I'll take care of it." Neel bent down and tightened his shoelaces, ready to leave.

"Be careful. He is pretty savvy." Stephen picked up his overcoat. "I'll walk back with you. Doug and Wasim must be apoplectic by now."

"How's that going?" Neel couldn't imagine his sister as Mrs. Senator.

"We have a good shot."

They arrived at the lab in a few short minutes. When they got to the building, Stephen was reluctant to say good-bye.

"What?" Neel had worked with Stephen in the field for two years and understood his body language and cues almost as well as Nina, if not better.

"I don't know," Stephen replied. "I don't know about all this." He made a sweeping gesture with his hands. "But Nina and I are convinced that this is the right thing to do." He stared at Neel. "I hope we don't step into more shit. We've barely recovered from the disasters of the last five years."

If Nina was the muse of Stephen's better nature and catalyzed all that was warm and tender in him, Neel was the navigator of his subterranean world, cutting through existential clutter and sorting out thorny ethical conundrums. Stephen had prided himself on this very trait, but recently things were less clear. Nina was eroding some of his most cherished, long-held beliefs with her peacenik ways.

"It'll be fine," Neel said. "In fact, if you are a senator, they'll be more cautious about messing with you. Too high profile. You'll have a security squad; I am sure. Don't worry."

Stephen's SUV drove up and haughtily flashed its lights from across the road.

"Neel, do you mind picking up Nina and bringing her to the fund-raiser? She doesn't want to come, but she's been on her own too much lately. You'll be able to convince her."

"Sure. I'll call her and tell her I'll be coming to pick her up."

He watched Stephen cross the road and get in the car and be immediately besieged by the staff. It was time for him to leave as well. It would take him more than an hour to drive to his sister's place.

TYLER'S MOVE

A slickly edited video, accompanied by an up-tempo piano, shows a fancy fund-raiser. Stephen and Nina are seen seated at a long, elaborately set table glittering with silverware and sparkling champagne flutes. A bevy of formally dressed waiters begins to serve dinner. The image dissolves slowly into a black-and-white photo of two hungry children foraging in a Dumpster. A woman says in a sad, weary voice, "How would he understand our pain?"

—TV ad, "Silver Spoon," Team Collins

The singer was gorgeous, with graceful caramel limbs and a halo of frizzy hair, swaying in a flowing black halter-neck dress slit well above her knee. Dramatic diamond earrings dangled and swayed against her swanlike neck. She plucked at a bass and filled the room with a plaintive song.

The mood was perfectly in sync with Tyler's spirits. He looked at his glass—it was empty. He caught the bartender's eye. She responded with a fresh drink and a bowl of peanuts. "Go easy," she said with a smile. "It's early." He shook his head and got back to contemplating his drink.

What happened, he wondered. His fame and success had proved to be amazingly short-lived, even in Twitter time. The public had lost interest in *The Daily Howl*, flocking instead to Stephen's official home page, which had suddenly become very chatty.

Stephen's campaign had hired a top-notch publicity team that turned the stodgy website into a hip, glitzy, hyperconnected hub bursting with multimedia. It had every new, shiny gimmick known to the Twitter world. The site was updated frequently and packed with vaguely personal factoids about Stephen, interspersed with Massachusetts trivia. Stephen's interview with the news anchor Sean was posted prominently, with little snippets popping up at unsuspecting readers—Stephen "Hi, sweethearting" his wife or staring into the camera and warning sternly about consequences to unfounded accusations.

Without tips from his readers and their Stephen-sighting photos, Tyler soon ran out of material and momentum.

Meanwhile, prominent members of both political parties had condemned the tabloid's allegations against Wasim Raja. The senior senator from Wasim's home state of Michigan took to the Senate floor and defended Wasim in the strongest possible words, calling *The Daily Howl* craven and irresponsible. The Collins campaign completely dropped Tyler and his tabloid from their publicity material.

Tyler drooped over his drink. What he desperately needed now was a scoop, a shocker, something terrible, something awful that would make the world sit up and restore him to his Internet top-dog glory. Even *he* was sick of *The Daily Howl* rehashing the same material over and over—privileged Stephen, disconnected from common man, activist wife, the Wasim-Nina "friendship." It had become very blah.

A girl came in through the front door of the club and sat down next to him at the bar. She looked Middle Eastern. She ordered a drink. He nudged the bowl of peanuts toward her with a smile. She beamed back. Wow, perhaps he wasn't completely out of luck. Don't be pushy, he told himself. Dial it down. They exchanged smiles; she sipped her drink.

"May I buy you a drink?" he said after a few minutes of encouraging silence. She glanced at the front door and then cut him off with an arctic look. He turned back to his drink, red-faced and resentful. She placed a ten-dollar bill under her glass, gave him another nasty look, jumped off the stool, and rushed to the front door. A young man had appeared there. The two kissed and walked out hand in hand.

Crazy bitch! Tyler swiveled back to the counter. The bartender cleared the girl's drink and brought fresh peanuts for Tyler.

He longed for Ashley's company. The last few days had been mind-numbingly boring and lonely without her lusty embrace. He texted her. *Are you back from your trip?*

Ping! *Yes*, came the immediate reply.

Meet me at The Grasshopper, he texted and sat back, tingling with anticipation.

The singer switched to more experimental fare, emitting birdlike coos and yips. She sliced the air with a bejeweled finger to mark each staccato note.

Meanwhile, his grilled cheese arrived, all fragrant and gooey, buried under a mountain of fries with a pickle perched on top. His stomach rumbled in response to the heavenly aroma of bread crisped to a golden brown by hot butter. He bit into it and eyed the barstool where the girl had sat. Something white lay wedged between the stool and the footrail. He leaned over precariously and pulled it out. A rolled-up newspaper! He opened it and was met by the stern countenance of Mr. Stephen James. According to the news item, the candidate was on his way to DC to address Young Republicans at a party shindig the next day.

That was his cue to get back to work. He pulled out his laptop from the backpack and set it on the counter.

While it booted, he gulped down his grilled cheese and asked for a coffee.

"Coming right up," the bartender answered.

Tyler nodded politely at her and returned to his screen to try, for the hundredth time, to find dirt on Stephen and his campaign team. Information was scarce, except for a few routine hits: Stephen's official web page, the Edward James Foundation for Women home page, public events, fund-raisers, the campaign Twitter feed—but nothing personal other than harmless nuggets, like "Mr. James loves spending the weekends hiking with his wife," and "Mrs. James spoke at a shelter for battered women." The vast Internet was devoid of any information, as if a rangy spider had scrubbed it clean. It probably had, in the shape of America's premier intelligence agency.

The bartender brought his coffee. She was not his type, almost a foot taller than him, but she seemed like a pleasant sort. Occupational necessity, he thought cynically.

Tyler opened the file he had compiled on Stephen. All it had was a brief account of the armed robbery that Stephen had interrupted at his neighbor's home around four years ago. According to Tyler's conversations with reluctant locals, Stephen was badly injured in that shootout, and the neighbor had disappeared subsequently.

However, there was a more interesting vein to the story, a vein of information that Tyler was reluctant to mine, afraid of tangling with the CIA.

One of Tyler's Indian friends, a former colleague at the chip-design company, had returned to India a few years ago, infected by the start-up itch. He had read about Stephen and his Senate run on Tyler's website, and written a note to Tyler: *Dave, I think your candidate is a CIA agent. He ran into some trouble here in India but it has been hushed up. I'll see if I can find some old newspaper cuttings. But check it out if you can—circa three years ago!*

Tyler looked at his computer without much hope. There was no evidence of any of this on the Internet. The Indian embassy had replied to Tyler's queries with a terse "No comment." Tyler had a vague memory of some altercation involving a CIA agent in India, but there were so many of those—the CIA and its contract employees were constantly testing legal boundaries all over the world. The newspapers that had published those articles had long ago scrubbed them from their archives and were very cagey. They did not respond to Tyler's calls or release the names of the reporters behind the stories. Stonewalling all around.

To clear his head and wile away the time until Ashley arrived, Tyler worked out a timeline on his napkin:

Oct. 2009:	*Stephen marries Nina*
Apr. 2010:	*Armed robbery at Sid Ali's in Massachusetts; Ali disappears; S is injured*
Nov. 2011*:	*Runs into trouble in India—suspected of CIA connection*

Mar. 2013:	*Buys the Ali property*
Apr. 2013:	*S. announces Edward William James Foundation for Women and appoints Nina as director*
Aug. 2014:	*Enters the Senate race in a special election*

*Need official corroboration

Tyler sighed and looked up from his list. The singer's warbling was a distraction. He folded the napkin and put it inside his bag.

Where was Mr. Ali now? Where was his family? Curiously, Stephen had since purchased that property from Mrs. Ali (according to public records). Mary Connor Ali was the sole owner of the property. There was no mention of her husband in any of the public records. The former Ali property was now a part of the guesthouse complex adjoining Stephen's impregnable compound.

Tyler could attest to the impenetrability of the James fortress. He and his friend Jimmy had walked by it several times when Tyler was looking to rent a house in the neighborhood. The James residence was set deep inside the property, far away from the road, enclosed, except along the waterfront, by a ten-foot-high concrete wall. It could be breached only through a solid metal gate overseen by conspicuous cameras.

Tyler picked up the phone and dialed Jimmy. His friend had parted ways with the Collins campaign after Tyler's Wasim-terrorist report and returned to DC to resume his lobbying gig. He was now an investor in *The Daily Howl.*

"Hi, Jimmy. How's it going? Have you got any names for me?"

Jimmy laughed. He and Tyler went back decades. He wasn't offended by Tyler's hectoring. "Soon, very soon. But be careful with him." They had decided not to mention Stephen by name, just in case.

"I know you think I'm crazy, but look at the man's home! Even the White House doesn't have such security…I don't think. What's he hiding from?"

Lore had it that the glass used in the James mansion during an extensive renovation was all bullet-proof: French doors, windows, skylights, and even the atrium were all redone with the new glass. The house had electronic security beyond belief—sensors, cameras, voice- and biometric-recognition locks, image- and pattern-matching technology that scrutinized every visitor to the house.

"Don't you wonder what demons drive this guy to such paranoid fancies?" Tyler demanded.

Jimmy just grunted in reply. When Tyler got obsessed, there was no reasoning with him.

Under the guise of Tyler's hunt for a rental home, Tyler and Jimmy had checked out the water-facing boundary of the James property as well. The estate stood out, even among the homes of indescribable beauty and opulence that surrounded it. A thick layer of trees shielded the house from inquisitive eyes.

But small gaps in the woods revealed glimpses of a lush garden and a wide terrace leading up to a majestic Victorian mansion. There was more than a five-hundred-foot stretch of waterfront, punctuated with warnings of underwater sensors and cameras and of dire consequences for trespassing.

"The man's dock looks straight out of a Bond villain's den!" Tyler couldn't even imagine such wealth. He came from a comfortable, middle-class family, the second of three boys, but he had to pay for his college education by working and taking loans. He had made a good living at his former job, but he could never afford to own even a tiny, little shack in this tony neighborhood—unless he could kick up a story of monstrous proportions.

"Jimmy, don't you think there's a big story here? What's this guy all about? He's running for the US Senate. We, the people, have the right to know."

Tyler had tried contacting the James siblings and Stephen's mother. The brother lived in Berlin and had not responded. The sister was a businesswoman based in London. She too had ignored Tyler's mail. Stephen's mother, who had remarried and settled in Crete, had her secretary send Tyler a curt reply: *Mrs. Nikolaos has not been in contact with her youngest son, Stephen Edward James, in over two and a half decades. She regrets that she can be of no assistance.*

"Dave, Dave, listen to me." Jimmy had to put the brakes on. Gossip and smut were standard publishing gimmicks, but the CIA was a different game altogether. "This is the CIA!"

"Maybe I'll have to go underground. I'll turn into a cult figure, like Assange or Snowden!" Tyler chuckled.

"It's no joke, Dave. I'll call as soon as I get the names," Jimmy said. "Don't do anything crazy in the meantime."

Tyler had been a good friend to Jimmy in high school, when Jimmy's parents had divorced in a very public fashion. Tyler had harbored Jimmy in his bedroom for an entire academic year. Without that support, Jimmy probably would have dropped out of school.

"Bye, Dave." Jimmy hung up.

Tyler was annoyed at his buddy's lack of enthusiasm. But he had very few options at this point.

The front door opened, and Ashley stood framed for a glorious instant. She knew how to dress and how to make an entrance, all blond hair and long legs, in a short black skirt and hot-pink top. Tyler noticed with pride that all the men had turned to look and all the women had straightened up, thrusting out their chests and sucking in their tummies, their hands flying to their hair.

Tyler closed his laptop and smiled as Ashley made her way across the room to him, the envy of every man there. She sat down on the stool next to Tyler and rested her hand on his with casual intimacy.

"Hi, Dave!" she said, through perfectly painted lips. Her teeth were small, even, and white, a miracle of dentistry.

He leaned forward and kissed her, watching the room through the corner of his eye. It was very satisfying.

"What will you have?" he asked.

"A mojito, please," she said.

"A mojito for the lady here," he called out cheerfully to the bartender.

"How was your trip?" He leaned closer to inhale the scent wafting up from between her breasts, which were barely contained by the flimsy blouse. He tried not to think about her trips. She had refused an exclusive contract or any type of long-term deal with him. It's not practical, she'd explained.

"Trip was good," she replied.

"I have a trip for you, if you are interested." He raised his eyebrows and gave her an arch look from underneath his lashes.

They paused for the bartender to deliver the drink. After she left, Ashley asked, "What kind of trip?"

He had been thinking about it for a while, in two minds. But he had to act now, before he lost more momentum and faded out of the public eye. It was hard to compete with singing babies and dancing cats on the Internet, not to mention the daily deluge of trashy celebrity antics.

"You know the guy I keep talking to you about?" She was about to say something, but he interrupted her by placing his finger on her glossy, silky lips. "Shush, don't say his name," he murmured.

She nodded and took a sip from her glass.

"I want to get some dirt on him." By now his hand was high on her thigh, playing peekaboo with the hem of her very short skirt, agonizingly close to where it wanted to go next.

She put down her drink, swiveled suddenly, knocking his hand off her lap in the process, and looked at him. "What did you have in mind?"

He was nonplussed by her directness but carried on. Come on, he thought, she must have seen and heard worse. He wasn't asking for some horrible, perverted thing.

"I want you to volunteer for his campaign," he said.

"Be your spy, you mean?"

"Yes."

"And? Do what? What would I be looking for?" Her eyes narrowed and bore into his.

"I am not sure…" He dragged out the last word, and then, as if it had just struck him, he exclaimed, "Maybe you could lure him and snap a picture with him!"

"You mean you want a picture of *me* in bed with *him?*"

"Yes."

She swiveled away and returned to her drink, sipping it slowly and systematically. He put his hand on her thigh once more. She didn't react. His hand just lay there, like a dropped glove on a cold concrete pavement. He took it back.

"I'll think about it," she said.

She had no intention of doing anything of the kind. Just yesterday, a young Indian fellow had come by, asking questions. Very charming and persuasive, a total flirt at first. She'd thought he was leading up to a business proposal. Her address book was stuffed with South Asian hedge funders and start-up moguls. But then he'd produced a badge and had her call a mysterious phone number to verify his authority. "We're not interested in making trouble. We just want information. Your boss has helped us in the past. Please call her and check." She had.

He'd wanted to know about Tyler. "What does he talk about? What does he buy? What does he read? Who does he hang out with, other than you?" It was clear to Ashley that he was from some type of secret service, even though his badge had mentioned a boring governmental agency, EPA, if she remembered correctly. From the way he sat and the way he asked questions to the way he stared at her with probing eyes, trying to read her darkest secrets, he was intimidating, yet it was a total turn-on. "Good-bye," he'd said with a parting smile, "we'll stay in touch. Naturally, this visit must remain our little secret."

Ashley had no desire to mess with the secret-service guy, even though she'd love to see him again.

She picked up her handbag and, always the professional, planted a perfunctory kiss on Tyler's lips and stalked away on irresistible legs.

He didn't know whether it was a kiss-off or whether she was really going to think about it. WTF, he thought, it isn't anything outside her normal business. What's she acting so insulted for?

The singer concluded her performance to vigorous applause. Tyler wondered if she had a boyfriend. Even if she didn't, she'd have to wait, because right now, he had to head to DC. Jimmy had just sent a text message: *Come to DC ASAP. I have data for you.*

THE SCOOP

"Mr. Stephen James does not pass our smell test. We believe that the lifestyle of his campaign manager, Doug Mayhew, is against nature and against God. Mr. James would do well to distance himself and his campaign from such unnatural choices, if he is serious about his political career."
—*Robert Wilks, the Conservative Coalition*

The bar in the trendy foyer of the *W* Hotel in Washington, DC, sparkled on this lovely autumn evening. Funky crystal chandeliers in elongated shapes dripped from the ceiling and glittered in neon purples and blood reds, morphing as the mood demanded. Leather sofas, coffee tables, and winged armchairs flanked by tall, elegant lamps clustered together in intimate groups.

The handsome bartender cleared the glasses and asked, "May I get you another drink, sir?"

"No, thank you," Tyler replied and settled the tab. His ex's ill-gotten wealth was bankrolling his jaunt. It doubled his enjoyment. His friend Jimmy had just left after delivering a list of phone numbers and names (first names only), along with a ton of caution and dire warnings.

Tyler watched the young power brokers mill around him and suddenly felt old and out of place. He debated for a minute but was not in a mood to start calling the precious phone numbers on his list yet. A walk would be a nice catalyst to get him going.

The White House was just across the street. He walked by the Treasury and then across the square and around the rear of the White House. Snipers, secret-service patrol cars, and uniformed guards stood warily at their posts. They watched over the crowds taking pictures.

There were only a couple of weeks to go before Thanksgiving. The place was crowded with festive tourists. Big, tight-knit groups of Chinese and Japanese visitors, smaller groups of South Asian families and children, they all pressed around him. Why were there so many little, howling, shouting, screaming kids?! He needed to get away.

A short cab ride later, he was strolling down the streets of Georgetown, enjoying the little bars, restaurants, and glowing shop fronts. This was Tyler's kind of crowd, with lots of eye candy. Tyler kept his eyes peeled, because in those packed streets it wasn't unusual to rub shoulders with an occasional luminary, like Robert Rubin or Tom Daschle of the tax-debacle fame.

To his surprise and shock, Tyler did pick out a familiar face in the throng, a face that was frequently seen next to Stephen James—that of his campaign manager, Doug Mayhew. The young man was hurrying down the street, checking his phone, dressed for a date, apparently, in a snazzy, tight shirt and skinny jeans. He had a wine bottle tucked under his arm.

Tyler was curious. Doug was gay. Everyone knew that. It would be fun to see who his date was...could turn out to be a find. Tyler followed him and kept a shield of two or three people between them, glad of the cover offered by the chattering mob.

Doug walked on, oblivious to his surroundings. He was too busy texting and smiling. Two blocks later, he turned onto a quieter side street that ended in a cul-de-sac. Several brownstone buildings overlooked the circular patch of garden at the center of the dead end, giving it a courtyard-like feel. Most of the brownstones housed fancy boutiques or lawyers' offices on the lower floors and bars and restaurants on the top floors. The glitziest building in the group bore a sign advertising a popular Indian restaurant. Doug paused, looked up at the sign, and then entered.

Tyler waited for a few seconds and went in after him. The doors opened to reveal a wooden stairway carpeted in red and gold. A heady aroma redolent of masalas and garlic swirled around Tyler. He climbed the stairs and came to a stop on the landing in front of carved mahogany double doors embedded with frosted-glass panels. Through the clear patches of design in the frosted glass, Tyler caught a glimpse of a hostess leading Doug to a corner table, where another man was already seated. The man rose with a big smile and greeted Doug. They embraced briefly and sat down.

Tyler stepped away quickly, before the glittering hostess could spot him and come to greet him. He rushed down the stairs, out of the door, and onto the street. He hastily picked up a free local tabloid from inside a metal box and sauntered over to one of the benches in the garden. Behind the cover of the newspaper, he contemplated what he had just seen, with a wary eye on the restaurant entrance.

Wasim and Doug. On the face of it, they were just two colleagues, getting a bite to eat while their boss hobnobbed with the powers that be. Why weren't they with their boss? Or lobbying whomever it was that they lobbied? Why weren't they hard at work back in Stephenland? How did they find the time for a leisurely dinner so close to the election? Their body language and attire did not hint at a business meeting.

The alley surrounding the garden was stifling. It trapped the smell of decaying autumn vegetation and spicy food with claustrophobic intensity. But Tyler waved it away. If Wasim turned out to be gay, and if

Tyler could catch Doug and Wasim in an interesting situation—wouldn't that be something! He would throw the "irrefutable proof" that Stephen had demanded right back in his smug, little face. Then he, David Tyler, would be back on top.

Inside the restaurant, Doug and Wasim were in the middle of a mini argument.

"You've already crossed over. What's the point of skulking around?" Doug said. "Don't you want to wake up together instead of rushing away and then spending every second longing to be with me? What's the point of denying yourself such a small pleasure when all that is standing in the way is your fear?"

Wasim stared at Doug while his mind churned away. He had to tell his parents; there was no going back. It was just a matter of picking the right moment when he visited them next. In the meantime, life was passing by. What *was* he waiting for?

"OK, Douglas," he said in a flawless imitation of Stephen. Doug laughed aloud. Wasim signed to the waiter to bring the bill.

Outside the restaurant, Tyler waited and waited. People went in, and people came out, but no Doug or Wasim. For a moment, Tyler panicked that they might have gotten away through a back entrance. But the building backed onto an overpass and a steep highway ramp; there was no exit other than the entrance. Meanwhile, he was hungry, and the smells wafting from the restaurant made it worse. What were they doing? How long did it take to eat dinner? He stood up to go in and check but then sat down immediately, because he caught sight of the duo exiting.

Wasim, tall, good-looking, with an easy smile lighting up the night, and Doug, sandy haired and impish, were having a whale of a time.

Tyler followed them. They walked around for a while, checked out a couple of bars, and then suddenly dived into a taxi.

Luckily, Tyler had done his homework and knew where Doug lived. It was just a block from his friend Jimmy's place. He flagged a taxi and gave the address and hoped desperately that was where they were headed. To his relief, he got glimpses of the other taxi at red lights.

"Could we go faster?" he asked his driver.

The man mumbled something and started weaving in and out of traffic, zipping onto side streets and avenues. Tyler anxiously clung to the door handle while he was tossed around like a salad. Within five minutes, the car pulled up in front of Doug's apartment building. He paid the cabby a big tip and hurried to cross the street, because he saw the other taxi as it turned the corner. A convenient tree offered a vantage point for surveillance. He stood behind it and watched, grateful for the deep darkness of the November night.

Doug stepped out first, and then Wasim stumbled out. They were both slightly unsteady on their feet. The taxi drove away. They stood facing each other, smiling and swaying.

Tyler got them in the cross hairs of his camera, perfectly captured in the center. "Kiss, damn it," he muttered. He willed them with all his mental powers, but the two men just stood and stared at each other with those silly grins. Finally they turned around and went inside the building, still with no incriminating physical contact.

"Morons," Tyler muttered. They were probably in there, doing God knows what, safe from his camera. He kicked the tree. He had no choice now but to wait and try to catch Wasim coming out of the building.

The tree looked climbable. He didn't want to be seen loitering outside the building and have the cops called on him. He pretended to check his phone and looked around. After a few minutes he was convinced that he was unobserved. He groped his way up the tree. The bark dug into his thigh through his pants, and a branch stabbed him in the back. Spiteful little twigs scratched his face. He squirmed around and finally found a comfortable position in a fork in the branches and waited.

Meanwhile Doug and Wasim took the elevator up to the sixth floor. Doug unlocked the door, switched on the lights, and threw the keys on the kitchen counter. His apartment overlooked an inner courtyard with its array of potted palms wrapped in spirals of twinkling lights. Faint music rose from below and added to an already-festive mood.

"Do you want something to drink?" he called out over his shoulder.

Wasim stood in the doorway, hesitating. Doug pretended to get busy. He cleared the sofa of books and began to open windows. He wasn't sure what to say to Wasim, whether to press him to come in or to let him take his time.

The music got louder once the windows were open. In the courtyard below, little bistro tables stood scattered under the illuminated palm trees. Couples sat at the tables, drinking and chatting. Doug leaned out to look at one couple that was energetically making out in the shadow of a tree.

"Come and look at this," he said to Wasim. But twisting around to look at Wasim, he lost his balance.

That galvanized Wasim. "Doug!" he shouted. With an enormous stride and lunge, he reached for Doug with long hands and pulled him up and away from the window. They staggered back, laughing, and collapsed on the sofa, tangled in each other's arms.

Outside, Tyler was getting cold, hungry, and tired. Around four in the morning, his eyelids began to droop, weighed down by invisible concrete blocks. He propped his lids open and banged his head gently on the tree to see if that would keep him awake. That didn't work at all. He browsed his phone until the battery died.

"Come out, come out, come out," he whispered fiercely. Thanks to the cold and lack of movement, his butt and legs were completely numb.

At 5:33 a.m., while it was still dark, the doors to the lobby of Doug's building slid open. Tyler sat up, shook the stiffness out of his body, and got his camera ready.

Wasim emerged first. Doug came out right behind him. Tyler's camera could see them clearly in the diffused light of the lobby.

Doug was in his shorts and house slippers. He and Wasim stood talking, waiting for a taxi presumably. They looked really happy.

"I'll pick up my things from the hotel and meet you at the airport," Wasim said.

"Aren't you glad you stayed over?" Doug couldn't stop smiling; he was so thrilled to have spent the night together.

"Yes," Wasim replied and swooped in for a quick kiss before the taxi appeared.

Astride a gnarly old branch, twisted at an unnatural angle at the waist, Tyler got his money shot—a split second of contact between two pairs of lips, an irresistible stolen kiss, still on fire from the night.

Tyler clicked in a frenzy. He was delirious at being at the right place at the right time for once in his life. The sharp pain radiating from his lower back was a small price. This story might not be on par with taking on the CIA from an underground bunker, but it would do nicely and keep the fish nibbling until he scored the big one.

AN INCIDENT

"Nina!" Stephen shook her awake.

She sat up in bed and looked at the clock. A bleary 3:33 a.m.

"What's wrong?" Nina asked in a panic. Her mother! Something must have happened to her. She had been complaining about an unusual stomach pain for the last couple of days.

"It's Wasim. He's in the hospital. I need to go and see what's going on."

She jumped out of bed and immediately felt dizzy and nauseous. Morning sickness, but she didn't have time for that now. She followed Stephen into the large dressing room just off the bedroom.

He looked furious. His lips were pinched together so tightly that they almost disappeared. He grabbed a pair of pants from his closet and pulled them on.

"I want to come," Nina said.

"No, it'll be too much of a strain. I'll call you as soon as I get there." He took a bottle of water from the fridge.

"What happened?" she asked.

"That's all I know. I got a text from Doug." He shook his head and went back to the bedroom to get his phone.

"Call me, please," she said, "as soon as you hear something."

Stephen gave her a hurried kiss and rushed down the stairs and into the car and screeched out of the garage into the cool night. "I am going to kill that piece of shit Tyler!" he muttered.

A few minutes later he realized that, back home, Nina would be sitting on the bed, brooding and worried. He got an update from Doug and called her.

"Any more news? Is Wasim OK? What happened?" she said.

"They're getting ready to pump his stomach."

"For *what*?"

"He's swallowed something to fucking kill himself. They're at Boston Memorial."

"Oh, my God!"

"Nina, it'll be fine. Don't worry." He tried to sound calm. He knew where her mind had gone at the mention of Boston Memorial. "Sweetheart, don't worry. I'll make sure that he is fine. I want you to try and go back to sleep. Bye." He hung up.

Sleep? How did he expect her to sleep? Nina pulled the covers over her head and hugged her pillow. How could she not relive the horrible night at Boston Memorial? That night she had gone to the cinema to watch a chick flick, while Stephen and Neel pounded out a squash game. She and Stephen had made up after their CIA-revelation quarrel and were in that mellow postmakeup mood. She was looking forward to snuggling up to him that night, inspired by the on-screen romance unfolding in front of her. Suddenly an usher had tapped her shoulder and said that she was needed outside. Stephen's mysterious boss, George Applegate, had been waiting for her in the theater lobby. Stephen had been shot and was at Boston Memorial.

She had listened, confused and stunned. She couldn't understand. No, no, she'd protested. But the police car's sirens were already approaching. She remembered getting into the car. George had hustled her down long hospital hallways to a prep room, where Stephen lay unconscious, wrapped in blankets on a gurney, attached to multiple intravenous drips. She'd been allowed a quick kiss, and her Stephen had been taken away to the mysterious void behind the double doors of the operating room.

A full three years later, at the mere mention of Boston Memorial, Nina's brain vividly conjured up the scratch of

Stephen's cold, gray lips on hers and flooded her nostrils with the ferrous smell of his blood. She threw off the covers and sat up. The black, paralyzing fear of losing him—her rock, whose strength she had taken for granted, who had driven her to hair-tearing exasperation with his recklessness and cockiness—that irrational fear returned from the depths of her memory. It took charge with renewed vigor, deceiving her for an instant that it was Stephen, and not Wasim, who was in the hospital.

She picked up the phone and called him. "Stephen?" she said anxiously, worried that some cruel twist of fate would return her to that night and that he would be unable to answer, lying senseless somewhere in the dark night.

He picked up right away. "Nina, sweetheart, it'll be OK," he said, and miraculously, just the sound of his voice steadied her heartbeat and the fluttering creature inside her belly calmed down.

"Stephen, do you think he did it because Tyler published those pictures?"

Tyler had posted the photos that evening under the pleasant title "Lovebirds!" The pictures were of Doug and Wasim kissing outside Doug's apartment and other variations on that theme.

The campaign had immediately gone into lockdown mode and canceled the remaining events scheduled for the rest of the night.

Stephen had issued a terse press release: *We condemn the unconscionable invasion of privacy of Mr. Mayhew and Mr. Raja. Our best wishes are with them during this ordeal. Our campaign has nothing further to add on this matter. We will resume our normal schedule tomorrow.*

The story was a major distraction, coming just a few days ahead of the debate with Congresswoman Collins.

Wasim had been devastated. His parents refused to return his calls. It was terrible that they had to find out in this humiliating, public fashion, all because he had been too much of a coward to confront them. His sister was on damage-control duty with friends and relatives. He had to stay off the family radar for a while.

Nina had consoled Wasim just hours earlier. "It will blow over," she'd told him. She should have stayed with him through the evening, she thought now. She shouldn't have left his side.

"Nina, don't worry." Stephen muttered into the phone. "I've got to go. I've arrived at the hospital. I'll call as soon as I hear something."

He pulled up at the rear entrance to the emergency room and ran in through the sliding glass doors. A receptionist directed him to a secluded room.

Inside, Doug sat on a couch with head bowed. He leaped up to meet Stephen as soon as he heard him come in. Doug was worn out—eyes rimmed with red, head tousled, rumpled, and tired—and looked young and frightened, like an orphaned schoolboy.

"They said they have to pump his stomach, but they won't tell me anything." He blinked at Stephen.

"He'll be fine," Stephen said firmly. "What happened?"

Doug was deeply shaken and couldn't believe that it was happening again, after losing his friend Jerry under frighteningly similar circumstances.

Doug had given the volunteers the evening off and sent the campaign staff to manage the press and photographers camped outside. He and Wasim had been practically alone in the guesthouse. Wasim had gone to his room and shut the door. Doug had decided to leave him alone for a while. But when hours passed and Wasim remained closeted, Doug had gotten worried. He had pushed the door open and found Wasim on the floor, vomiting and shuddering.

"Who else knows about this?"

"Nobody. There was no one in the office."

"Did the media see you or follow you here?"

"No, we left through the garden exit. I had a volunteer bring a car there. We came to the rear entrance of the hospital."

"Good man!" Stephen was relieved. He didn't want the distraction to turn into a soap opera. "You didn't call 911, did you?"

Doug shook his head. "I asked for privacy at the registration desk when I came in with Wasim. They knew I was connected with you, so they've promised to keep things quiet."

Stephen took a deep breath. "Let me see if I can find out what's going on." He patted Doug on the shoulder. "Call Nina. She wants to talk to you." He went out of the room and slammed the door behind him.

Nina imagined Doug in the gloomy waiting room, on the same lumpy couch that she had sat on three years earlier. It was amazing how strongly those feelings of misery and helplessness came back now. The surroundings had been branded on her memory during her eight-hour vigil to hear from the doctors—the clock on the wall, the pile of dog-eared magazines, the impersonal furniture and fake plants in the corner. That terrifying night, George had asked her to wait until the morning before calling her parents. She remembered the looping prayer in her head: "Please, God, please let him live." Is this love, she had wondered, this sickening terror? Until that point in time, their marriage had been uneven, filled with extremes of sweetness and aloofness, the tectonic melding of two polar temperaments and cultures.

Now, she gave a little shudder, got out of bed, and went to the living room to switch on the TV. It proved to be an ineffectual distraction. Her thoughts wouldn't leave Doug. He must look the way she had, as if the facial muscles could no longer sustain themselves and had succumbed to the power of gravity. Her phone rang. She answered at once.

"Doug, it'll be OK. You'll see," she said.

"It's my fault," he replied from the hospital waiting room. "I pushed him to go out to dinner with me in public. I thought it was the right thing for him, to begin being himself." His other friend had given up his life because the secrecy he had clung to as a lifeline had snapped. He had wanted to avoid that with Wasim, to have everything in the open so that there were no secrets to fear.

He looked at the phone as if it were Nina. "It's my fault. He wasn't ready."

"It's not your fault," Nina said. "Why don't you go get something to drink? Water? Tea?"

He shook his head but clasped the phone tightly. "I'm glad you are here."

"Me too," she replied. "Talk to me."

Nurses and aides passed through occasionally. He looked up with expectation each time, only to be disappointed.

An hour later Stephen bustled in and sat down next to Doug, who was still on the phone with Nina.

"I spoke to the doctors. He's going to be fine." Stephen smiled at Doug. "They pumped his stomach. It was a mixture of alcohol and sleeping pills. We can see him now."

"That's wonderful!" Stephen heard Nina exclaim over the phone.

He leaned toward it and said, "All's well, Nina. Doug will call you back. We have to go now, bye!"

The elevator bank was just outside the waiting room. They entered, pressed the seventh-floor button, and watched the floors flash by in red digits on the panel. After a minute, the doors separated to reveal a long hallway guarded by the nurse's station.

Stephen didn't recognize any of the faces there, none from three years ago when he had spent two weeks in a morphine fog, drifting in and out of pain.

On that awful night, he had walked into the Ali home, acting on Sid's request for a meeting. Sid Ali, his neighbor, had just been traced to a major terror attack in India. It turned out that he was the one who had anonymously tipped off Stephen and Nina in time for them to escape from the targeted hotel. Stephen's boss, George, was convinced that Sid would contact Stephen for a plea bargain. Stephen had entered the Ali home cautiously, but he had not expected to be ambushed and almost killed. If it hadn't been for Neel, who had heard the shots and rushed over, Stephen would have bled to death.

His big memory of the hospital stay was of lying with his cheek on Nina's heart, absorbing her warmth and strength, trying to ignore the pain in his mangled limbs. The prospect of disability and disfigurement had hung like Damocles's sword, a bitter pill for a man who took such pride in his physical strength and toughness. But Nina had been there to mitigate it with her smile, ready to wrap him in her arms, sing to him, tell him endless stories from Indian mythology, do anything to comfort him and distract him from thoughts of the future.

He had felt humbled and small, after the I-need-my-space stunt he'd pulled on her in the early weeks of their marriage. He had been such a stuck-up, arrogant prick. In his drug-addled, sentimental state, he had dubbed her his guardian angel, and to this day that was how he thought of her in his innermost thoughts.

After his discharge, his in-laws had taken turns babysitting him, because Nina wouldn't hear of an impersonal stranger being in charge of his care. It had been a whole new world, the intense family dynamic, awkward at first, but soon the sound of their voices in the next room became a comforting hum that he listened for as soon as he woke.

His mother-in-law, Deepa, had taken charge of him with irresistible maternal authority. His father-in-law, Ravi, who hadn't quite approved of Nina's choice of husband, had watched over Stephen with gruff affection, despite rancorous debates over gun control and taxes.

Stephen shook his head free of the past.

"Here it is, seven oh three," Doug said. His voice trembled. Stephen pretended not to notice.

In a large, bright room with a couple of chairs, a sofa, a TV, and a huge window, Wasim lay propped on a bed. A nurse finished settling Wasim, checked the intravenous drip and a beeping monitor next to it, and wrote her name on the whiteboard in the room. "Ring the bell if you need me, honey," she said to Wasim and waved them into the room.

"How are you, Wasim?" Stephen asked as soon as the nurse was out of earshot.

"I am OK," he replied hoarsely. He looked at the IV drip and the clip on his finger and then at Doug.

Stephen pulled a chair up close to the bed. Doug stood near Wasim on the other side of the bed, between the IV and the monitor. His hands gripped the bed rail.

Wasim's haggard face and the hospital bed, with its cold, industrial geometry, took Stephen back to a time that he'd rather not recall.

"That was a stupid thing to do," he said to Wasim without any ceremony.

Wasim nodded, his tired, dark eyes still on Doug, who seemed to be gulping for air.

"Why did you do it?"

Wasim didn't answer immediately. "I don't know," he said. His speech was slow and thick. "I started drinking… and then I thought I should try and sleep…but…before I knew it, I had swallowed the entire bottle of pills."

"You didn't plan on killing yourself?"

Wasim shook his head. "No. I started thinking of my mother and couldn't fall asleep. Her life must be hell right now. My father is a terrible, violent man." His mother's face haunted him, her eyelids heavy with unshed tears, every day a minefield of navigating her husband's spite and cruelty. She was the fragile shield that stood between the monster and his children. "I just kept taking those pills and tried to fall asleep… trying not to think of what must be happening to her."

"Wouldn't it be much worse, a permanent hell for your mother, if you had died?"

Wasim turned to look at Stephen, stricken.

Is this really Stephen? Doug wondered. The man who refuses to speak to his mother or siblings, even after the passing of twenty long years? Stephen had shot down every attempt at mentioning his birth family in the campaign, other than Grandpa James. But at this moment he was kindness itself.

Wasim nodded—it was incredibly stupid of him to allow a jerk like Tyler to get to him. His mother would surely have died of grief.

In a way Wasim was relieved that the truth was out. There was no scope for self-deception anymore. He was free. Left to himself, who knew—he might have settled for a barren, loveless life just to please his parents.

Stephen patted his hand. "It's lucky that Doug found you in time."

Wasim looked over at Doug and finally cracked a faint smile. His eyes said it all. Weak-kneed with relief, Doug bent down and hugged him.

Stephen looked away, slightly embarrassed. "What do we need to do campaignwise? Do we need to put out a media release about this?"

Doug pulled up the other chair and sat down. "No. If anyone asks, we'll say that Wasim was treated for exhaustion. Can we trust the hospital staff not to leak?"

"I'll take care of that." Entire wings in the hospital were named after his grandparents. He could get them to do anything.

Stephen pushed back his chair and picked up his jacket. "Guys, I'll leave now. Nina's waiting for me. Call us if you need anything. The doctor will discharge you around noon."

Stephen took a peek as he closed the door on them. A few years ago he wouldn't have known how to handle such an emotionally charged situation. He would have just shut it out and gone off for a grueling swim. But the last five years with Nina had been a rough training ground. Love, tenderness, desire, guilt, shame, and most of all, the terrifying fear that he would inadvertently cause her death, had seasoned him. That black grief when he'd held her in his arms on their return from the doctor's office after the miscarriage—he could never forget that. He felt a little bit of that guilt now, as if he were directly responsible for what had happened to Wasim and Doug. Their lives would never be the same, and their private moments would be forever archived in the bottomless memory of the Internet.

On the way home, Stephen called Nina. She demanded every little detail—what did Doug say, how did Wasim look, did they declare their love for each other?

After fifteen minutes of answering her questions, Stephen said, "Now that we've straightened everything out, I'm going to destroy Tyler."

"Stephen!" Nina, who had been listening with teary-eyed relief to the Wasim-Doug saga, sat up in alarm. "Don't be hasty."

"Don't worry, my love. I won't be breaking any laws. I promise," he said and glared at the traffic.

She didn't answer.

Stephen couldn't be stopped once he had made up his mind. His dislike for Tyler went beyond concerns about Nina's safety or damage to his political campaign.

"Nina, you know that I am right. That piece of shit needs to be punished. Wasim almost died because of him. Tyler is low-class trash that thrives on other people's misery. He *needs* to be punished."

"What are you going to do?" She clutched the phone tightly.

"Me? Absolutely nothing." He grinned. "Anyway, I'm almost home, sweetheart. I'll see you in a couple of minutes."

MACHIAVELLI

If an injury has to be done to a man it should be so
severe that his vengeance need not be feared.
    —*Niccolò Machiavelli*

George Applegate, Stephen's former boss, was
badly in need of a cigarette. The debate rehears-
al was almost over. Stephen and a political strategist
standing in for his opponent, Ms. Collins, had been
sparring for almost two hours.

George was amazed at the transformation in
Stephen. He could see now that Nina had been the
missing ingredient in his ambitious plans for Stephen.
Gone was the brittle, hard-edged, cynical man whose
loneliness and sense of betrayal had turned him

sour on humanity. Stephen was a family man now, a father-to-be, with an effervescent Indian American wife. She had made him electable! In fact, George had been the one to convince Nina that it was in Stephen's best interest to make this Senate bid, to stop him from running off on another dangerous adventure.

"Excuse me," Stephen said to Doug and Wasim, when he saw George standing by himself. "I'll be back in a minute." He walked away despite protests from the two young men.

"Hi, George. Thanks for coming. What did you think?" He shook George's hand.

"Not bad."

"But?"

George looked at him. "I've told you my opinion, Stephen. I've nothing more to add." They'd been discussing this ever since Tyler broke the story about Doug and Wasim. In fact, George had warned him at the very beginning not to take on Doug as a campaign manager, even though Doug was from George's home state of Louisiana and shared a common political network.

"George, I am not going to fire Wasim and Doug. Our party is making a huge mistake by making gay marriage a big deal. Most of the world has moved past it. I personally don't care one bit who sleeps with whom, as long as it's consensual."

"Stephen, *nobody* cares who sleeps with whom. It is a political necessity if you want to have the donors and the media moguls on your side. They are fighting a proxy religious battle, and we are all fighting the same enemy."

"Not really, George. We are fighting terrorists, not religion. Whereas, *they* are fighting a religious battle. I don't care about that. You know me."

George was losing credibility with some of the Republican power brokers. He'd convinced them that Stephen was the perfect candidate and that he could be coached. While Stephen had been reluctantly accommodating in some matters, like ending his speeches with "Gob bless" or not explicitly speaking up in favor of same-sex marriage, he'd been stubborn about not letting Doug, and now Wasim, go.

"Well, all I can say is that you're being incredibly naïve."

George had to stop himself from saying anything more. Religion had never been on Stephen's radar, and he had distanced himself from it during the campaign, saying that it was his personal matter. The electorate seemed perfectly happy with that. There was no point in arguing with Stephen once he'd made up his mind. George needed to conserve Stephen's goodwill. There'd be many occasions in the future when he'd have to push back harder, because, after all, he planned on being heavily involved in shaping Stephen's political career.

Despite their frequent arguments and disagreements, Stephen was really fond of George. The older man had thrown him a lifeline when he had been thrashing around for a mooring. George had turned him into a compulsive reader and polyglot, exposing him to places and cultures that had never crossed his path earlier…South Asia for instance. Of course, it had turned out that George had planned on recruiting him all along, but that hadn't bothered Stephen. He had a high regard for George and his cold and implacable pursuit of anybody suspected of endangering the country. If only he hadn't turned into such a damned kingmaker!

George took out a cigarette from its pack and held it between his fingers. It gave him some comfort even if it wasn't lit. "Anyway, if you are going to hang on to those two, you should at least retaliate and silence Tyler. Otherwise you will come across as weak."

"I agree. What would you suggest?"

"I'd go with shock and awe. Slam him."

"How? I can't just go and beat him up though I'd like nothing better."

"He is reckless and impulsive—he will slip up. Neel tells me that Tyler is desperate to get hold of that hooker. She's been ducking him. We'll listen in to see what's going on."

Stephen winced. It seemed impossible to wean himself from George and his political machine. George would surely demand his ransom at some point and Stephen wouldn't have a choice. He had tried to get away from George in the past, only to find himself in a cruel Pakistani prison or in a shoot-out on foreign soil.

It always seemed to end that way, with George bailing him out of some deadly predicament.

Wasim waved to Stephen from across the tent and fiercely pointed to his watch.

"I've got to go, George. Give my love to Ginnie. But come and say hello to Nina first. She's been looking for you."

They were inside a big, white, heated tent, where Stephen and select members of the campaign staff had retreated for debate prep. It was pitched in the shelter of a cliff, protected by the outstretched rocky arms of the coastline. Stephen had a special attachment to this beach. It had been his safe haven during his turbulent teenage years after his father and grandfather had died. He would come to this hidden beach to read, to swim and be alone, and to work out his unbridled anger and unhappiness.

Stephen and George went over to a corner of the tent where Nina sat huddled in an armchair, ensconced in a cocoon of blankets. She jumped up when she saw George.

"Hi, George!" She gave him a big hug.

He smiled down at her. "Careful now," he said. "We don't want to crush little Stephen."

"Stephen thinks it's a girl."

George and Nina had a love-hate relationship. He was her only connection to Stephen's pre-Nina years, and she knew that he loved Stephen in his own perverse, manipulative, self-serving way. Nina remembered how shaken and worried George had been on that fateful night three years ago; they'd waited for eight long hours to get word on Stephen's condition after his surgery in the wake of the shooting at Sid Ali's. George had moved heaven and earth to see to Stephen's recovery and Nina's comfort during their prolonged hospital stay—he must've flown in every trauma specialist in the country to oversee Stephen's surgery.

On the other hand, George had been instrumental in putting Stephen in dangerous situations, and when Nina had found that even Neel had been inducted, she had been absolutely livid. But her kid brother was an adult, and he had willingly chosen that path, and there was nothing she could do except pray.

But overall, she loved George, and she loved his wife, Ginnie, even more. "How's Ginnie?" Nina returned to the warmth of her blankets.

"She's well. You'll see her at the debate. She's very excited about the baby."

George was happy to see Nina looking so radiant and happy. Barely a year ago, during Stephen's Pakistan misadventure, she had almost starved herself to death, waiting for him to come home. It was a miracle that she was still by Stephen's side, given all the insanity that he'd put her through. The CIA had a high divorce rate, and not many spouses lasted more than a few years.

"Bye, Nina. I have to go now." He gave her a parting peck on the cheek and put on his jacket. He shook hands with Stephen and walked away.

Meanwhile, Wasim was getting desperate. They had a crushing schedule to keep, but everyone seemed to be moving in slow motion. It would take them at least two hours to get back to the campaign headquarters from this godforsaken spot that Stephen had chosen.

Granted, the secluded beach was an ideal getaway from the ever-present media. The last two days had been a circus: reporters, photographers, and party operatives were breaking down the doors to get an interview. Some in the party demanded that Stephen's gay staffers step down. Rumors flew fast and thick that there had been some kind of an incident. The official explanation of "exhaustion" for Wasim's brief hospital stint was being deconstructed daily into new hypotheses, despite Wasim's public presence on the campaign trail.

Wasim was a little wan but indefatigably worked the phones, trying to cram in as many events as possible in the few days before the imminent Thanksgiving holiday. He was subdued, unable to work up his usual energetic banter, still trying to figure out how he could have done something so desperate.

He'd look up once in a while from his work to find Doug scrutinizing him anxiously. Ah, he thought, I understand now what Nina meant when she said that it takes a crisis to find out how you truly feel. One of

Wasim's fears in the immediate wake of the incident was that Doug would break it off with him. After all, who'd want to knowingly get involved with an unbalanced, suicidal man? But Doug was much more overt in his affections and commitment now that everything was out in the open. It was a good thing that they were all breathlessly busy and didn't have the time to brood about what might have happened had Doug waited a little longer before checking on Wasim that night.

Some forward-looking Republicans were now flocking to Stephen. Here was a fresh face, an MIT engineer, well connected, with deep pockets and an Indian American wife. He was exactly what they needed after last year's shellacking at the polls, where they'd lost the presidential race as well as precious Senate seats, thanks to the extreme right-wing positions taken by some of the candidates. Wasim was constantly fielding calls from Republican midlevel luminaries wanting to campaign for Stephen.

Despite all the good news, Stephen was still getting hammered on likability, according to their polling guru. Congresswoman Collins was almost a foot shorter than Stephen, but with her bubbly, spontaneous personality and merry laugh, she could easily command the stage and overshadow Stephen. Her campaign repeatedly painted him as aloof and isolated, a patrician loner.

"We need to get his pregnant wife on the road with him," a political strategist said to Doug.

"We'll work on that today. It's only for a couple of days now. We'll convince him."

Doug sent the campaign staff back to the guest-house, where a lavish lunch buffet awaited them. He had chartered a big catamaran to ferry people back and forth, because there was no ground access to the beach. He looked around for Stephen and Nina. He saw Wasim gesture angrily that they had to get moving.

Nina and Stephen had wandered toward the beach. In summer, the pale, sandy beach cloaked itself in a colorful mix of purple thistle, Queen Anne's lace, goldenrod, and fragrant pink puffs of red clover. Clouds of white butterflies flocked to sip the nectar.

The day after their first encounter, Stephen had taken Nina around his gardens to make up for his rudeness the previous day. At the end of the tour, on a whim, he'd suggested that they should sail down to the beach to see the wild flowers. It had been one of the happiest days of his life. She had been easygoing, quick to smile, and perfectly natural with him, like she'd known him for ages. And, when they had stood together and looked down from the lighthouse at the world's beauty beneath, he had felt a strange, new sensation, a lightness and warmth that he hadn't experienced in decades.

He'd remembered the words of Milan Kundera, sent to him by a former girlfriend long, long ago, words that he had tossed aside because they had meant nothing at that time but that had suddenly surfaced in his brain, which stashed away everything, like a superefficient database, to be retrieved when needed: "Love begins at the point when a woman enters her first word into our poetic memory." He had known then, if only instinctively, that Nina was the key to his happiness. Neither of them could have dreamed that five years later they would be standing on the beach together, married, pregnant, and campaigning for a Senate seat!

They stood talking at the edge of the water, looking out to sea. Doug and Wasim hurried toward them.

"What?" Doug asked after watching a nonverbal exchange between Stephen and Nina.

Wasim joined them. "Let's go! We need to move!"

Stephen looked at Nina. "We came here on our first date. She was terrified to be alone with me in such a secluded spot."

"I wasn't!" She turned pink. "Besides, it wasn't a date."

"How did you two meet?" Doug asked. "You've been awfully mysterious about it."

Wasim threw up his hands in exasperation. He pointed at his watch for the hundredth time. Nobody paid any attention.

"He was trying to recruit me," Nina said.

Stephen laughed. "It took me all of two seconds to know that she'd make a lousy spy."

Nina buttoned up her coat and pulled her scarf around her neck and ears. "Then why did you bring me here that day?"

Even Wasim was curious now. He'd never seen his boss in such a mellow mood.

Stephen reached out and took her hand. "She was like an old friend, even though we'd just met. All the noise in my head melted away, and I felt…at peace." He turned to the two young men. "I was very selfish, I'm afraid," he said with a touch of sadness. "I've caused her a lot of pain."

Nina looked away. What was going on with Stephen today?

Wasim took advantage of the pause to discreetly herd them toward Stephen's personal boat, docked at the slip.

"Why did *you* agree?" Doug asked Nina. He was curious about this interracial odd couple, so different in temperaments and background, from such opposite family cultures. The crisis of Wasim's hospitalization had brought clarity to many issues Doug had been skirting in their relationship.

Nina put her arm around Stephen's waist and looked up at him. "He was very charming. He was well informed, was well-read, and made an effort to find out what I was all about, instead of going on about himself."

"Do you guys ever disagree, or are you always so… compatible?" Doug asked.

Wasim raised his eyebrows. Don't overstep, dude!

Both Nina and Stephen laughed at the question, much to Wasim's relief. Stephen helped Nina get onto the boat from the dock.

Whenever they disagreed, Nina would throw a fit and get on the phone with her mother. She wouldn't complain or say anything, but just the sound of her mother's voice would calm her down. Stephen knew that Deepa could sense when they had quarreled and would casually bring up something nice Stephen had said or done, and Nina would grin sheepishly at him while still on the phone with her mother. His mother-in-law was a major stabilizing influence on both of them, and he was grateful that she was a part of their life.

"We've had our arguments," Stephen said.

Nina shook her head, as if to say, "What an understatement."

When they were all settled in, Stephen took the wheel and started easing the boat out into the open water.

"How about race? That was never an issue?" Wasim asked. That had been on his mind lately, now that the big secret was out—how Doug's family would receive him at the upcoming Thanksgiving holiday. The Mayhews of Louisiana were, after all, famous for their plantations and all the rancid history that went with it. His own family had yet to acknowledge his existence postincident.

"Nina had a huge chip on her shoulder," Stephen said. "She saw racial slights in every social encounter we had."

"Of course! Everybody was so condescending. I wanted to shout, 'I come from an aristocratic family; judge me by my accomplishments not by my skin color.'"

"I don't think anyone really thought that, Nina. It was what *you* assumed they thought."

Nina shook her head once more.

"What about you? Was it a culture shock?" Wasim turned to Stephen.

Shock! Their Indian wedding, his first prolonged exposure to Nina's family and the Indian community, was utter chaos—eardrum-shattering music, tongue-scorching food, inquisitive relatives, and the unimaginably shimmery fabrics. Despite having spent so much time in South Asia, it was still a jolt to his senses. His brother-in-law Neel's constant company was his only connection to sanity.

"Not really," he said, "we didn't have time for all that. A lot of bad things happened to us in quick succession. If it weren't for my in-laws, we would never have made it through. That sped up the bonding thing considerably. Straight to matters of life and death, you see."

They continued in silence for a while, each lost in his or her private universe.

"Well, now that we have only a couple of days left, do you think we could take Nina on the road with us?" Doug ventured.

"No." Stephen responded with his usual finality.

These days he was constantly reminded of Nina's earlier pregnancy. They were both alarmed at every cramp and pain. On that awful day two years ago, she had been in a taxi and had removed her seat belt to reach across for her handbag. A big SUV had hit the taxi from behind and sent her flying into the plastic partition. Immediately after the accident, Nina had called Stephen at his office and had gone home to sleep it off. He had been in the living room, working, waiting for her to wake up, when he'd heard her call for him. The sight that met him when he entered the bedroom had been forever branded on his brain: Nina had stood by the side of the bed, holding onto the headboard, bent over, her pajamas soaked in blood. The crimson pool collecting at her feet had terrified him more than any horror he'd seen in his career.

Stephen tried to drown out the image and fiercely focused on the healthy, smiling woman sitting near him. There was no doubt in his mind that it had not been an accident and that she had been followed and watched to the point where they knew exactly when she had removed her seat belt and was vulnerable. The offending SUV had driven off, and by the time the police and the Agency had tracked it down, the crew that had driven it had long disappeared, after trashing the van and pushing it into a swamp on the outskirts of the city. The wreck had revealed no secrets. The vehicle had been stolen a week earlier from a small side street in a New Jersey suburb. The Agency was still working on tracing the vehicle and combing it for clues.

"C'mon, Stephen, it's only for a few days now," Nina said.

"Let me think about it."

THANKSGIVING

Stephen Edward James @stephenjames . Nov 25
We are honoring the brave acts of police officers in the wake of
the Boston Marathon tragedy. Please join us.

Katherine Collins @kathycollins . Nov 25
Mr. James, please tell your party to stop blocking aid for
veterans and first responders.

S tephen and Nina's limo was stuck in Thanksgiving
traffic. They'd just dropped Wasim and Doug at
Liberty International Airport in Newark, after attending a fund-raiser in New York City. The two young men
were going to spend the holiday at the Mayhew home
in New Orleans. The whole team was due back at the

campaign headquarters on Friday for more debate prep and the hectic homestretch of the race.

The car soon left the madness of the highways and sped through picturesque woods and horse country, cut across a national wildlife preserve famous for birding, and finally entered a gravel driveway that went up a hill to the open gates at the edge of a large property. A Frank Lloyd Wright–style home hugged the contours of the land, like a cubist snake made of glass and wood. The grounds of the house were occupied by acres of a Zen-like natural garden of native plants and tall trees.

The first time Stephen visited, Nina had watched his startled reaction with sly amusement, because she knew that he had expected a modest home in a typical, suburban cookie-cutter development. She had done nothing to disabuse him.

He wouldn't admit it, but now, five years into his marriage, Stephen enjoyed his visits with his in-laws, particularly during the holidays. The front door was already open, and the entire clan stood ready to welcome them home. The Sharma children were given the same extravagant greeting each and every time they came home.

"We're home!" Nina sat up in excitement when the limo came to a stop in front of the wide stone steps that led up to the entrance. The chauffer opened the car door for Stephen, who, in turn, held it open for Nina. When she stepped out and caught sight of her mother, Nina burst out laughing and waved to her. This was her first time coming to her parents' home after becoming pregnant.

"Congratulations!" Ravi shook Stephen's hand, while Deepa and Nina remained locked in a prolonged hug. Neel grinned at everyone. Nina's grandparents beamed from inside the house.

The sprawling house was already decorated for the holidays, a long stretch of several months that began with Diwali, the Hindu festival of lights in October, and ended with the Indian harvest festival in January. Thanksgiving, Christmas, and New Year's were sandwiched in between. Strings of Diwali lights were artfully tucked away and sparkled golden from unexpected corners and surfaces, filling the house with warmth.

Neel and Ravi hustled Stephen to the family room, where the large-screen TV was gearing up for endless football.

"Are you expecting a big crowd?" Stephen asked. His in-laws were notoriously social, with a large circle of friends and relatives, and were very active in the local Indian community.

"No, it's just us. We thought we'd wait until after you two leave before we invite the mobs over. We have all weekend to do that." Ravi turned to Neel. "Why don't you get Stephen a drink?"

"I'll come with you." Stephen followed Neel to the bar off in a corner. Neel poured him a glass of wine. Stephen asked in an undertone, "Got a few minutes?"

Neel nodded. "Let's go out. I need to fix one of the lights outside."

Once they were out of hearing, Stephen said, "I need someone to watch Tyler."

"You mean physically watch him, like a stakeout? Because I am already watching his e-mails, credit cards, and bank accounts." Neel took down a string of Christmas lights and draped it on the ladder and found the faulty bulb.

"Yes. What he did to Wasim and Doug can't go unpunished. I want to send him a message before he tries another stunt."

What did you have in mind?"

Stephen located the correct bulb and handed it to Neel. "I am not sure yet. George wants him destroyed. But I don't want to do anything too drastic at this point in the campaign. For now, just have him watched. All the time. Let's see what we find. Even if we don't catch him doing anything, maybe we can spook him."

"There's a former security guy I know. He's very discreet. And a huge fan of yours." Neel put the lights back up and switched them on. They came on with a jolly ping.

It was almost five in the afternoon by the time they sat down to dinner. The dining table was set in the hexagonal hub where three different wings of the house came together. Wide glass-walled hallways led from the hub to other parts of the house.

The meal was an Indian interpretation of Thanksgiving staples, like yams, sweet potatoes, corn, pumpkin, and cranberries, supplemented with traditional Indian curries, dals, and raitas. It was arrayed like an Impressionist painting on the crisp white tablecloth. Parathas of different kinds were stacked in a dish in the middle, all wrapped in a soft white cloth to keep them moist, ready to melt on the tongue. A silver tray on the side was piled with a fragrant mountain of ghee-soaked basmati rice cooked to fluffy white perfection. Stephen's stomach rumbled in response to the aroma; he hadn't realized how hungry he was.

Nina's grandparents were served first, then Stephen, the son-in-law, then Ravi and Deepa, and finally Nina and Neel. This was the traditional hierarchy, to be followed with scrupulous care at every meal, despite a cosmopolitan approach to other matters.

The Sharma clan loved their food. Cooking and eating were social affairs where everyone contributed any way they could—chopping, blending, cleaning, grocery shopping, tasting, stirring. And when they sat down to eat, everyone was highly animated and talked at once.

"Stephen, how is the campaign—" Deepa began.

Ravi jumped in before she could finish. "Yes, I've been watching the polls closely—"

Suddenly Grandpa announced loudly over the din, "I WANT RICE AND..."

Both Deepa and Ravi ordered Neel, "Serve *Dadaji* what he wants…"

But Grandma interjected, "It's not good for him, don't…" only to have Nina say, "*Dadiji*, it's Thanksgiving, let him…"

In the meantime, Neel served a generous helping to Grandpa and asked "Stephen, did you watch the—"

This caused Nina to scold, "Neel, stop checking the scores."

Ravi rounded it off with an emphatic "Denard was AMAZING!"

It never ceased to amaze Stephen that the family managed to not only have a conversation but to have cogent discussions and to make important communal decisions in this chaotic manner. Stephen never understood how. He had given up trying long ago and developed a strategy of joining in randomly. The family complained all the while that another morsel would kill them but continued to dig in any way.

Deepa got up after the main dinner. "You guys go watch your game. I'll bring dessert and coffee."

Nina was about to rise to help her, when Stephen said, "You stay. I'll help Ma."

The family had a deep-seated antipathy to live-in help. "It's a pain to have strangers puttering around, no privacy," Nina had said to him. It had taken her several years to get used to Mrs. Brown, Stephen's housekeeper.

Stephen followed his mother-in-law to the kitchen. It was a sleek, modern affair, with everything hidden behind wood panels that blended seamlessly with the rest of the house.

Deepa pulled a large tray out of the oven.

"You made Christmas cookies!" Stephen exclaimed. His grandfather used to leave a basket of Christmas cookies by Stephen's bedside every Christmas Eve. He had mentioned it in passing to Deepa once, and now every Christmas he got his cookies. Today was an early bonus.

"Least I can do"—she smiled at him—"given that you are forced to eat a vegetarian Thanksgiving dinner with no turkey. Want some coffee with your cookies?"

"Not right now, thank you," Stephen replied. Deepa was resplendent in a magenta silk sari with subtle gold embroidery. The sari reminded Stephen of the one that Nina had worn for their Indian wedding ceremony.

"How is the campaign? How are you holding up?"

Her question had its usual effect on him. It was never asked casually, as a matter of form. She wanted to get to the bottom of whatever was inside his head and know whether all was well or not. It had been hard for him in the beginning, when she had come to help them during his recovery after the shooting at Sid's. He had pulled his hand away, too proud to let her change his oozing bandage. But she'd cut through his reserve firmly.

"You kids are our lifelong responsibility," she'd said. "It's not a favor; it's not quid pro quo." That was his place in the family order—one of the children, to be cared for and protected but also to be corrected and taught when needed. He had never had a maternal figure in his life and hadn't known how to deal with it. But it was the look on her face that had rendered him defenseless, her shock and sorrow when she'd seen his wounds underneath the bandages, as if he were her own son.

"You poor child!" she'd exclaimed and cleaned the wound with great tenderness. He'd been unable to breathe from the unfamiliar emotion that had constricted his throat.

Over time, he'd found himself increasingly looking to her for comfort and reassurance, just like Nina and Neel. She was a highly intelligent and intuitive woman and could negotiate his angularities with tact and kindness.

He considered her question for a few seconds. How *was* he holding up?

"I don't know. I wish I could look into the future," he said.

They were both startled, because he had used exactly the same words a few years ago, the night he had come from testifying in front of an investigative committee in Virginia. He had been expelled from India after his encounter with an Indian photographer, and the State Department had lodged a complaint with the CIA. His future was uncertain—he could be dismissed, imprisoned, or worse.

Deepa had asked him, just like she'd today, how he was doing. He had looked at her with sorrowful eyes, his heart in the grip of a steel vice. They had been sitting at the table, eating breakfast. Nina had been giddy with happiness that he had returned after three long weeks, singing while she served *aloo parathas*. Her happiness had only deepened his melancholy; he worried that it might be too short-lived.

Deepa had seen that look and replied with her usual gentleness and affection. "We're here for you now; you don't have to slog this road alone. Let go of your pride, anger, guilt, regret—they just sap the life out of you. Be with Nina. She adores you. She'll make you happy." She had reached out and patted Stephen's hand, something she did routinely with her two children. And miraculously, the knot in his chest had disappeared, and he had breathed lightly for the first time in months. She still had that effect on him, the proverbial cool hand on the fevered brow, to quote her favorite writer, P. G. Wodehouse.

Deepa took the warm cookies from the tray and arranged them on a dish. "Are you concerned that you will lose the election?"

Stephen had an ultracompetitive streak. Deepa noticed it whenever he played chess with her or tennis with Neel. One time, she'd thought he was going to explode with self-recrimination when he missed a shot. "C'mon, Stephen," he'd muttered to himself. "What the hell are you doing?"

"Actually, I am worried that we will win."

She laughed. "What! Really?"

"Yes. I am always anxious about safety. You know that."

It had been a shock to Deepa and Ravi, those headlines in Indian newspapers a couple of years ago. Their son-in-law was suspected of working for the CIA; their daughter, Nina, had been in the cross hairs of danger because of that. Ravi was sure that it was all true, but Stephen had explained that his engineering company worked on classified projects, joint missions with the Indian government—it was nothing more than that. Nina hadn't said a word on that matter.

Deepa looked up from arranging the cookies.

"You know, I always worry about you kids. So many things could go so wrong." She walked across the kitchen to the large, concealed fridge and extracted a cheesecake from its capacious interior. "I had a heart attack the first time Nina crossed the street by herself when she was five."

Even Deepa's voice was soothing to Stephen. She had a calm cadence and an Indo British accent that he found both charming and amusing.

"But that's no reason to stop living your life." She cut the cake into slender slices. "Don't take foolish risks. That's all."

She had her suspicions too, about Stephen and his profession. Nina, her sunny lark of a daughter who could never stop singing, had shown signs of extreme stress and anxiety ever since her marriage to Stephen. At first Deepa had thought the problems were caused by quarrels with Stephen, or other marital tensions, but as time passed, she realized that Nina's anxiety was on his behalf.

"Here, carry this for me, please." She handed Stephen the cake and picked up the dish with the cookies. "The others must be desperate for dessert by now."

When Stephen made no sign of moving, she said, "It'll be fine, Stephen. Don't worry. We—all of us together, collectively, I mean—will be able to deal with anything that comes your way."

That was another quality he loved about his mother-in-law. She was a strong woman and surely must've had opinions, but she never lingered on negative thoughts or judged, just offered encouragement and reassurance.

They returned to the table. A raucous debate was underway, Nina and Ravi against Neel on the topic of legalizing pot.

"What do you say, Stephen?" Ravi asked.

"Sure, why not?"

"Stephen!" Nina protested. "What kind of a Republican are you?!"

"Small government and all that, we don't want to tell people what to eat, smoke, or who to sleep with." He smiled and sat down to enjoy his cookies and cheesecake, gazing out on the beautiful snow-covered surroundings outside the glass walls.

The dining area overlooked a large, paved inner courtyard, where illuminated trees stood like ballerinas, glittering arms stretched to the heavens. The festive lights and atmosphere brought back bittersweet memories for Stephen, memories of the Christmases when his grandfather had been alive.

Nina tried to reinstate as many traditions as she could. She had to drag the information out of him and infer from old albums and journals hidden away in locked rooms and forgotten closets, whenever and wherever she could find them. Time had come crashing to a halt for Stephen when his grandfather died, and he, in turn, had cursed it to rot away unseen inside the James mansion. Nina would wander through those haunted floors, looking for clues to his childhood. She had no other way to learn about it, because he had forbidden her to get in touch with his mother or siblings. "That's all I demand of you," he had said the night they'd been married, "no contact with my family whatsoever."

"Stephen, let's go. The game is about to begin," Neel's voice urged. Stephen excused himself and joined Neel, Deepa, and Ravi in the family room, while Nina continued to gossip with the grandparents at the table. Even though he'd been overwhelmed by the boisterous and social Sharma clan at the start, he now felt completely a part of the family. He had learned to smile back at Grandma Sharma's chanted blessings and exchange firm handshakes with Grandpa on every arrival and departure.

After a long, leisurely evening of eating and talking and more eating, Stephen and Nina went to bed around midnight. They were to sleep in Nina's room, as usual. The queen bed always felt way too small to Stephen, accustomed as he was to his grandfather's galleon of a bed. He kept fidgeting and tossing, trying to find a comfortable position without jabbing Nina with his elbows.

His phone buzzed.

"Hello!" he answered immediately. Nina opened her eyes. Her antennae were always keyed to danger.

"Hi Wasim! What's up?"

Stephen laughed at something Wasim said and finished with a good night.

Nina sat up. "What happened?"

"Wasim's drunk." Stephen's phone plinked pleasantly, and a video clip came through. He showed it to Nina: Doug playing the clarinet in a band at some club.

He sounds fucking amazing! said the text from Wasim.

NEW ORLEANS

Wasim and Doug arrived at the Mayhew residence in New Orleans just in time for Thanksgiving dinner. Their taxi pulled up in front of a picture-postcard home that sat like a candy-colored confection in a lush nest of flowering trees, shrubs, and vines.

They had barely climbed the front steps when the door flew open. "Hello!" Doug's mother welcomed them. "Come in. Come in. We were just about to sit down for dinner. Freshen up, get dressed, and come down quickly, boys! We are hungry!" She hugged her son.

Doug gave his mother a noisy kiss on the cheek and introduced Wasim.

"Pleased to meet you, Wasim. I have heard so much about you," she said.

She was older than Wasim had expected, with white hair and gnarled, veiny hands. But what he noticed at once was her remarkable voice and sparkling eyes and Doug's impish smile. Colorful bangles tinkled musically on her wrist when she shook his hand.

"A pleasure to meet you too, Mrs. Mayhew."

"How's the campaign going, fellas?"

"It's a lot of work. We don't get much sleep. But I wouldn't trade it for anything!" Wasim replied. Doug had already disappeared into the crowd in the next room.

The house was full of relatives and friends. Doug was hugged and greeted loudly as they made their way through the packed rooms and up the ornate staircase to his bedroom. "How's the election," people asked. "How's your man doing? Will he win? Go get 'em, Dougie!"

Wasim was met with a cautious courtesy, as if they didn't know what to make of him, this tall, good-looking man with a funky name. Where's Mr. Mayhew, Wasim wondered. Doug had warned that his father had been diagnosed with Alzheimer's a few years earlier. Perhaps he was too ill to be a part of the festivities.

Doug opened the door to his room. "Welcome!" He stepped aside to let Wasim enter.

"Oh man! What's *this*?!" Wasim exclaimed.

In one corner of the room stood a massive collection of clarinets, at least fifty or so, in different styles.

Some were antiques. An entire wall was dedicated to shelves of music—binders, sheet music, books, CDs, LPs. A piano occupied the wall next to the clarinets. Several music stands stood in readiness, awaiting their turn.

"I play the clarinet, always have, since I was five years old," Doug said. "I know, I know…it's dorky, but I love it."

"No way!" Wasim knew that Doug was an avid music listener and frequented jazz clubs and concerts late at night, but he had no idea that Doug was a musician as well.

"I'll play for you tonight, with some of my friends. But we'd better get dressed and go down."

Doug went to the bathroom to shower.

Wasim walked around Doug's room, picking up and putting down things. It was a beautiful room, with high ceilings and tall plantation-style doors that opened onto a wide balcony. Wasim, who had grown up in a modest split-level home bereft of any architectural grace, was highly appreciative of such beauty. During his career as a communications director he had seen many wealthy homes and always admired Stephen's for its stately Victorian dignity and sparse, tasteful interiors. But this was a different type of beauty, the kind that grabbed you by the collar as you walked by and made you look again. The house was not on a grand scale, like Stephen's, and lacked the scenic setting of the New England coast, but it was a work of art, both inside and out, with its jewel tones and regal wrought-iron flourishes, an architectural stunner set amid cascading bougainvillea and honeysuckle.

The room itself was an extension of Doug, playful, fun and full of life, and completely genuine—no affectations or pretense. Every object in the room was a part of Doug, his story and his life.

Wasim was so deep in his daydream that he didn't notice that Doug had emerged from the shower and was getting dressed.

"Wasim, my man, snap out of it!" Doug said. "Go get dressed, or my mom will have your head on a platter!"

Wasim picked out his clothes from the suitcase but couldn't tear himself away to go get dressed. He sat down on the bed and smiled at Doug, who was whistling away. Being home had turned Doug into a happy little boy, far away from the crushing responsibility of creating America's future statesmen. It was such a joyous sight.

When Wasim was dressed and they were ready to go downstairs, Doug turned to him. "How do you want me to introduce you—boyfriend, partner, or friend?"

Wasim was taken aback at the question. "I don't know...whatever you like."

Doug opened the door a crack and was about to step out but then stopped and closed it, shutting out the din of voices. His hair was slick from the shower, and his face was scrubbed to a pink.

"Wasim," he said, "you are it."

Wasim looked blankly at him. "I am what?"

Just then Doug's mother called for them, making it impossible for Wasim to quiz him any further. What had just happened? Was it a declaration of love? What was it?

They went down the stairs and were immediately subsumed into the large crowd sitting at the vast table. A battalion of uniformed waiters began serving dinner.

Wasim sat between Doug's uncle and cousin and barely paid attention to the conversation. His mind was still on what Doug had said. He forced himself to concentrate and give civil replies, and keep his eyes from wandering to Doug, sitting across the table.

The faces around the table were a different make from what he was used to on the East Coast and in the Midwest—there was more olive in the skin, more honey in their eyes, and a caressing lilt in voices coming from fuller lips. It was all very interesting. But all he could think was, I wish I could be alone with Doug.

He had to endure another hour at the table before everyone rose and moved to the other side of the house for music and coffee.

"This is our chance to slip away," Doug whispered. "Let me get my mom's car keys."

And in less than twenty minutes, they were in a section of "N'awlins," as the locals called it, where music was literally in the air. Small knots of people formed spontaneously at street corners, performing and improvising. Mellifluous notes from saxophones, clarinets, and trombones wafted onto the street from wide-open doors and windows of small buildings and shacks. It wasn't clear whether they were homes or bars or shops. But it didn't seem to matter. Each hall had a big crowd outside, fans craning their necks to see the musicians and hear them playing.

There wasn't an inch to move. Yet, the crowd throbbed to the beat in unison, like a surreal sea coral undulating in the ocean currents. It was electric. Wasim had never experienced anything like that.

Doug grabbed Wasim's hand and pulled him along through one such crowd to the doors of a small, brightly lit hall. A band was playing inside on a small, rickety wooden stage elevated barely a foot off the floor. The room was packed, with people crowding around the stage. There was not enough room for the musicians to even move their instruments. But no one, least of all the musicians, seemed to mind.

A young black hipster stood behind the ropes at the entrance to the hall, collecting cash and preventing overcrowding inside. When he saw Doug, he greeted him enthusiastically and showed them both to a back entrance.

They entered the room from the other side and emerged right behind the piano. The musicians beamed at Doug and waved for him to join in.

Doug seated Wasim on a little stool next to the piano, picked up a clarinet, and, without missing a beat, joined the band on the stage.

Wasim's jaw dropped when he heard the first note that Doug played. It was pure, resonant, and effortless. He listened in utter disbelief.

That was just the beginning. After a few numbers, they moved to another venue and then another and another and continued on, imbibing free drinks and smoking free smokes along the way. Doug was like a crazed dynamo, switching from clarinet to sax and back to the clarinet, occasionally pounding out a rousing piece on the piano. All Wasim could do was watch and listen and try to keep up with his manic energy.

As the night wore on, Wasim's recollection grew fuzzy, and he barely remembered returning home and crashing on the couch in Doug's room.

Hardly an hour must have passed when they woke to the jarring alarm on Doug's phone. It took a huge effort just to open their eyes. They washed, packed hurriedly, and went downstairs. Their taxi would arrive any minute.

The house was quiet. Where is everybody, Wasim wondered. Back in his parents' home, relatives and guests camped out for days and weeks when they came to visit.

"We're here," Doug's mother called out from the dining room. "Come have breakfast before you leave."

Doug and Wasim left their bags near the front door and went to the dining room.

The large Thanksgiving table had been replaced by a normal-sized dining table. Doug's mother sat at one end in full makeup and formal attire. An older gentleman that Wasim hadn't seen earlier was at the other end of the table, in a wheelchair. A helper of some sort sat next to him with a feeding bowl and spoon.

The room was bright with sunshine. A wayward breeze brought in the fragrance of early morning flowers. It was a scene straight out of a painting—vases filled with extravagant blooms, a crisp white tablecloth, gleaming china, antique rugs, artwork everywhere, and a grand piano at the far end, the epitome of gracious living.

Except for the gent in the wheelchair whose mouth had gone slack. The last spoonful of food dribbled down his bib.

"Wasim, this is my father, Peter Mayhew. He was away yesterday because the crowd is too much for him to handle."

Doug knelt before his father and looked into his eyes. "Dad?" There was no recognition. He rose to his feet and took Wasim's hand and put it in his father's. "Dad, this is Wasim. Remember I've been writing to you about him? Can you say hello?"

No response. "Not today, sweetie," his mother said. "It looks like an off day today."

But Wasim thought he felt a pressure on his hand. He bent down and said, "Pleased to meet you, sir." This time the pressure was a little more pronounced.

"I think he said hello." He turned to Doug. "He pressed my hand."

Doug gave a lingering look to his father and then kissed him on the cheek. It hadn't been this bad during his last visit. The old man had managed to smile at least. His mother had warned him that it would be worse this time around, but it wasn't enough to prepare Doug for this total blankness.

"Sorry, Doug," Wasim said once they were in the taxi and on their way to the airport. He took Doug's hand and held it in both of his. It was a first for him, this public display of affection. He looked defiantly at the cab driver, who stared at them from the rearview mirror.

"Thanks." Doug was touched. He knew how difficult it was for Wasim, even this small gesture. It took a lot of effort to overcome the mental and physical taboos one was brought up with. His thoughts returned to his father, the awards and plaques that filled his study, a lifetime of accomplishments that he had cherished and strived for rendered unrecognizable and meaningless to him by a cruel disease.

TABLOID LOVE

I t was just by chance that Tyler saw her. He had worn out his sneakers and had stopped off at this particular mall because it was on his way. It was the Saturday after Thanksgiving, and the mall was insufferable. The long weekend had been miserable. His mom had asked him to come home to Texas, but he hadn't felt like it. He had stayed back in his rented home and eaten pizza in front of the TV, feeling lonely and utterly sorry for himself. It was his first Thanksgiving in twenty years without Claire. To make matters worse, Ashley had claimed she had other engagements and had refused to see him. But here she was, standing in front of the Zara display.

As usual, she was a treat for the eyes. The mannequins couldn't compete with her in her hip-hugging jeans and her trademark heart-stopping red sweater. Red was her favorite color. Its effect on men was well known, and she used it to the best advantage—red nails, lips, underwear. She had been difficult to reach ever since he'd suggested that she sleep with Stephen and get it on camera. And after the Wasim-Doug story, she had completely cut him off. He had no idea where she lived. This was an unexpected stroke of luck, running into her like this.

He was about to walk up to her when it struck him that he should follow her and see where she lived, just for future reference. That would be more useful than a one-time showdown in the mall.

He followed her discreetly while she wandered around window-shopping and talking on the phone. Whoever was at the other end was clearly a very close friend, not a client. She was unguarded and super chatty. She made stops at Starbucks, Saks Fifth Avenue, Furla, and Neiman Marcus, and then, just as Tyler was about to give up and accost her, she looked at her watch and rushed out of the mall to the parking lot. He followed her car for a good thirty minutes on the highway, until she peeled off and sped toward a high-end condo complex on the water.

The parking garage was multitiered and, surprisingly, accessible to the public. She drove into a section that was protected by a security gate. Man, I hope I don't lose her, he thought and parked in the public area while desperately twisting around, trying to keep an eye on her car. He got out of his Miata and watched for her between the gaps in the pillars as she trawled for open slots. She finally found one and pulled in.

After what seemed to Tyler like an eternity, she got out of the car and made for the elevator, weighed down with shopping bags. He slipped behind her and tried to walk as quietly as he could. He needn't have bothered, because she was busy with her iPod and didn't even notice. She stopped near the garage elevator and waited, humming to herself, adjusting her hair and looking at her phone.

"Hello, Ashley," he said when he was within feet of her.

She turned around, startled.

"Hello," she said and pulled out her earphones, not at all happy to see him. "What are you doing here?"

"Nothing, I just followed you from the mall." The elevator rang, and the doors opened, but she didn't get in.

"Why didn't you return my calls?" he asked.

The elevator gave up, closed its doors, and went away. She turned around and jabbed the elevator button to summon it again.

"I was busy," she answered without looking at him.

"Bullshit!" He couldn't contain the anger and resentment of the past few days and perhaps of grudges of even greater vintage.

"Well, you were going crazy. I thought I'd get back to you after you had time to cool down."

He could see her mind whirring. How can I get away from this punk, she was probably thinking.

"More bullshit!" He tried to ignore the pounding in his ears and chest.

She looked uncomfortable now. The cavernous parking garage was deserted. "There's a café downstairs," she said. "Let's go there. We can talk."

She walked toward the stairs and was about to open the door, but he grabbed her hand.

"Dave! Let go!"

"Listen, all I asked was that you cozy up to that prick and take some pictures. What's so crazy about that?"

With a quick move, she freed her hand. Then she pulled out a Mace spray from her bag. "I don't want to make a fuss. But if you touch me or call me again, I am going to get a restraining order against you."

She glared at him. "In my business, there are people who handle difficult situations for me." She turned away.

Tyler sneered. "You are threatening me now, is it? You going to set your hounds on me?"

She gave him a contemptuous look and opened the door to the stairs.

A dark rage exploded in his head. He followed her through the door. Why did these women treat him like shit? His ex was the same way, the same look of scorn. And suddenly he realized that Ashley looked a lot like his ex. When he'd selected her from all those luscious photos, some Freudian urge must have pushed him to pick her.

His mind was numb, but his hands, without his bidding, shot out and pushed her just as she stretched out a foot to take the first step down the stairs.

He must have used a fair amount of force, because she lost her balance, not surprising given the heels she was wearing, and tumbled down the stairs and came to a stop at the feet of a young couple who was on the way up.

"He pushed her!" the woman shouted.

Nosy bitch! Tyler stood there, unable to move, disbelieving of what he had done.

Ashley sat up. She was unhurt but stunned.

The couple helped Ashley to her feet and asked her if she was OK.

Tyler slumped down at the top of the steps, still in a daze, looking without seeing, listening without hearing. He didn't resist when the male half of the couple stood guard over him and called the cops or when the cops cuffed him and took him to the police station.

Ashley didn't look at him once during the entire proceedings. Even in the midst of that fracas and humiliation, his mind registered her long blond hair in disarray and that sullen, pouty look that drove him to distraction.

He didn't say a word in the police car and continued to sit in silence at the police station. What was going to happen to him now? Was this the end of even this trashy career that he had been reduced to? He felt really sorry for himself. What he'd give to be back in his old job in the dignified and silent halls of chip design.

The law-enforcement machinery churned around him; phones rang, officers talked and joshed, and there was constant chatter on the walkie-talkies. A clerk handed him a phone and said, "Make your call."

Tyler sat staring at it for a long time. He tried to pick up the courage to call his friend Jimmy in DC. What a fucking idiotic thing to do, to land in this ridiculous mess. His hand refused to press the buttons and make the call.

An officer took him to a tiny holding cell that smelled of urine and slammed the door on him. His shame and humiliation were complete. His ex, Claire, would've loved to see him in this state, clutching his head, sitting next to a toilet bowl that had serviced murderers and rapists.

The next morning, the cell door opened and a professional-looking woman, a cross between a lawyer and an accountant, entered with an officer. Tyler sat up. He hadn't slept at all, and his middle-aged body was hurting and creaking from the unaccustomed rigor of the hard bed.

"I am Ashley's attorney," she said to Tyler. "My client doesn't want to press charges."

Tyler couldn't believe his ears. He stood up and thanked her profusely—thank you, thank you, thank you. "How is she doing?" he asked.

"Fine," the woman replied curtly.

Once they were outside the station, she turned to him. "Mr. Tyler, I will drive you to your car. But if you try to contact my client again, you will be in a whole lot of trouble." And during the twenty-minute ride to the parking lot where his car was, she did not answer a single question, nor did she volunteer any other information.

He watched the red taillights of the woman's car disappear after she'd dropped him off. He opened the door of his Miata, slid in behind the wheel, and slowly began driving back home.

What if the story got out? The whole world would know David Tyler stalked and attacked a high-end call girl. Dave Tyler, the pitiful bastard who couldn't get a woman to sleep with him without paying. If some tabloid or TV station paid Ashley a shitload of money, she would readily tell them that Tyler had asked her to frame Stephen James, Republican candidate for the US Senate. That son of privilege would once again be the cock of the walk, while he, Tyler, would be back where he was when he first met Stephen, crushed under the cruel heels of a coldhearted bitch.

By the time he got home, showered, and had a drink, things had started to look less bleak. Tyler convinced himself that he was safe. Ashley had very little incentive to jeopardize her thriving business. Discretion was absolutely critical for her roster of clients. That was the reason why she had dropped the charges in the first place. As for the young couple that had helped her up, they probably had no idea who he was. Not many people did.

He'd be wise to get working on getting that big scoop before other shit got in his way, as it almost always did. The debate was just a few days away. That would probably be his last opportunity to get to Stephen James before the election.

TYLER'S SURPRISE

Stephen Edward James @stephenjames . Oct 25
Come to our debate party! Join the discussion through our
social media stream.

The camera focused on Stephen, Nina, and Neel. They stood to one side of the auditorium stage, along with the campaign staff. For some reason, the sight of the trio unsettled Nina's father, Ravi. He still found it hard to digest that Nina had chosen such an odd husband. Admittedly, Stephen had wonderful qualities. He was principled, fearless, and truly concerned about being of service to the country. And there was absolutely no doubt about his devotion to Nina. But this whole CIA thing was too crazy, and it put Nina in danger. Now, even Neel seemed to be drawn into Stephen's orbit. He'd given up his job at a prestigious global civil-engineering company to run Stephen's "research" outfit that consulted for the Department of Defense.

Nina's mother, Deepa, on the other hand, was thrilled. She kept up an excited commentary, watching her children with pride. She chose not to think about Stephen's past but focused on the future. "Come on, Ravi," she said with a laugh. "We could be the parents-in-law of a US senator! How funny is that!"

Ravi and Deepa were in their family room, settled comfortably in front of the big HDTV. It was a large glass-walled room with glimpses of other parts of the house and the courtyard. Deepa pulled a blanket around her and moved closer to Ravi on the leather sectional. She was excited from head to toe—their son-in-law was about to debate his opponent in the Senate race, Congresswoman Katherine Collins.

Under normal circumstances Ravi and Deepa would have loved for their friends and relatives to watch the debate with them. But they were uncomfortable discussing Stephen, because he raised awkward questions in the Indian community. Many people in their circle were familiar with the story that had gotten Stephen expelled from India. So the Sharmas had decided to watch the debate without company, without even Grandpa and Grandma. The elders had gone to bed hours earlier, retired to the warmth and comfort of their temperature-controlled room, maintained at a steady eighty degrees Fahrenheit.

The moderator called the crowd to order. Stephen and Congresswoman Collins took their places on the stage. The congresswoman was confident and cheerful. She was a plump little woman who smiled and waved constantly, at friends, at the audience, at strangers. Stephen, in contrast, looked inert and expressionless. He read and reread his notes, visibly impatient for the bout to begin.

Despite her maternal image, Katherine Collins was no easy opponent. She launched right in.

"Washington is not like your ivory-tower world of privilege, Mr. James," she began. Her team had told her to get to him and make him lose his cool. They reported he was said to be very thin-skinned. She taunted him. "Mr. James, you can't always count on family connections in the real world."

He countered her calculated offense with a point-by-point, precise rebuttal. He smiled at her. "But I don't need family connections, Congresswoman. I have built a viable business based on my inventions and hard work. I didn't need anyone to pull strings for me. It was the government that came to me to buy up my patents! I understand that's difficult for you to fathom, being the Washington wheeler-dealer that you are."

Stephen affected a gentle, friendly manner for the debate. With his hands planted firmly on either edge of the podium, he smiled at the cameras and frequently looked over at the audience to co-opt them.

Nina sat in the front row with her brother, anxiously watching the stage. She was worried that Stephen would lose his temper or get into his hypercompetitive mode and become too aggressive.

"*Excuse* me for having actually served two terms in the Congress." Ms. Collins placed her hands on her hips and stepped away from the podium with a bow.

But Stephen was disciplined and stayed on message, thanks to hours of preparation and rehearsals. "But what have you accomplished in those two terms? Your voting record is all over the place, because you are beholden to special interests," he said politely to Ms. Collins. "And all those contracts," he said with great reluctance, "they seem to always end up with your friends!"

"You are just another Republican," she said dismissively and turned to the audience. "He is progun, even after the horrendous shooting that we've witnessed in our neighboring state."

"Now, now." Stephen smiled. "That's not entirely true, and you know it. I have vocally advocated for closing loopholes at gun shows and have pushed for background checks, even before I decided to run. You know that, Congresswoman. But you are a Washington insider. You just ignore inconvenient facts!"

"Mr. James," she shot back, "you can talk when you have served a few years in the government. Right now, you haven't served a single day. Why should the people of Massachusetts trust you?"

"Because," Stephen replied courteously, "you have nothing to show for your years spent in Washington, other than parroting your party's positions. You haven't accomplished anything...initiated a single bill, debated any issue, or stood up to your party...nothing. You have voted in lockstep with your party. You seem to lack a mind of your own! And you are held hostage by special-interest groups; you know, your unions, your lobbies. What is the value that you bring to Massachusetts?"

"You might not know it, walled off in your palace, Mr. James, what I've done for teachers and veterans."

"You know as well as I do that most Republicans voted for the same measures for veterans and teachers that you did. You do whatever the DNC tells you to do." His glasses glinted with cold efficiency. "I, on the other hand, am a true independent and can vote the values I stand for. I have parted ways with my party on abortion, climate change, and even taxes."

"There you go again. That's your inexperience talking." She turned away from him.

"That's really sad. You are so entrenched in your Washington ways that you are not even willing to *try* to change the status quo. That's why I want to institute term limits on House members and dock their pay if they can't perform essential duties, like passing a budget. I am fed up of the Congress holding the country hostage!" Stephen was actually animated.

As the evening wore on, no matter what question the moderator asked, the congresswoman simply kept repeating the same mantra—he doesn't understand the common man, he has no experience, he has no track record of accomplishments. Stephen, in turn, kept pivoting to the same talking points—her flip-flopping voting record, ties to special-interest groups, and political favors to friends and family. Back and forth it went, with partisan applause from the audience.

Nina watched stiffly, every muscle taut with anxiety. Neel leaned over and said, "Nina, relax. He's doing great." She gave a brief smile but didn't let up on watching Stephen. On one occasion she detected subtle signs of a temper, when Ms. Collins alluded to Stephen's grandfather's clout and connections, but he gripped the podium and let it pass.

After ninety minutes under the hot lights on that stage, after small skirmishes on gun control and wire-tapping, after verbally pummeling each other, the weary candidates delivered their prepared closing statements.

The moderator thanked everyone, and the university's auditorium filled with applause. Large groups of supporters from both camps swarmed the aisles to greet their candidates. The PR teams immediately went into spin cycle: our candidate won the debate!

Tyler stood listening at the back of the auditorium. He watched Stephen, Nina, and Neel through his camera's telescopic lens. He had his hat pulled down and had discarded his all-black ensemble so as to be inconspicuous until he chose to be recognized.

Nina had seemed nervous to him, especially at the beginning of the debate, but she had settled back into her adoring-wife mode once Stephen finished his opening statement. Now, Tyler watched her make her way to the stage. Her brother helped her up the steps and remained close, watching her and the surrounding crowd. A bit too intense, Tyler thought, almost like a bodyguard. Why? Who would want to hurt Nina? He had tried in the past to reach Nina's family members to dig up material about Stephen, but they were well insulated from the public, their information carefully protected. He had no way to reach them, short of following Nina in the hope that she'd lead him to her parents' home.

On the stage, Stephen and Congresswoman Collins shook hands. In a gesture that brought her much positive publicity later, Ms. Collins went over to Nina. They spoke for a few minutes under the greedy eyes and ears of the media. "What a lovely young lady," the congresswoman said afterward to the members of the press around her, "*and* she's a Democrat!"

Stephen, on the other hand, had relapsed into his stiff and formal ways. He shook a few hands and hastened to get Nina out of the crush of people. The cameras flashed, and after posing for the briefest of photo ops, Stephen and Nina left the stage.

Tyler got up and hurried to where he could be within feet of the couple when they walked by. There was the usual throng of volunteers, campaign aides, and the general public surging to the aisle to greet the candidates. Stephen came first and stopped frequently to shake hands. Nina was secure between him and his brother-in-law. Doug and Wasim followed a few feet behind, busy talking to the reporters.

Tyler got his camera ready. He could frame the candidate in a nice, tight close-up.

Stephen spotted Tyler when he was still twenty feet away. Without breaking his stride and with only a quick look, he continued down the aisle. Nina saw him next and started visibly. The crowd picked up on it, and a hubbub rose around them as people became aware of who Tyler was.

Stephen continued at an even pace and then stopped abruptly, right in front of Tyler, and half turned toward him with a sharp movement. He was about to say something but then decided to steer clear. The last time he was in a spat with a member of the media, it ended in his expulsion from India.

Tyler said loudly and clearly, "Mr. James! Did Wasim Raja try to kill himself? Was there a delay in bringing him to the hospital?"

Stephen paused to put his arm around Nina and walked on. He glanced at Wasim behind him.

Wasim was stone-faced and walked with a fixed stare of concentration. Doug switched sides and positioned himself between Tyler and Wasim as they passed him.

Tyler had his camera ready and was clicking away. "Is it true that you tried to cover it up? The hospital staff has been told not to talk about it?"

The whole media circus had congregated around them by this time. Tyler loved the attention. He was part of the story now, perhaps the story itself. But he only had a couple of seconds before he would lose the opportunity. Stephen was already several feet away. Tyler had to say something that would make him react.

"When is the baby due? Girl or boy?" he called out. The pregnancy had not been officially announced, even though Nina was beginning to show.

Stephen gripped Nina's hand firmly and continued to walk toward the exit.

Tyler played his trump card. "Did you refer to your opponent's "claws" and suggest that she bake cookies and watch *The Golden Girls*, Mr. James?"

Everyone stopped. An unaccustomed silence reigned. All phones were immediately set to mute, all conversations came to a stop. Tyler held up his cell phone and played an audio snippet.

"Would future Senator James authorize drone attacks?" Wasim's voice asked.

"Of course!" Stephen's clipped accent answered.

"What about civilian deaths?"

"Collateral damage."

"Even children?"

"Yes."

"Stephen, you can't say that!" Doug's voice piped in.

"Why not?'

"Because Collins will be all over you."

"I am not afraid of her claws. What does she know about drone attacks? It's not like sitting around baking cookies and watching The Golden Girls."

Sound of men laughing.

Tyler switched it off.

Stephen let go of Nina's hand. That conversation had taken place at the very first debate prep session at Stephen's campaign headquarters. Someone must have recorded it. Stephen tried to remember who else had been in the room. George, Wasim, Doug, a couple of political consultants, and his two debate coaches—no one else that he could think of. Had there been any interruptions? Yes! A young volunteer had brought in a FedEx for Doug to sign. He must have been in the room for perhaps five minutes.

It was an unfortunate coincidence. Stephen was normally very guarded, especially in the presence of people he didn't know well enough to trust. But that first practice session had been a disaster, with Stephen having had to modify almost all his answers. He had been irritated and frustrated with the coaches and the words had slipped out.

The reporters clustered around Tyler and Stephen who were now facing each other like boxers at the beginning of a prize fight.

Doug and Wasim rushed in and pulled Stephen away. Wasim whispered in Stephen's ear. Stephen's face turned red. He gave a curt nod. He looked over to the side of the auditorium and saw that Nina was safe in Neel's custody, close to an exit. She looked angry but he didn't have time to deal with her right now.

He turned to the reporters and photographers who were jostling and pushing around him.

"That was a private conversation." He gave a forced smile. "Ms. Collins is a tough opponent and a seasoned politician. I am confident that she can handle my ill-chosen words said in a moment of frustration. However, I do apologize on Mr. Tyler's behalf for the conversation having been made public, and for whatever grief and inconvenience it might have caused her. That's all I have to say."

A cacophony broke out while all the photographers and reporters rushed to jab their microphones at Tyler for a response. None of them caught the look that passed between Neel and Stephen, or the grim smile that graced the Republican candidate's face for a split second.

Neel pecked something on his phone with a finger.

The next instant there was a collective gasp from the crowd. A news story had just popped up. An eager, young reporter turned to Tyler. "Is it true that you were arrested last week, Mr. Tyler? Why? Would you like to share that with us?" He held up his phone so that Tyler could see the story.

George Applegate had sent Stephen and Neel the entire file on Tyler's arrest, and they had prepared their move just for such an occasion. Neel had pushed out the story untraceably via Tor, the anonymized Internet router service—not the entire story but just enough to ignite people's imaginations and make them suspect the worst. The story hinted at a crime involving sex and Tyler's overnight jail stay but nothing more. People's imaginations are far worse than the truth, George had said.

Tyler was paralyzed. He couldn't move or talk, frozen in nightmarish immobility.

Everyone saw it. Cell phones, cameras, and other digital snoops recorded his stunned face, to be flashed around the world with humiliating efficiency to e-mail addresses, websites, and social networks.

Tyler's ears burned hot. He managed to regain control and pushed his way through the tittering, snapping mob. The photographers were crowding around him, but he forced himself not to run.

"Would you like to comment on that, Mr. Tyler? Why were you arrested?" Reporters pushed microphones and recording devices into his face. The political gossip sphere was on fire. What could it be, they wondered. An underage girl? Another man—wouldn't that be ironic, after outing Doug Mayhew and Wasim Raja! OMG, a boy, an intern? The speculation went viral and covered every deranged possibility that a human brain could think up.

Tyler got into his car with what he hoped was dignity and drove away before he could be blocked by other traffic.

Back home, Deepa and Ravi watched in dismay. Controversy and conflict seemed to always erupt around Stephen.

"I bet Stephen had something to do with it," Ravi said. He looked angrily at Deepa. "Your daughter's been a nervous wreck ever since she met this guy!"

Even though he had come to terms with Nina's choice, Ravi was still wary of Stephen. For one, Stephen had an inexplicable influence over his normally level-headed daughter. She had jumped into marriage after barely a few weeks' acquaintance. She had brought Stephen home one day, after a single phone call on this important matter, to inform them that she had agreed to marry him. They wanted to be married as soon as possible. The family had no say or choice in the matter.

Both Deepa and Ravi had been surprised. Stephen wasn't the usual sensitive, soulful, poetic type that seemed to catch her fancy. And when they learned about Stephen's family history, they were not at all happy. Barely a year later, they were shocked once more when they'd heard of Nina's plans to move to

New Delhi with Stephen. Why did she have to go live in India? Why couldn't she just visit her husband? She had such a phenomenal future ahead of her; why did she have to jeopardize her career in deference to Stephen's? Then came the CIA scandal in India and now the latest insanity, this Senate run.

The camera caught a last glimpse of Stephen, Nina, and Neel exiting the building, while on a split screen, another camera chased Tyler's little Miata on a highway.

"The man is crazy!" Ravi switched off the TV and flung the remote on the couch.

Deepa continued to stare at the blank TV screen. She paid no attention to Ravi. Her mind was busy with disaster fantasies. Tyler was evil. He had already pushed Wasim to the edge of death. What if Tyler did something even more extreme? What if he hurt Nina and she lost her baby?

Ravi watched Deepa's face as one emotion chased another and immediately regretted his unjustified outburst. He had upset her. All said and done, Stephen was Nina's husband. She loved him. And there was no denying it; Stephen doted on Nina and made every effort to please her and her family. He was fundamentally a good and decent man and a man of incredible courage and bravery.

Ravi sat down next to Deepa. "They'll be fine," he said. "They have to get used to this sort of thing. They will be in the public eye all the time now."

"What do you think Tyler will do?" she asked Ravi.

He shrugged and switched on the TV once more to watch the postdebate yammering.

Tyler was livid. He gripped the steering wheel violently as he drove, a lurid stream of invective flowing from his lips.

The past weeks, after the gay photos, had been quite interesting. A conservative faction of the Republican Party had come courting. "We love your website. We love the values you stand for. Come and be our advocate," they'd said. "We will give you a broader platform with greater reach. We have billionaire backers, and we need your help in taking down lip-service conservatives like Stephen James. The primaries for the next election cycle are barely months away!" Tyler was on the verge of signing a contract with a prominent right-wing rag that belonged to the Conservative Coalition group.

Now, all that would be impossible. The conservatives would not take kindly to hookers. They would eventually find out; the whole world would. The Internet made it impossible to keep secrets, even if the mysterious breaking story hadn't mentioned any details. Of course, Stephen must've been behind the leak. How could that son of a bitch have known about the arrest? Wasn't that shit supposed to be confidential? Was he really that powerful?

A MAN AND A PLAN

Tyler opened his eyes a slit and shut them immediately. He dropped his face back into the dark, funky-smelling recesses of the sofa. His mouth tasted sour and smelled like a mouse had died in it. A prodigious hammer worked away at his head. Stop, stop, he pleaded, but it continued its insistent rhythm.

He sat up slowly and attempted to open his eyes once more. Even though the blinds were down, the filtered light proved to be too strong in his fragile state. He stumbled toward the bathroom with his eyes shut.

It was in worse shape than he was. He quickly flushed the toilet to rid it of its contents and kicked his way through the debris on the floor to the shower.

The water hit him like a sandblaster, ice-cold at first and then with maddening extremes of temperature as he desperately fiddled with the knob. His boxers and T-shirt hung on him like deadweight. Once he got the temperature under control, he peeled off his clothes and fumbled for the shampoo bottle. Empty. He hurled it across the room in a fury.

By the time he came out of the bathroom, a savage, acidic hunger twisted his stomach into knots and led him to the kitchen. He grabbed a fistful of Cheerios and stuffed them in his mouth. The fridge was bereft. A solitary piece of cheese stared at him. He bit into it and grabbed the can of orange juice. On his way to the living room, he saw a bag of potato chips and emptied it into his mouth. The chips scraped his cheeks and the roof of his mouth. He sent orange juice to the rescue, to soften the chip fragments on their way down into his writhing intestines.

Where were the goddamned pain-killers? He returned to the bathroom, located the bottle, and swallowed a mouthful with the juice.

Dressed and sober, he went into the living room in search of his computer. My God, did I do this? he wondered, arrested in the doorway. Bottles and cans were strewn everywhere, and the place smelled of stale booze. Must've been quite a bender! Had he used something stronger than alcohol? He couldn't remember. He examined the carpet and was relieved that there were no spills or vomit stains.

His laptop and phone were buried under a pile of cushions. He couldn't possibly work here with the state the room was in. It would take him at least an hour to get it back to habitable. He grabbed the two devices and retreated to the relative tidiness of his bedroom.

By now his eyes had adjusted to the daylight. He pulled up the blinds and opened the windows. The lawn outside had been freshly mowed, and the raw smell of chlorophyll overwhelmed him, dredging the orange juice back up his throat.

The laptop beeped that it was ready for work. But he dared not look at it, terrified at what was out there. His enemies must be reveling in his humiliation. His ex would lap it up, cackling with glee.

He took a deep breath and forced himself to look, his head still tender and achy.

Every website on his list of favorites had that picture of Tyler flinching while his camera slid out of his grasp.

Tyler shuddered. Growing up a middle child, he was the weakest of the three siblings and physically intimidated by his more athletic brothers. He remembered when his mother had just returned to work after fifteen years of child-rearing and hadn't been at home to stand between him and the two belligerent boys. His brothers had taken every opportunity to get back at Tyler for his academic preening, without leaving a mark on his body but maiming him nevertheless. That childhood fear had never left him. And in an unguarded moment, when the reporter had mugged him with an unexpected question, Tyler had relapsed into his middle-school days and cowered.

Where's the outrage? That arrogant prick had been so dismissive of his opponent, a grandmother and professor. And nobody cared—not the media, not the Twitter world. Even the Collins campaign had waved it off, saying "The women of Massachusetts heard him loud and clear." Feminist groups made some feeble attempts but nobody paid any attention. Everybody was in love with the second coming of Kennedy, their fucking perfect candidate, even after he'd called children "collateral damage". How did the story get buried so easily? And how come all the heat was turned on Tyler instead?

He picked up the phone and called his good friend, the only friend he had, the man who had gotten him into the business of political gossip in the first place.

"Jimmy, it's Dave. Call me back."

Jimmy called back within minutes.

"How are you, Dave?"

"Terrible, I fucked up big time." Of course, Jimmy must know by now. It was all over the Internet that he had been arrested. But because no charges had been filed and Ashley's powerful friends had hushed things up, nobody knew why he had been arrested. Stories and rumors popped up afresh every few hours.

"What happened?" Jimmy's voice was faint, lost in crowd noises.

Tyler gave a short but honest summary of what had happened with Ashley. Jimmy whistled. "Dave, you need to calm down, man. You've been losing it ever since Claire left you."

Tyler didn't answer. There was too much truth in that statement. Worst of all, he realized finally that he still loved his ex-wife and that there was no replacing her. Twenty years of his life had been savagely cut out of his heart.

Jimmy, his childhood friend, who knew him best, understood. "Sorry, Dave."

Tyler sighed.

"That's OK. Can't do anything now. But I *really* need to get to the bottom of this Stephen guy's career at the CIA. Nobody on the list you gave me ever called back."

"These guys are hard to crack. Dave, you need to be careful. This is scary stuff."

"I know. But I have no other option. There must be a way. There is something weird going on, Jimmy. How come the story disappeared so quickly from the news cycle? The guy dismissed children as collateral damage! Someone's hushing up things!"

This was how every one of Tyler's misadventures started, with utter conviction. But Jimmy listened patiently.

"Jimmy, we need to find the one disgruntled person who is willing to talk."

"Let me see what I can do," Jimmy said. "But it will take a few days." Jimmy had cultivated a powerful network during his twenty years in DC and could do miracles.

"Thanks, Jimmy, but remember the election is less than a week away."

When he hadn't heard back from Jimmy after two days, Tyler began to get worried. The election was in another three days. Timing was everything in news; there was nothing more ephemeral.

Finally, around six in the evening, Tyler's phone buzzed in his pocket, and it was Jimmy...at last.

"You need to meet Rob at Café Beethoven in an hour." Jimmy's voice was exultant.

"Who's Rob?"

"I don't know. But that's the message I'm supposed to give you."

"OK, thanks, Jimmy. This is great."

An hour later, Tyler was at Café Beethoven, a large pastry shop just outside the main town square. In keeping with its name, the café played classical music over its music system. A preppy middle-aged couple tended the counter in soft, caressing NPR accents. He picked up a Linzer torte cookie and a cup of coffee from them and sat at a corner table with a view of the entire dining space. He had no way of recognizing Rob.

There was quite a crowd. It was sunset, and the café had a head-on view of the water ablaze with the fire of the setting sun. Tourists, older folk, and honeymooning couples sat around enjoying the view while they munched pastries and downed steaming cups of cappuccino. Tyler tried to guess if one of the men there was Rob, but none of them made eye contact.

A very tall man, with a slight paunch and a rolling gait, like a kite in shifting winds, walked in. He wore thick glasses, sported spiky blond hair, and had an abstracted look, like a professor gearing up to deliver a complicated lecture. His roomy, checked shirt was tucked into high-waisted pants that stopped an inch too short of his ankles. As if to complete the caricature, he had a yellow writing pad in one hand and a noticeable set of pens in his shirt pocket. He saw Tyler and made for him across the café floor.

"Mr. Tyler, I am Rob. I am here to talk about the contracting job for remodeling your house," he said, sitting down, his head cocked to one side like an attentive sparrow. "We spoke over the phone about the stone you wanted to use in your kitchen. I thought I'd take you to a store near here to show you some samples."

Tyler gaped.

"Stop staring, and do what I tell you. We don't have much time," the man snapped in an undertone.

As instructed, Tyler made small talk, pored over some diagrams that the man drew on the yellow pad, and then stood up.

"Drive to Moonlight Bay's lookout point, near the cliff," the man said as soon as they got into the car. The paunch disappeared, as did the look of abstraction.

"Where's that?" Tyler asked.

"Keep driving. I'll tell you." While Tyler drove, Rob smiled and chattered, about absolutely nothing.

Moonlight Bay's lookout was a secluded vista point at the end of an off-road trail. Tyler pulled into a dirt clearing.

"Now what?" he asked.

Rob got busy checking for surveillance with a little gizmo. He grabbed Tyler's cell phone and pulled out the battery and threw it into the bushes.

"Why'd you do that?" Tyler snatched his phone back, before it too was tossed out.

"Where's your laptop? Do you have it with you?"

"No! Who are you?" Tyler was truly alarmed now.

"Nobody. Stop talking, and listen," the man snapped. Then he proceeded to thoroughly pat down Tyler.

"Is this necessary?" Tyler asked, squirming.

"You've no idea," he replied and continued frisking with rough efficiency.

"What are you looking for?" Tyler pushed away the man's hands.

"Anything that might have been planted on you."

"Who'd do that? And how?"

The man gave a derisive guffaw. "I'll bet my life that he knows, down to the last ounce, how much you peed yesterday."

"Who? Who does?" Tyler looked so shocked that the man laughed once more.

"Who?! Are you kidding me?"

Tyler saw a serious flaw in the man's logic.

"If he is keeping an eye on me, how come he couldn't stop me from publishing those stories?"

The man directed a look of utter contempt at Tyler. "Do I really have to explain that to you?" He paused. "Because, you couldn't have helped him more if you tried. When you published the fake charges against Wasim Raja, you gave James an opportunity to posture as a champion of American Muslims. Oh the irony! And, when you published the kissing photos, he came out in full support of his gay boys, and now he is the darling of the LGBT lobby. You, single-handedly, made him a national figure. He is going to win in a landslide, my friend."

He stared at Tyler for a minute longer and continued. "Don't interrupt me. I will not repeat anything. You understand?"

Tyler nodded. He tried not to show how mad he was.

"I worked with Stephen James in Pakistan and in India, for almost ten years. We ran many missions in Kashmir. I have seen the things he has done and the things he is capable of."

The man stopped to poke his head out of the window and look around. "He is a violent, arrogant sod who gets away with murder because he is so fucking well connected. He has abused his authority so many times and has not once been held accountable. Your typical Ivy League—"

"He went to MIT," Tyler objected.

The man leaned toward him and brought his face really close and muttered, "Same difference. The man is a murderer."

"But isn't that your job?"

"Killing innocent children? No, Mr. Tyler, that's not our job."

Tyler prudently decided to keep his mouth shut. Nobody said anything for a few minutes.

"George, our boss, jumped through hoops to cover up Stephen's bloody messes. Nobody, other than the precious Mr. James, got that kind of protection. No, no, he even got promoted to be my boss! Do you know why?"

Rob sighed and answered his own question. "Because his fucking grandfather had given a boatload of money."

"To whom?"

"To the right people."

The man stared at Tyler through his thick glasses. "Two years ago, when he was head of operations for South Asia, James sent me on an overseas mission. And when it ran into trouble, he refused to give me diplomatic immunity. I managed to get out of the country, but now, I am wanted by Interpol for kidnapping in seven nations, including the country where my mother lives, because he refused to get me diplomatic immunity. I can't visit my mother, even though she is dying. The funny thing is he has claimed that same immunity to save his ass so many times."

"Was this in India?" Tyler asked.

The man did not reply.

"I have to go now. If you want to know the whole story of Stephen James, talk to Binodini Roy."

"Who's he?"

"She. You are a big boy; you figure it out. Bye now." Rob was suddenly in a big hurry. "Drop me off at the cul-de-sac near the end of that drive."

It took them barely a minute to get there. Rob kicked the door open.

"My friend, I'll give you a tip and a warning." He got out, closed the door, and bent down to look through the window at Tyler.

"First, the tip. Have you ever wondered why James would buy his neighbor's property? It must hold such terrible memories for him, literally soaked in his blood, the place where he almost died. Why would he do that?"

He laughed. "And now the warning, if I were you, I'd make damn sure that my wife and kids were provided for."

He stepped back and disappeared into the night.

Tyler sat in his car, confused and terrified. After a few minutes, he gathered himself. A disgruntled employee…that's all that man was, he told himself. There was no way that Stephen could still be employed by the CIA and run for the US Senate and no way that he could snoop on Tyler.

He drove back slowly. His eyes darted to the rear-view mirror every few seconds, searching for...what? They were all just headlights; he couldn't tell one car from another.

After a stressful drive of trying to elude phantom trackers, he entered the garage and stepped warily inside the house, looking at everything through suspicious eyes. Smoke alarm or hidden camera? Motion detectors...who were they sending the information to, whenever he moved? He shook his head. He shouldn't let Rob get to him like that.

He poured himself a glass of Scotch and sat before his computer. It was his gateway to the whole universe. He typed variations of the name that Rob had mentioned and finally hit on "Binodini Roy." Screen after screen scrolled past—activist, social worker, communist, rabble-rouser, professor, and general watchdog of Indian intelligence services. He clicked on Google Images and waited. And waited. Nothing happened. His computer just froze.

He swore and rebooted his computer. It went blank and refused to reboot. Damn! He got his tool kit and opened it, hooked it up to another laptop, and tried to see what was wrong. Nothing, not a clue.

Time was running out. He needed to get in touch with Binodini Roy and see her in person in the next two days, before the Senate election. But how? Rob hadn't given him any leads other than her name.

Frighteningly on cue, he heard his mailbox in the driveway open and close. How odd, the mailman didn't usually show up at nine thirty at night. Who'd open his mailbox? Tyler rushed to the window just in time to catch the red taillights of a car exiting the cul-de-sac. He ran out to catch the driver's attention, but the vehicle was gone. Should he follow the car or check his mailbox? There wasn't any point in trying to chase down that car. What'd he do, even if he caught up?

He walked over to his mailbox, took a deep breath, and opened it. At first he didn't see it, because it was deep inside, just a single sheet of paper. He reached in and pulled it out. There wasn't enough light for his tired eyes to read it. He took out his phone and turned on the flashlight.

It was a boarding pass. It had his name and everything. Shit! The flight was in three hours. Who were these people? Why were they buying him a ticket to India? Who cared? His life had crapped out completely; there was nothing to lose. He ran to his bedroom, packed a change of clothes, and grabbed his passport and car keys. It was time to go to Hyderabad, India, where Ms. Roy lived.

HYDERABAD

Collins
Experience Matters

Katherine Collins @kathycollins . Nov 30
Diplomacy and peace are our best weapons against terrorism, not rendition and torture.

This is not too bad, Tyler thought. The Hyderabad airport looked like any other modern airport, except it was shiny and new. He had just gotten off a twenty-hour flight, spent sandwiched between two matrons who resented having him in the middle seat. They stared at him, mumbled angrily across his chest at each other, and battled him for the armrest.

Rajiv Gandhi International Airport swarmed with people, even though it was four in the morning. Flights from the Arabian Peninsula disgorged men and women in traditional Muslim attire, who walked solemnly behind carts hauling mountains of luggage. Porters, janitors, travelers, flight crews, and vendors added to the din.

Tyler scanned the crowd and spotted, with relief, a large placard that said, *Mr. David Tyler.* It bobbed up and down on the other side of the customs gate. An earnest young man was attached to it. He was Tyler's driver and interpreter, identified by the travel agency only as Gopi.

"Welcome, Mr. Tyler," Gopi said and took Tyler's meager suitcase. "No more luggage?" he asked in disbelief.

Tyler tried to keep up with Gopi as he elbowed his way through the crowd to the exit and to a wide access ramp outside, where a long line of cars snaked up a hill in single file and crept past the entrance and away into the distance on a sweeping overpass. Gopi ran to his car, which was just about to be ticketed by a baton-wielding security guard. Gopi slipped him a few notes, and the man walked away.

The interior of the car smelled musty. Something tiny buzzed and settled on Tyler with a little sting that soon turned itchy. Mosquitoes! Tyler tried to swat them away, but there were just too many.

Tyler strained his eyes and peered out of the clouded window. Occasional piles of burning garbage dotted the slums that they drove through. Then, all of a sudden, as if someone had drawn a line on the map and said, "No slums beyond this point," the landscape became gentrified, with parks and gardens and even a lake.

The city emerged under a brightening sky, and the streets filled with cattle, vehicles, and people going about their daily chores and quarrels. The car drove on through a warren of progressively narrowing streets and pulled into a compound guarded by a cement wall and an ornate metal filigree gate.

A six-storied apartment building occupied the center of the compound, while a tidy garden ran along the perimeter, with large shade-giving trees here and there. Women walked in tight little groups, heads close together while they gossiped and whispered to enliven their morning walk. Round and round the building they went, as if on a hajj, casting curious glances at Tyler, who, although a mere five eleven, towered over the locals.

Gopi and Tyler got into a rickety elevator with an iron grill door. The ancient cage creaked its way up. Tyler was nervous; it didn't look like it could hold the weight of a baby, let alone two grown men and a suitcase.

The lift, as Gopi called it, stopped at the fourth floor. They stepped out into a hallway that was open to the elements on one side—more a long common balcony onto which the flats opened. The sun had gathered strength by this time and bounced harshly off the polished cement floor, blinding Tyler. The doors bore the numbers *401, 402*...Almost all the doorways were festooned with colorful garlands and the occasional string of lemons. To ward off the evil eye, Gopi explained, as if it were the most obvious use of lemons.

They stopped in front of the penultimate door, numbered *404*. It was one of the few doors that did not have the colorful garlands, festooned instead with green leaves strung together on a piece of twine. *The Roys*, a small brass plaque declared in dignified black letters to the left of the doorframe, just above the bell.

Gopi knocked. Light footsteps, clicking locks, and a swish later, the door opened to reveal Binodini Roy.

She appeared to be in her early sixties, with kohl-lined eyes and a diamond stud sparkling on her left nostril. Her frizzy gray hair was pulled back in a bun, and she was dressed with the cultivated carelessness of an Indian intellectual, in a cotton sari. She smiled and said with great warmth, "Come in, come in!" A gray-bearded gent appeared next to her, clad in similar humble clothing. "My husband, Suren," she introduced.

Tyler was welcomed into the small living room of a tiny but immaculate apartment, with cool marble floors, slender rosewood furniture, and lace curtains in two doorways that probably led to bedrooms. A table was set for three in the dining part of the L-shaped room. The kitchen gleamed in the morning sun just beyond the table.

"Please have a seat. You must be exhausted!"

Everyone shook hands and sat down and exchanged looks. After a brief, awkward pause, Tyler requested to go to the restroom. Ms. Roy seemed puzzled for a second and then exclaimed, "Oh, bathroom." She showed him to a tiny bathroom and handed him a fresh white towel.

He could barely maneuver in the tight space; the sink was too low, and the faucets twisted the wrong way. When he managed to finish washing up, he was shocked at the amount of dirt that came off his face and hands onto the snowy towel.

"Let's have breakfast before we start," Ms. Roy said when he came out. "I know you don't have much time, but I think we can squeeze in a couple of good Bengali meals!"

She went inside the kitchen and returned with a big dish piled with freshly fried puris. Steam unfurled in fragrant tendrils from the golden puffs. Suren fetched a silver dish of fish and vegetables in creamy gravy and a pitcher of water.

"Please, get some grapes from the fridge," Ms. Roy instructed her husband.

Is this the infamous America-hating, tree-hugging, rabid activist who suspects CIA conspiracies behind every world event? Tyler wondered. She seemed so mellow and warm. She reminded him of his mother, the way she hovered and made sure that everyone had enough to eat.

The food was too rich and heavy for Tyler's stomach, already confused by the time change, but he ate enough to allay doubts. Suren ate in grave silence punctuated with abstruse questions about American foreign policy. Tyler's answers were clearly unsatisfactory. Suren nodded politely and retired to one of the curtained-off rooms as soon as he was done.

Gopi ate separately on the balcony, all by himself. He excused himself once breakfast was over. "I'll pick you up at seven this evening, sir, to take you back to the airport," he said with a deep bow.

Tyler returned to the restroom, this time to get the greasy food off his fingers and provide relief to his agitated stomach. By the time he came out, Ms. Roy was seated at the dining table, which no longer bore any traces of food. It was now covered with neat stacks of files and folders.

"Would you like to rest a little before we start?" she asked.

"No, ma'am," he replied with a reflexive flash of his old Texan manners. He sat down on a chair that for some reason felt low.

"Coffee?"

"Yes, please!"

She laughed and went to the kitchen and brought back two steaming cups. Milk and sugar were already mixed in. It was too sweet for Tyler, but he was grateful for any form of caffeine. "Suren, do you want coffee?" she called to one of the lace curtains.

"Nah," came the answer.

Her duty done, Ms. Roy turned to Tyler. "Mr. Tyler," she began in a low, soft voice, "what I am about to tell you is completely off the record. I will not share any documents with you, but I will let you look at them so that you can convince yourself that my story is true. You cannot make copies—no recordings, no photographs, nothing. Is that acceptable?"

She had a singsong cadence that Tyler recognized from his Indian colleagues at his old chip-design company.

"Yes, ma'am."

"Please, call me Binny," she said, but her regal bearing made anything less than "Ms. Roy" unthinkable. The diamond on her nose caught a ray of sun and arrayed a rainbow of stars on her cheek.

"I am the head of a group called the Third Eye. It is a watchdog organization that monitors intelligence agencies around the world, particularly in their dealings with their Indian counterparts. I focus on the CIA."

She shuffled the file folders and aligned the edges into a neat stack. "We have known of Mr. James since 2001, when he started operating in Pakistan and Afghanistan. That was almost fifteen years ago. He must have been very young, early twenties perhaps?"

Tyler nodded, since she seemed to be looking for confirmation.

"He was brash and arrogant and often worked outside the law. He went too far on many an occasion and got into trouble with local authorities in Pakistan. The US government would bail him out. He would come to India, cool his heels for a few weeks at the embassy, and return to Pakistan after things had settled. He had an engineering company that dabbled in surveillance equipment, and that was his excuse to go in and out of Pakistan."

Binodini must have been a beautiful woman in her youth. Even now, she had the comportment of a woman accustomed to being admired for her looks.

"In 2010, there was a terrorist attack on a luxury hotel in New Delhi. Three hundred and sixty-two people were shot and killed in cold blood by armed men who had crossed over from Kashmir."

She sighed. "It was one of the most brazen attacks of all time."

She flashed an arch look at Tyler. "Did you know that Mr. James was in the hotel at that time?"

"What!" He sat up, his attention no longer on his roiling stomach.

"Yes, he was in the hotel with his wife, who was in New Delhi on a business trip."

"What happened?"

"He and his wife left the hotel just minutes before the assault."

"How do you know?"

She opened a folder and showed Tyler a series of pictures captured by a security camera. The photos showed an unconcerned Nina and Stephen in various parts of the hotel, just a few hours before the attack, annotated dramatically in red marker, *T-120, T-90,*

T-65. When he finished examining them, she returned them to safekeeping and brought out what seemed like a guest list at a hotel. One item was highlighted in yellow: *Room 1203, Nayantara Sharma + 1 guest.*

"Nayantara?"

"Yes, that's Mrs. James's first name. By the way, that item has been removed from all official records since."

"How did you get these?"

"I'll get to that later. But the question is, how did the couple escape?" She put that folder away. "A year later, in 2011, James was back in New Delhi. This time as a military attaché to the US embassy."

She looked out the window, at the gulmohar tree, aflame from tip to tip with glowing orange-red blossoms. "At first we thought his wife was an operative herself. But it became clear that she was a civilian and that he was paranoid about her safety. She always traveled with heavy security, more so than other embassy spouses."

A young woman let herself in through the front door and stopped when she saw Tyler.

"It's OK. Come in, Gita," Ms. Roy said. The girl gave a shy smile and hurried away into the kitchen. Ms. Roy called out instructions in Bengali.

"She's my helper, Gita. God bless her," Ms. Roy said. "Where was I? Yes, Mr. James and his wife. We wondered why she had so much security and what had caused him to be so nervous."

Tyler was distracted by Gita, who had brought out a plastic bucket full of water and had begun to mop the floor with a wet cloth. She squatted and scooted simultaneously, in quick bursts. It was an entirely new mode of locomotion. She caught him staring and finished up quickly and moved on to the curtained room. Immediately, Mr. Roy emerged, looking irritated at being disturbed. But he was dressed to go out.

"How is it going?" Mr. Roy asked. He sat down on a bench near the front door and began to put on his shoes.

"Good!" they both replied.

"I am going to the university. I won't be home before dinner." He got up and looked at Tyler intently. "Nice to meet you, Mr. Tyler. Please convey my inquiries to Barack." He laughed at his own joke and went out of the flat chuckling, rattling a cigarette pack in his left hand.

Ms. Roy waited for the front door to click into place and took out a photograph from another folder and laid it flat for Tyler's perusal. "*This* was what made James nervous."

It was a glossy eight by ten of Mr. and Mrs. James in an ecstatic embrace, crushed together in a deck chair, clad in very little.

Tyler's mouth went slack. He laughed aloud in surprised delight. His eyes jumped greedily from detail to detail, trying to memorize it all—the polished deck, the high-end mast and sails, the brilliant ocean, and her shapely golden-brown leg being caressed by his long, pale fingers, wedding ring glinting in the sun. But the stars of the photo were two angry red scars, front and center, one running down Stephen's left arm while the other wrapped around his left leg from hip to calf, like a spiny crocodile.

"Had your fill?" she asked.

He whistled and shook his head in amazement. No wonder the man was never seen in anything but a suit. The fashion police had speculated about Stephen's formal buttoned-down style, which he maintained even during the muggy summer days of Massachusetts.

She put the photo away and looked at him. "I have many more photos like this, but that is the most egregious one, taken on his private schooner while he was vacationing on the Goan coast. They must have shot it literally from under his nose."

"Who's 'they'?"

Just then Gita came and whispered in Ms. Roy's ear.

"Let's move to the balcony. She wants to clean here and set up for lunch."

Ms. Roy carefully packed all the papers in a leather suitcase and brought them with her to the balcony that was half the size of a beach blanket. A tiny table and two chairs were wedged on it. A luxuriant climber, laden with thick bunches of brilliant magenta bougainvillea blossoms, vied with an aggressive jasmine vine to form a bower around the chairs.

Tyler squeezed himself into the chair. Once settled, he found it surprisingly cool and tranquil inside the verdant cocoon of flowering climbers. Ms. Roy reached out with nimble fingers and picked off wilted leaves.

"I love sitting here," she said.

"Who's 'they'?" he repeated.

"Remember that terrorist attack of 2010? On that luxury hotel? James was sent to India in 2011 to help Indian authorities hunt for the people who did it. It was a joint mission between Indian and American agencies. You know what they say: terrorists practice in India what they want to do in the United States."

She turned to Tyler. "The terrorists, in turn, were trying to ward off James. They snooped on the couple and took pictures of them at unguarded moments as they went about their daily routine—dining, shopping, going to the movies—and sent them back to James as a message. 'Look, we can get *this* close to you. Be careful. Keep away from us.' Threats."

She must have been a dancer, he thought, or some exotic sign-language specialist, because she compulsively illustrated her conversation with graceful hand gestures.

Gita brought a tray with two perspiring glasses of a pink drink and set it down on the table. She whispered in Ms. Roy's ear and went away.

"Please." Ms. Roy gestured for Tyler to take the drink.

He hesitated, because he had been warned about the water.

"Don't worry," she said. "It's made with distilled water."

Tyler picked up a glass and took a sip. It was revoltingly sweet, with a cloying, sickly rose scent. But as it washed down his throat and into his stomach, a cool sensation radiated from within and spread through his body.

"This is amazing!" he said, genuinely surprised.

Ms. Roy, who had been watching his expression closely, was highly amused. "It's an herbal drink dating back to the Moguls. It's made with mint and rose-petal syrup."

They drank in silence. A chatter rose from below, where a group of senior citizens had gathered in the courtyard to gossip and wile away the time until lunch.

Ms. Roy resumed their conversation. "The day after that picture on the schooner deck, when James was completely on edge and ready to explode, the militants sent two men in a speedboat to pull up alongside his boat."

She took out two more photos from inside the suitcase on her lap. Tyler wiped his hands on his pants (there were no napkins) and gingerly took the photos with his fingertips.

The first one showed Stephen on the deck. He had a rifle pointed at a man in a small boat alongside the handsome schooner. The man held a camera with a long telescopic lens trained on Stephen. Another man was at the wheel of the boat, a holster at his waist. A woman in a bloodied white dress lay flat on the deck near Stephen's feet, shielded from the other boat by the side of the schooner.

The second photo showed what must have happened a few minutes later. Stephen was midstride, running toward stairs that led belowdecks. He dragged the woman by the wrist with his left hand, his rifle held high in his right hand. The long lens of the man in the boat continued to record their flight. The woman was Nina. Her lower leg was covered in blood from a gash above her knee, and her white summer frock was soaked in blood.

"Who took these photos? How did she get hurt?" Tyler asked. His hands trembled, and his voice shook with excitement.

Ms. Roy continued as if she hadn't heard. "According to witnesses, a shot was fired. Mr. James swore that it wasn't him, and ballistics support his claim, but nobody believed it. There was a huge furor."

She looked dreamily into the distance with half-closed eyes. "The press was furious. How dare an arrogant power-drunk American threaten an Indian citizen on Indian soil! Eager reporters did some frantic digging."

Her voice became very quiet, almost inaudible. "They found that back in Massachusetts, James had a Pakistani American neighbor named Sid Ali. And that Sid Ali was the victim of a mysterious armed robbery a week after the terrorist attack in New Delhi and had not been seen since."

Tyler listened in awe. "What else did they find?"

She paused and smiled at him. "Was Ali's disappearance from *his own home*, a week after the terrorist attack, just a coincidence? The Indian media didn't think so. They dug deeper into Ali's background and found that he not only had connections to banks that fronted for terror networks but that he had made several trips to India and scouted the New Delhi luxury hotel prior to the terrorist attack."

A faint breeze stirred the leaves around them. She ran her fingers over the flowers and continued. "Immediately, the media went crazy with wall-to-wall, round-the-clock coverage. They speculated that Sid Ali was a double agent and worked for both the CIA and the ISI, the Pakistani intelligence agency; that Mr. James was his CIA handler; that Ali had tipped off James at the very last minute about the attack, facilitating the couple's escape from the hotel, but without giving James an opportunity to stop the attack; and that Mr. James, furious at the double cross, personally took out Sid Ali a week later, under the guise of an armed robbery gone awry."

She emphasized each point by tapping her finger on the table. "That was the end. It didn't matter whether it was true or not. The Indian government came under great pressure and expelled Mr. James, deaf to the protests of the US State Department."

"How come this never came out in the US press?"

"Mr. Tyler, Americans have no interest in anything outside their shores. Your media is only too happy to oblige with celebrity stories. Besides, the CIA would have made sure that this did not come out in the United States."

"What happened to Mr. James after that?"

"Ah! It gets really interesting now," she teased.

Tyler smiled. He really liked this woman.

"We don't know the details, but what we do know is that there was some kind of inquiry into Mr. James's episode here. He was absolved. And just a few months after that, he was appointed the head of operations for all of South Asia."

"How do you know all this?"

At that moment, Gita came in and whispered once more to Ms. Roy, who replied in Bengali. The girl nodded and went away.

"We'll have lunch in half an hour," she said after Gita was gone. "I think Mr. James was really frustrated that he had been pulled out of India when he was so close to catching the mastermind behind the New Delhi attack. When he returned to work at the CIA, Mr. James went after the terrorists with a savage fury and instituted one of the most brutal programs in Kashmir, in collusion with the Indian intelligence agencies. Kidnappings, assassinations, you name it. Even children weren't spared, particularly boys."

She tapped her fingers on the suitcase. "Once his wife was on American soil, he felt emboldened. We are told that he spared no effort in extracting information from the young men captured in his neighbor's home. But they got to her."

"You keep saying 'they.' Who's 'they'?" Tyler asked in exasperation.

"The terrorists from Kashmir who launched the attack on the luxury hotel, the ones he was trying to hunt down." Isn't that obvious, her singsong tone implied. She waited for more questions, and when there were none, she continued.

"They crashed his wife's taxi in New York City. As you know, a majority of taxi drivers in New York are from this region. It was easy to arrange."

She tapped her fingers on the table. "It isn't clear what her injuries were, but Mr. James resigned a few weeks after that."

"Wow." Tyler whistled.

"I'm not done yet, Mr. Tyler. I have some more red meat for you."

Tyler tried to lean forward but was arrested by the edge of the table in that tight space.

"A few months after the resignation of Mr. James, the mastermind behind the New Delhi attacks was blown up in Peshawar, Pakistan, in a small, suburban house. You might have read about that; his name was Zia Akhtar. You know, top terrorist leader killed in Pakistan, etc."

Tyler had a vague recollection of that.

"Akhtar was supersecretive and hadn't been seen in public in over ten years. It was an amazing coup for the CIA, though they never took credit."

She looked at him. "Isn't that odd, Mr. Tyler?

"What we do know," she continued, "is that a man, an American matching Mr. James's description, who was in Khairpur's prison in Pakistan for assaulting a local, had escaped two days earlier, in a well-orchestrated rescue, after killing several guards. He and two companions were spotted around Peshawar hours before Akhtar was killed. Peshawar is but a hop, skip, and a jump from the Afghan border and American bases."

"You are saying that James killed that Akhtar guy?"

"Yes, Mr. Tyler, and with plausible deniability for the CIA if things went wrong. He was no longer their man."

"Wow," Tyler repeated.

She took out a fat binder from her suitcase. "Here are some documents that pertain to various cases and operations run by Mr. James in Kashmir."

Tyler took them from her and looked through them. He had no way of knowing whether they were real, forged, or fabricated; they just looked like any official document. He returned the binder.

"How did you get them?"

"Mr. Tyler, leaking classified information is a capital offense in India. Both you and I could be in a lot of trouble. Hanged, if you will."

"You can count on my discretion."

"Every organization has whistle-blowers. People disillusioned and disgruntled, for personal or ideological reasons. I have two independent sources, one driven by personal reasons and the other by ideological. They have been in remarkable agreement, unbeknown to each other, on the story that I just told you."

She stared at him intently, as if to gauge his character.

"My first source is a Kashmiri freedom fighter, whose fifteen-year-old son disappeared from Mr. Ali's house on the night of the armed robbery. The boy's father is the source of the photographs."

"The second source is an American, a person with access to these documents."

Tyler wondered if it was his informant, Rob. Ms. Roy watched him in silence.

"Why did you choose me?" he asked, finally.

"Because I heard that you were hungry. And that you took risks." She answered without hesitation.

He wasn't so sure about that now.

"Why are you interested in getting this story out?" He stalled.

"Oh, Mr. Tyler, where do I begin?" she laughed. "We are concerned that Mr. James, if elected, which we think he will be, will have great influence on putting in place hawkish, warmongering foreign policies and will hand even more power to intelligence agencies. Our studies have him as a good bet for the US presidency by the time he is fifty, in a dozen years or so."

"What!" Tyler guffawed.

"Laugh if you will, Mr. Tyler. But be careful around Mr. James. He is not what he says he is."

She gathered the documents, put them in her suitcase, and twisted the combination lock.

"Do you have it in you, Mr. Tyler, to be the hero we need?"

"Not without evidence, Ms. Roy," he retorted.

"Unfortunately, I can't help you with that." She looked at him for a long time, as if sizing him up. "But I will give you a tip. Find Sid Ali and that boy. They will lead you to your evidence."

"But where do I look for them?"

"I don't know. What would you do with them if you were the CIA?"

She got up from her chair. "I'll print your boarding pass now. Please give me your confirmation number. It might take a while—our printer is really old." She took the information from him and left.

While Tyler waited, he noticed that a sheet of paper that had fallen to the floor. It must've slipped out of her folder. Tyler picked it up. It was a photo: four frightened children huddled in some sort of a holding pen. They were squatting on the floor, and one little girl was crying. The kids were quite healthy and well-groomed, dressed in traditional Pakistani salwaars. Not your orphans or street urchins. In one corner, a man's shoe was visible, the rest of him hidden by a concrete pillar. But, at the far end of the room, behind the children's cage, a blacked out window dimly reflected his face.

Tyler recognized the shoe immediately. It was the same fancy kind that Stephen James favored.

He took out his phone and snapped a picture and slipped the document back under the table where Ms. Roy had dropped it. Inadvertently, perhaps.

STRANDED

Tyler was frantic. He couldn't find his passport. He was sure that he'd had it on him when Gopi dropped him off at the entrance to the airport an hour ago. He had been holding it in his hand, along with the boarding pass Ms. Roy had printed for him.

The lady at the counter sweetly asked him to step aside so she could take care of the others. There was a long line behind him.

Tyler ran back, retracing his path to see if he had dropped it anywhere. No, he couldn't find it, not even in the restroom. He rushed to find the security office.

The office was in a remote corner of the airport, and finding it was a challenge in itself. Each person he asked helpfully pointed in a different direction. When he finally found it and knocked on the door, it took them five minutes to let him in.

A swarthy young man in a khaki uniform, with a bushy moustache, led him to a small room and asked him to sit down at the desk and wait for the inspector.

"No! Don't you understand? I have to leave. I have a flight!" Tyler stamped his foot for emphasis. He couldn't afford to miss the flight, he gestured repeatedly at the gate. "Has anyone turned in an American passport?" he demanded.

The young man, whether he understood the words or not, certainly understood the tone. He looked at Tyler with large, hard eyes. Even his moustache seemed to have doubled in size. He left the room abruptly and shut the door on Tyler, leaving him alone in that tiny, airless room.

"What the fuck! Come back!" Tyler yelled after him. He tried to open the door, but it was locked. The handle wouldn't budge.

That frightened Tyler more than the thought of missing his flight. He had heard of Americans being incarcerated in foreign countries. India, if Ms. Roy was to be believed, had a nasty record regarding the human rights of prisoners. He collapsed in the chair, holding his head in his hands. Rivulets of sweat made their way down his shirt and collected in an uneven stain around his belt. He sat up and tried to use his phone, but there was no reception in that heavily walled room.

At least fifteen minutes must have passed before the door opened. Tyler stood up, prepared for the worst.

An older man, also sporting a fierce moustache, a gray one, walked in with a brisk stride. He too wore a khaki uniform, but with many decorations, and he carried a gun at his waist and, for good measure, had a baton in his hand. Two armed minions came in behind him.

He looked at Tyler for a second and said, with incongruously crisp diction, "Sit down, Mr. Tyler."

"I..." Tyler was about to launch into a tirade, but the man quelled him with a sharp look. "Sit down," he said, while he took the throne-like chair behind the desk.

Tyler sat down.

"You have lost your passport?"

"Yes, I..."

"When?"

The inspector sat like a small potentate dispensing justice. One of the minions filled out a form, while a recording device captured Tyler's story, step by step, elicited brusquely by the inspector. The three officers paused to talk to each other in a barrage of sharp, short words.

Suddenly one of the minions snatched Tyler's laptop.

"Hey!" Tyler stood up. "Give that back!"

The inspector got up from his chair and leaned across the desk and rested his baton gently on Tyler's shoulder. "Sit down." The baton became more assertive on Tyler's shoulder.

Tyler sank back into the chair.

The other lackey hooked up Tyler's computer to a big screen and started running a software program on it. Tyler wanted to jump up and shout, "Don't mess with my computer! Keep your virus-ridden software out of my machine," but he didn't have the nerve. The baton was not to be slighted.

The program ran on, spewing all kinds of bogus warnings and errors, and came to a halt with a flashing red box.

The three men turned to Tyler and stared at him.

"What?" Tyler asked.

"Mr. Tyler, we have to impound your computer. We have found objectionable material," the inspector replied.

"What!" Tyler tried to stand up once more but was pushed down by the henchman standing behind his chair.

"Yes. We have found illegal material. We have to confiscate your hard drive."

They shut down his computer and, right in front of his eyes, removed the hard disk, and locked it in a safe box, with a sticky red tape around it. They returned the laptop, sans hard disk, to Tyler.

It was an empty gesture, as everyone in the room knew, but dramatic nevertheless.

The inspector took out a phone from a locked drawer and placed it in front of Tyler.

"Call your consulate."

"But I have to leave!"

"Not without a passport. Call your consulate. Have them pick you up. And return when you have a replacement passport."

"Don't you understand? I have to leave, sir," Tyler persisted weakly, barely managing to choke out the honorific at the end.

"Would you rather spend the night in jail?" the inspector asked in an icy voice.

"I don't have the number." Tyler made one last feeble attempt.

The inspector sighed and asked one of the minions to fetch a binder from the recesses of a cabinet. He opened it to a page and handed it to Tyler and marched out of the room while the assistants saluted.

There was nothing Tyler could do. He called the number and waited under the watchful eyes of the armed guards until a cheery staffer from the consulate arrived to pick him up. The man introduced himself as John and retrieved Tyler from the custody of the surly Indian officials.

John seemed to know the airport down to the last hallway, staircase, and door. He led the way at a canter, through passages, stairways, and finally through a vast parking lot enclosed by a high barbed-wire fence.

Tyler's brain was exhausted and wasn't really focused on what the man was saying. How long would the whole process take, he worried, and what if he missed the election? Perhaps he should just head back to Ms. Roy's place.

"Could you drop me off at a friend's place?" he asked, turning to his rescuer.

"No, sir," the young man replied. "I can't let you out without proper papers." He smiled at Tyler and continued to drive. It was only then Tyler noticed that the kid looked like a marine or some other military type.

"Are you with the army?" he asked.

"No, sir, former marine. I am a part of the consulate's security detail now."

"Does the US consulate need a lot of security?"

"Oh, yes, sir! There is a big Muslim population in this city, and religious tension leads to law-and-order breakdown frequently. The US consulate is often a target of demonstrations and riots. We can never be too careful."

"Do you take such good care of all Americans who lose their passports?" Tyler laughed to show that he was only kidding.

"No, but the airport has lodged a complaint against you for unruly conduct. I am not sure you want to spend the day in an Indian jail. We're helping you out, sir."

"How long do you think it will take?"

"A couple of days at the most. We should have you out of here by tomorrow night, early Wednesday morning."

Wednesday! The election would be over by then!

Tyler shook his head in disbelief. Was it possible that Stephen had arranged for this whole fracas with the help of his friends at the Agency?

There was bright sunshine outside now. His flight must have taken off two hours ago. The roads were crammed with people going to work. The heat and glare were unbearable.

They arrived at tall metal gates. The heavy gates swung open after the guard checked the driver's papers and scanned the car's undercarriage with a mirror.

A beautiful, pale sandstone building, with tall arches and verandas, rose a hundred yards away. They drove around the sparkling fountain and stopped at the wide steps of the building.

"Wait here," his guardian said and disappeared inside. Two guards kept an eye on him. Their fingers were on the triggers of their weapons, in incessant readiness.

The marine returned and hopped into the car and drove around the back to a cluster of white buildings. He pulled into a carport. "Here we are," he said.

Tyler picked up his suitcase and followed him into the closest building. It looked like a cross between a hostel and a motel, with no lobby to speak of, only long hallways with rows of doors on either side.

The young man showed Tyler to a small room on the third floor. "These are the staff quarters, sir, and this is one of our guest rooms. Here is the bathroom.

Here is a phone. Please call me, if you have any questions. I'll be back in a few minutes." He left with a nod and closed the door behind him.

The room was small, but it was air-conditioned, much to Tyler's relief. He washed in the tiny bathroom and was amazed once more at the amount of dirt that came off his face onto the towel. He went back into the room. It had a single twin-size bed and a little desk with a chair, nothing else—no books, no pictures on the walls, no TV. But there was an old-fashioned phone with a rotary dial. A square of light lit up the drapes from behind. He opened the curtains and looked out through the window, wincing as the sunlight poured in. The room overlooked a black rooftop and faced a wall, the side of the next building, possibly. That wall had no windows or markings, just a tall, bright white wall awash in the harsh sun. He pulled the curtains closed.

There was a knock, and his friend entered with a tray. He was a solid fellow, with bulky arms, a thick neck, and a buzz cut. He looked a little like Matt Damon.

"Here, Mr. Tyler, you must be hungry." He put the tray down on the bed.

"Can I leave this room, or am I a prisoner?" Tyler tried to sound jocular.

"Of course you can go out, but almost every part of this building is restricted entry, so there are not many places that you could go to, even if you wanted to. Please call me if you need anything."

He stood for a minute, looked around the room, and left. The door closed behind him with a firm click.

Tyler tried the door. It opened easily. The hallway outside was deserted. But a security camera was brazenly pointed right at the doorway where he stood. He shut the door in a hurry.

He came back inside the room and examined the food tray. Buttered toast, omelet, coffee, juice, water bottle, and a banana. He started eating quickly, suddenly spurred by a hunger that he hadn't noticed. Since there was no TV or computer, he tried to read the news on his smartphone while he ate. It acquired a signal but needed a password.

He picked up the phone in the room, and immediately John replied, "Hello, sir."

"John, how do I get on the Wi-Fi network? Is there a password?"

"You can't, sir. This is a secure network. Sorry."

"But I need to!"

"Sorry, Mr. Tyler."

Tyler hung up.

Now he was certain that he hadn't lost his passport. It was too much of a coincidence. Everything had gone like clockwork. The security office, the inspector, the conveniently available consulate emergency number. In fact, John, if that was really his name, had appeared at the airport in less than twenty minutes, while it had taken them more than an hour to drive from the airport to the consulate. Had he known ahead of time that he had to pick up Tyler, and was he already on the way to the airport? Perhaps he didn't live at the consulate; perhaps the traffic had slowed them down on the return journey, perhaps, perhaps, perhaps.

He felt really tired and lonely. He lay down on the bed and stared at the ceiling. Maybe his friend Jimmy was right. How "retired" was Stephen? He either was still active or had enough contacts that he could pull off a stunt like this. In any case, the man was not to be taken lightly.

He sat up. Did he really want to be the hero Ms. Roy was looking for? Did he have the courage to take on such a task, to spend the rest of his life turning the spotlight on secrets and ferreting out bodies buried consensually by governments around the world? Where would it take him? What was in it for him?

A chill swept through his body. At that moment, Tyler knew that his course of action would change his life completely and possibly the lives of Stephen and Nina. It was an astonishing feeling that gripped his heart with a fist of ice.

He got off the bed and paced the room. Normally, he'd have poured his thoughts out to his computer. But it had been disemboweled and was lying wounded in its case. Maybe he could put down his thoughts on paper, the old-fashioned way, no password needed. He opened his suitcase for his writing pad and pen. And what should drop out onto the floor but the napkin that he had scribbled on a month ago, while waiting for Ashley in the bar. He must have stuffed it inside the writing pad in his hurry.

He picked it up gently and smoothed it out on his lap. It was the timeline he had put down while trying to piece together Stephen's enigmatic life.

Oct. 2009:	*Stephen marries Nina*
Apr. 2010:	*Armed robbery at Sid Ali's in Massachusetts; Ali disappears; S is injured*
Nov. 2011*:	*Runs into trouble in India—suspected of CIA connection*
Mar. 2013:	*Buys the Ali property*
Apr. 2013:	*S. announces Edward William James Foundation for Women and appoints Nina as head*
Aug. 2014:	*Enters the Senate race in a special election*

*Need official corroboration

Was the universe sending him a sign? For the first time in hours, he smiled. That crumpled piece of recycled paper was just the catalyst he needed. Thanks to Ms. Roy, he now had so much more information to fill the list out.

He took his writing pad and pen set and sat at the tiny desk, feeling like a schoolboy about to write an exam. He put the pen down on the paper and began. His pen flowed silkily (he had a weakness for collecting expensive writing instruments) on the smooth ruled paper of the yellow writing pad.

2001:	*S. joins the agency, posted in Pakistan and Afghanistan*
Oct. 2009:	*Stephen marries Nina*
Apr. 19, 2010:	*Terror attack at Le Meridien, New Delhi (S. & N. were THERE!)*
Apr. 26, 2010:	*Armed robbery at Sid Ali's*
	Ali disappears
	S. is injured (fifteen-year-old boy missing?)
Sep. 2011*:	*S. is posted to New Delhi (as military attaché)*
	Begins hunt for Zia Akhtar, leader of Le Meridien terrorist attack
	Akhtar's guys try to intimidate S. with snoopy photos of S. & N.
Nov. 2011*:	*Threatens Indian photographer while on vacation*
	Claims self-defense, photos on schooner prove it
	Accused by Indian press of running a CIA agent, Sid Ali (same neighbor of S.), who is suspected of also working for the Pakistanis and aiding in Le Meridien attack
	S. is absolved in inquiry back in the USA and reinstated
Jan. 2012:	*Appointed HEAD OF OPS, SOUTH ASIA*
May. 2012:	*N. is in accident (Bad guys suspected)*
Sep. 2012:	*S. resigns*
Oct. 2012:	*Man fitting S.'s description arrested in Khairpur, Pakistan*

Nov. 2012:	*Mastermind Zia Akhtar dies in explosion in Peshawar*
	Man fitting S.'s description seen in the neighborhood with <u>two companions, day before the explosion</u>
Mar. 2013:	*Buys the Ali property*
Apr. 2013:	*S. announces Edward William James Foundation for Women and appoints Nina as head*
Aug. 2014:	*Enters the Senate race in the special election.*

*Need official corroboration

Tyler stared at the paper for a long time. He had underlined the two companions because he could guess who they were. One could have been Rob, his secret informer and fellow Stephen hater. And the other?

A crazy theory popped into his head. The second companion could have been Nina's brother, Neel. Tyler had watched him stand near Nina during her campaign appearances. When Tyler thought back, it was clear that Neel had special training. For one, he ran Stephen's company that was, for all practical purposes, an extension of the NSA. You needed all kinds of special clearances for that. It was quite possible that Neel was Stephen's link to his past. From his research, Tyler also knew that Neel had worked for a global civil-engineering company that had major construction projects in Pakistan and Afghanistan. Therefore, it was also possible that Stephen had recruited him at some point. That would also explain why Stephen trusted Nina's safety to Neel.

He got up from the chair in a daze, put the writing pad away inside his suitcase, and went back to lying on the bed and staring at the ceiling.

He must have fallen asleep, because the next thing he heard was a voice calling, "Sir! Sir!"

Tyler sat up. He had been in an almost coma-like state.

"How long have I been asleep?"

"Fifteen hours. That jet lag's a bitch."

Tyler looked at the meal that John had brought him.

"Good news. The airport authorities have recovered your passport. They are holding it for you. You can leave on this evening's flight."

"Man! I've lost track of time. What's today?"

"Tuesday, Mr. Tyler. You'll be home by tomorrow afternoon. Lucky you."

Tyler nodded. He drank the coffee gratefully. A good, strong cup of American coffee!

On the way to the airport, there was but one thought in his head—should he? He was so preoccupied that he barely answered John's questions. But by the time John saw him off at the security clearance at the airport, Tyler knew the answer.

He should, he could, and he would be Ms. Roy's hero. However, in order to do so, he would have to become invisible and be outside the grasp of Mr. Stephen

James until he had gathered all the evidence. But first, he had to take one parting shot.

He had planned on generating election-eve excitement with Ms. Roy's interview, writing his story on the plane and pushing it out as soon as he landed. But now, he had nothing, not even a computer, and the election was probably well underway.

Tyler's phone had been mysteriously rendered useless, fried by the feral Indian electricity that had coursed through the charger. He hoped fervently that the precious photo was intact. He remembered seeing an Internet kiosk just outside the security waiting area. He hadn't been able to go to it while John was with him, keeping watch. Now that John had left, after making sure that Tyler had passed through security, Tyler eyed the kiosk with interest. It seemed sound and offered high speeds and "exciting web-surfing opportunities."

Tyler got up and went to the security guard. "May I go out for a minute? I'll come right back and pass through security again." He had picked the youngest, most friendly looking guard, a girlish woman. She looked at his American passport, his expensive clothes and luggage, and, after a brief display of hesitation, nodded him out.

He thanked her and went out through the gate. After pretending to buy a cup of coffee, he sauntered over to the kiosk. The clerk said, "Ten minutes only, five dollars." Tyler plunked down a ten-dollar bill and rushed to the nearest available computer terminal.

After around eight minutes of furious keyboard acrobatics, he created a rudimentary page to be pushed to his website:

The Daily Howl

Dear Readers:
Greetings!
You must be wondering what has become of me during these most critical, final days of the election and on the big election day itself.

I am writing to let you know that I have some stunning news about Mr. Stephen James, news that will stop your blood midflow and chill you to the core. No, I am not talking petty scandals of sex or money.

I am talking BIG news—of murder and kidnappings, of assassinations and torture, of an unbridled lust for power, of terrifying ambition of unimaginable proportions.

I am more motivated than ever to uncover the truth about "the perfect candidate," even if it means risking my life. I will come to you when I have gathered all my evidence, which I promise will be very soon.

So, stay tuned for some shocking (to say the least!) revelations about Mr. Stephen James of Massachusetts.

In the meantime, here is a question to ponder: How did Mr. James occupy himself between 2001 and 2011, other than intervening in armed robberies at neighbors' homes?

Cheers!

Dave Tyler

He hit "Upload." The familiar spinning disk popped up. They were calling his flight. Move, move, move, he urged the invisible data streams. But the disk kept churning. A dialog box popped up. *Retry later?*

"Damn," he muttered. But he had no choice. He hit "OK," logged out of his account, and ran to the security gate.

PERCHANCE TO WIN

Stephen for Senator

Stephen Edward James @stephenjames . Dec 2
Listen to @NinaSharmaJames, of Edward W. James
Foundation. Educate our girls and save the world!

A large orange moon popped out of the ocean and shimmered over the horizon like a magic cantaloupe. Within seconds, it turned a brilliant white and sprinkled the ripples below with magnificent silver sparks. Stephen stood on the balcony, transfixed.

"There you are," Nina said, stepping out. She closed the glass door behind her. The December night was chilly, and she had come out in her flimsy nightdress. She put her arms around his waist and hugged him close for warmth. He enveloped her inside his robe.

She was warm and soft and cuddled at his side like a kitten.

"We're going to win tomorrow, you know," he said.

"You don't sound too happy about it."

"We'll see." He squeezed her closer.

Her fingers reached under his T-shirt and felt for the scars that crisscrossed his back, particularly the nasty one that stood out like a ridge. It had become such a habit of hers that neither of them noticed it anymore.

The scars hadn't always been there. In fact, in their early days together, she used to laugh that for such a tough guy, he had baby-soft skin. All that had changed in a hurry. Within six months of being married, the big medical-suture scars had appeared on his arm and leg, after the shootout at Sid's. But those scars were nothing compared to the ones that had appeared almost two years ago now, during a two-week stint in a Pakistani prison.

The night that he had returned, as usual with the briefest explanations about his unexpectedly long "trip," a mission gone awry, he was just about to step into the shower when she had come in to give him fresh towels. She'd stared at the big, fiery welt on his back, prominent in a filigree of smaller lacerations, and at his knees and calves that had turned blue and purple with bruises. Her heart had stopped. His feet had deep cuts from the glass shards atop Khairpur's prison wall.

That instant was forever branded on her brain. She'd imagined what he must have endured with every cruel mark.

It was getting chilly on the balcony. She withdrew her hand from under his shirt and sighed. She always did that—she would touch his scars and immediately get glum, thinking of what he had been through.

For him, it was the opposite. That instant was one of the happiest moments of his life, coming home from that wretched prison to see her lovely, angry face and feel her gentle fingers on his poor, raw skin. He'd thought he'd never see Nina again. In that terrible hellhole in Pakistan, he had known for the first time what it was to be homesick. Home was where Nina was, waiting for him, and that was where his mind had flown to during those hopeless hours and days. The thought of what would happen to her if he gave up had forced him to get through the days at Khairpur's prison. Standing in front of her in that sparkling bathroom the night of his return, he had been grateful to whatever mysterious forces had helped him make it back to her.

He had spent those long, lonely nights in Khairpur thinking about all the things he'd do, should he ever make it out. He had known that George would send reinforcements, but it was possible that time would run out. The Pakistani jail warden, a terrible, cruel man, had been waiting for papers from the headquarters. Stephen would've been executed within minutes of their arrival. Meanwhile, the warden had lost no opportunity to physically and mentally hurt Stephen, goaded by Stephen's pride, silence, and strength.

From his dirty, stench-filled cell, Stephen had watched the sad parade of young girls, barely in their teens, brought in by their own fathers, no less, to be sold for the night to the wardens or prisoners who could arrange for the money. He could hear their cries and screams, and it hurt him terribly that he hadn't been able to help. That was why it had been such a joy to choke the warden to death with his bare hands while escaping.

Nina's words had rung in his ears at that time: "Education is the only hope for girls in third-world countries." Otherwise they'd be reduced to sexual slavery and domestic drudgery, and they would die in childbirth by the time they were twenty-five. He had decided then that he would use his inheritance to set up a foundation for educating girls and women in third-world countries, under Nina's direction. It was also an effective way to stem the rise and spread of terrorism in the dirt-poor countries, which were proving to be such rich recruiting grounds for the enemy. An educated mother had better odds of preventing her children from falling into the hands of charismatic preachers of violence and death.

He shuddered. The moon had risen higher in the sky and brought him back to the present. He felt Nina's round belly against his side and leaned his head on

hers. On his return from Pakistan, he had been horrified at how ill she had become, first with the miscarriage and then his disappearance. All the energy and
liveliness had been driven out of her face, eyes dull and
swollen from weeks of crying. He'd never let it happen,
ever again, he'd sworn to himself.

Was he reneging on that now, with this Senate run?
Did the future hold more blood and tears, or had they
paid their dues and now a benevolent fate was ready to
shower them with joy and happiness?

"Are we asking for trouble, Nina?" he asked in an
uncharacteristic admission of doubt.

"What's the alternative?" she said immediately. She
had been debating the same question in her head for
months now. "I think this is the lesser evil. I am afraid
that you won't be happy just running the foundation
or sailing around the world and that you will slip back
into your old profession and end up in a ditch, dead."

She paused to take a breath. And then there
was her private fear that he'd follow in his father's
footsteps—alcoholism, depression, and suicide.

The moon disappeared behind a puffy little cloud.
"Let's go in," she said. "My feet are freezing."

They went inside. It was four in the morning, and
egged on by Stephen's smart timers, the fireplace burst
into welcoming flames and cast dancing shadows on
the walls.

HOMESTRETCH

The election results trickled in slowly. The atrium of the Edward W. James Memorial Library was decked out with big-screen TVs and hummed with subdued conversations. Supporters and campaign staff were milling around, their numbers increasing by the minute as they trickled in from dinner.

Stephen, Nina, and senior campaign members were cloistered in a smaller room off the atrium. They were monitoring the results via TV, computer, and direct phone lines to volunteers in the polling stations.

Nina couldn't take the tension and got up to leave for the tenth time.

Stephen pulled her down to sit next to him. "Come on. You have to watch with me."

She shook her head. The waiting and uncertainty were wearing her down.

"I thought you didn't care about the outcome and that you were happy either way?" he teased.

"I know. But I don't want you to be unhappy."

"I won't be. We'll win."

"How can you say that?" She pointed to the screen.

Stephen trailed by ten points, with 1 percent of the precincts reporting.

"Your good friend Amazing Nate has predicted that we'll win decisively. You should have faith."

"I'll be back," Nina said and got up from the sofa and walked toward the restroom at the other end of the building. She couldn't make up her mind as to what she really wanted. For Stephen's sake, she wanted a victory. Losing would send him into a prolonged spell of moody silence. But if he won, they would not only be under the microscope of public scrutiny but also be in the cross hairs of enemies that Stephen had left behind in the wake of his fifteen-year career.

She entered the restroom and paused to look at her reflection in the mirror. Tyler's snippet where Stephen referred to children and civilians as collateral was just the beginning. Journalists and investigative reporters built their careers by taking down men like Stephen. She looked away from the haunted face in the mirror and washed her hands in the sink and came out into the hallway.

Doug and Wasim were waiting for her. The results were beginning to arrive and Stephen had sent them to fetch her.

At the sight of the two friendly faces, she felt the energy drain out of her. Her head started to spin and she felt all her weight bear down toward her abdomen. She leaned on the wall to steady herself.

"Nina! Are you alright?" Doug asked, and grabbed her arm. Wasim grabbed her other arm and they walked her to a nearby bench. She sat down and closed her eyes.

"Nina! Should I get Stephen? Do you need a doctor?" Wasim asked.

The two men looked at her and waited anxiously for her to say something.

She shook her head and covered her face with her hands. "Just give me a minute."

At last she opened her eyes and looked up at them. "It's Tyler."

"What has he done? Did he hurt you?" Wasim asked.

"No! No! It's not that." She struggled to get the words out.

Wasim squeezed Nina's hand.

"What is it?" Doug kneeled in front of her.

"I feel disloyal even saying this, but if anyone would understand, it is you two."

She looked at them. "Tyler is going to tear him down. You guys have no idea. My husband has done some really, really terrible things. He has been in untenable situations and has had to make decisions that are simply beyond our comprehension, so far beyond a normal person's experience."

She stopped to take a deep breath. "It is hard to imagine that we humans are capable of doing such things…but when it is a matter of survival, all of us have hidden savagery in us. That part of his experience will never go away. I have seen him struggle so hard to deal with those contradictions…but it is a big part of who he is. If that part of his past ever comes out, he will be torn down…turned into a monster… condemned. He will not survive that!"

Stephen and she had discussed this so often, and it always ended in assurances from him. "That *will not* happen," he'd say. "How do you know? You're not God," she'd reply. And now, with a possible victory around the corner, her fears had taken the shape of Tyler.

"Don't worry, Nina," Doug reassured her. "Nothing will happen. Stephen's past is classified. Nobody can get at it."

Wasim had doubts but he nodded. "I agree. Come on, we should get back. We can't leave Stephen to monitor the election results by himself."

They walked back together to the accompaniment of rings and buzzes from the many phones the two men carried.

Nina had regained her calm. All things considered, it is better that he should win, she decided.

They would take care of the rest later. But for now, he must win.

They joined Stephen who had perversely put the TV on the most liberal channel. The host, Rachel, bashed him on a regular basis—plutocrat, son of privilege, disconnected from the common man—and vocally advocated for the Collins campaign. It amused him, this ineffectual effort to stop him.

The congresswoman had appeared on Rachel's show many times, often to cast aspersions on Stephen's ability to lead. What has he got to show for himself, she'd ask, other than an engineering firm that uses his grandfather's government clout to get business? What has he done?

The Collins campaign had tried to undermine Stephen in many ways, but his biggest advantage was the lack of a voting record. They couldn't hammer him on that, while his campaign routinely brought up Ms. Collins's questionable votes on issues that she claimed to espouse. Perforce the Collins campaign had to bring up character issues. Can we trust a man who has no loyalty to his own mother? Is he a man of faith? Is he a Hindu? Has he converted? One of the surrogates would ask this in every show she appeared on. Or is he a Christian? Why doesn't he come out and say what he believes in?

While the Collins campaign ran on emotion and old-style TV advertising, Doug and Wasim had expertly exploited the fragmented cable-TV market to microtarget their ads. During the last week leading up to the election, they had played up Nina and the foundation's work for underprivileged girls. Interviews, press conferences, fund raisers—Stephen and Nina were suddenly everywhere.

The more Stephen was seen with his pregnant wife, the more his likability ratings improved. The campaign events at which Nina appeared were carefully orchestrated. She would appear exactly five minutes prior to when Stephen's speech was scheduled to end. Neel would walk her over to Stephen. At the end of the event, Neel would recover Nina and drive her away. Some media outlets commented on the strange routine, but the campaign was able to spin it as a necessity, due to Nina's schedule and her "health."

Most of all, Stephen's staff was surprised by his sudden turbodrive to reach out to people. He was relentlessly in public, shaking hands and dandling babies. "I am going to win this fucking thing," he told Wasim and Doug, and off he went to another suburban train station or ball game.

Having spent more than four months with his team, he was now as concerned about letting them down as he was about his own future. All these young people who had worked so hard for him in spite of his unpredictable tempers and moods, he owed it to them.

So, in the closing weeks of his Senate race, Stephen Edward James went on the campaign trail with exhausting determination. He crisscrossed the state like a maniac, summoning the training of his past, dazzling his team with his endurance and toughness. They watched, with mouths agape, as this almost middle-aged son of old money stood in ice and rain, gave speeches, built homes, served meals at nursing homes, and read storybooks to elementary-school kids.

But what was even more shocking was that he was enjoying himself thoroughly.

Now, all they could do was wait for the polling stations to close across the commonwealth.

Stephen's phone chimed for his attention. He looked at it and got up to go to a quiet corner of the room. "Yes?"

It was Neel. He'd just intercepted an update that was waiting to be pushed to Tyler's website. He read the contents of *The Daily Howl*'s teaser to Stephen. What should he do?

Stephen thought for a while. He had hoped for a little peace, now that they had managed to stall Tyler in India for a couple of days. But the battle was underway. Tyler had fired the first shot.

"Neel, hold it until midnight, and then release it."

Neel was silent.

"It's OK," Stephen assured him. "Let it come out. It has to. We'll handle it."

"Stephen?"

"Yes?"

"I think he must have some proof. He wouldn't stick out his neck like this unless he has something."

"What could it be?"

"He met that Roy woman. Who knows what she's given him?"

"But why now? She had all these years to leak those documents."

"You know why. If you win, you will have real power. That's why."

"I can't talk now, Neel. I'll call later."

"OK. Bye."

Stephen returned to sit with Nina. She asked, "Who?"

"Some press person." He smiled. "Not important."

The results remained maddeningly close as the night wore on.

"It's a bloody media conspiracy to keep us in suspense," Doug muttered. "They're withholding Republican-leaning districts until the very end, the assholes!"

Wasim shook his head. "Doug, come on. Calm down, man." He handed Doug a bottle of water. "No more Red Bull for you."

Doug took the bottle. "Do you think he will win?"

Wasim looked at him. "Well, all our polls point to a win. But you can never be sure. Anyway, let's hope for the best."

Doug looked so glum that Wasim smiled. "It's OK, Douglas," he said. "If not now, the next time around. Stephen's not one to give up. He'll be back."

"So, you don't believe he'll win?"

"That's not what I'm saying at all, dude." Wasim stood up. "All I'm saying is that even if he doesn't, this is not the end—not for him, not for us." He clinked his water bottle against Doug's. "Anyway, I am quite sure that we will win tonight."

Sure enough, as more and more precincts checked in, Stephen closed the gap and finally moved past Ms. Collins.

The atrium exploded when Fox called it for Stephen, the first TV channel to do so.

Nina sat down, overcome. This was it. It was done. It felt unreal, the people, the noise, the clapping, and the bright lights.

Stephen hugged her and clasped her hand tightly. "It's going to be great," he said to her. "You'll see." He pulled her up gently. "Come. Let's go. They're waiting for us."

Doug and Wasim walked ahead of them and got the crowd worked up. "Stephen, Stephen, Stephen," they chanted, and the crowd joined in, with clapping, hooting, and noisemakers.

"All credit to you two," Stephen said when they caught up with Doug and Wasim. They walked to the hall together, the same one where they had announced Stephen's candidacy.

Stephen walked the familiar route to that familiar podium flanked by the familiar flags, Nina next to him. This time around, it was a completely different feeling. He felt powerful and strong, like the master of the universe, master of his fate. Nothing could stop him.

The ocean of uplifted faces beamed back at him. "Stephen, Stephen, Stephen." And there it was—that old rush of adrenaline, that indescribable high that flowed through his body when he managed to elude the grasp of death. He put his arm around a very dazed Nina and started speaking.

After that, things moved very quickly. Congratulations poured in, and the all-important concession call came from the surprisingly gracious Ms. Collins.

As soon as that call was done, Stephen turned to Nina and said, "Call your parents," and was immediately swept away on a flood of greetings and blessings from his in-laws, gliding down the cellular network in happy digital packets.

The rest was a blur. So many calls, so many people to thank, so many hands to shake, and so many smiles.

Around one thirty in the morning, Wasim said to Stephen and Nina, "You guys go home. We'll take care of the rest. Tomorrow will be a busy day. Go get some sleep." There was a raging party in progress in the decorous confines of the Edward W. James Memorial Library.

With a final round of thank-yous and good-byes, Nina and Stephen left and drove home by themselves. It was a rare luxury, just the two of them.

Neither said a word, content at this rare saddle point of anticipation and apprehension, where there was the happy sense of achievement, the consequences and hardships ahead were still far enough in the future, and the pleasure of being together was a joy in itself. They went to bed cocooned in the same amicable silence.

TYLER VANISHES

Tyler looked around the rented home. There was nothing left there that belonged to him. The furniture was part of the lease; he had cleared out everything else, carefully burned all documents, and wiped the place down to a shine. His ex would have turned green at his diligence. He had never bothered to help her keep their place clean, which was one of her many gripes. "Why are you such a slob?" she'd say. He used to shrug it off with good humor. He'd taken it as a sign of familiarity rather than a genuine complaint.

He took a deep breath. It had been an exhausting few days. His lightning trip to India had left him with a bubbling stomach and seriously disrupted sleep patterns. It was three days since his return, two days since Stephen had become senator-elect.

Tyler was getting ready to disappear, to become nonexistent, to become a phantom and slip through Stephen's fingers, which would surely reach out to crush him before he broke the story. But he had a lot of work ahead of him, to piece together Stephen's violent and secret past. Without evidence, he had no story and nobody would take him seriously. This time around, he wanted to do it right. He would create an irrefutable body of evidence that would convince even the fucking *New York Times*.

This disappearing business wasn't easy though. Everything he did left a trace, right from his phone and laptop to security cameras at stoplights and tollbooths, not to mention credit cards and other digital IDs. He had gotten rid of all his credit cards, trimmed down his wardrobe to basic jeans and plain T-shirts, and sold his few belongings through an intermediary for whatever he could get. He still had his bank account, driver's license, and various e-mail accounts. He'd have to figure out what to do with them.

The Internet had all kinds of information on how to disappear. He had been careful to use untraceable search engines, like DuckDuckGo and Tor, to figure out how to go "off the grid." But reading about it was

quite different from actually doing it. Short of enter-
ing a witness-protection program, he couldn't think of
a foolproof way.

But he had set up a deadman's handle. If something were to happen to him, any material that he'd
put in a safe electronic account would be immediately
published to e-mail accounts and Internet sites he had
designated ahead of time. Also, if that account wasn't
accessed every week, the files would be automatically
released. The only problem was all he had in that account was speculation. No proof yet. He really needed
to get a hold of Sid Ali, to find out exactly what had
happened at the shootout and find the fifteen-year-old
boy who had been captured along with him. Perhaps
the boy's grateful father might be willing to share photographs or documents or lead Tyler to people in the
Kashmir valley who would provide some corroboration.

The antique clock in the hallway struck four in the
morning. Tyler rose from the sofa reluctantly. He'd
probably never lived in any place this beautiful. His
short stay in the rental home had been almost perfect. An English garden grew all around, tended by
the owner's gardening crew. The house wasn't quite
on the water, but all he had to do was cross the quiet
country by-lane in front and stroll past a few properties
to a small gravel path that took him to the coastline
in a matter of seconds. And, of course, rousing memories of the luscious Ashley were inextricably tied to the
place. Naked nights in the infinity pool, drinking and

sitting in the hot tub at all hours, her lovely body snaking around his. Man, how he missed her.

He locked up the place and got into his little Miata. He was going to miss it too. He had just sold it on Craigslist and was scheduled to deliver it to the new owner in New York later that day.

The roads were deserted. He was on I-95 in no time at all and halfway to New York well before sunrise. Tyler turned on the defroster and thanked God for heated cars. It was miserably cold outside. His childhood home in Texas would be nice this time of the year. He'd thought of staying with his mother there, but that was too traceable, should he need to disappear quickly. They had probably staked it out by now. Or not. He wasn't completely unaware of his tendency to exaggerate his importance.

Tyler had given much thought to where he should go to lie low. If Uncle Sam really wanted to find Tyler, there was no escaping. But barring that, there were several options for making it difficult for Stephen James, junior senator from Massachusetts, to keep an eye on him.

Tyler could go to Maldives, Montenegro, or Vietnam. They had no extradition treaties with the United States. Or, Iceland, a country that frequently offered refuge to asylum seekers. But what was there in Iceland other than ice, volcanoes, and failing banks? It would be boring as hell. He could go to a paradise, like Costa Rica, where living was cheap, and be relatively close to the United States, should he need to come back. But then, South American countries weren't very good at resisting pressure from the United States. Not many countries were. Or, he could go off the grid right here in the United States of America. Given a choice, he'd rather stay in America than flee to another country. At least here, he understood the system. He could count on public outrage, should something happen to him. In a foreign country, he was completely at the mercy of governments that had their own agendas and axes to grind. He'd be just a pawn in their games with the United States.

A sign for McDonald's flashed by. He spotted the golden arches off the exit and took the ramp. His stomach, in its current delicate state, demanded familiar comfort food.

He picked up his order and sat in a corner, looking out onto the highway. The traffic was heavy now, with the beginning of rush hour. The generous pats of butter on his pancakes melted into an inviting puddle. He doused the stack in synthetic, sticky syrup; took a sweet bite; and felt his childhood slide warmly down his throat, those Sunday-morning outings after church.

Should he get another order of pancakes? This one had disappeared alarmingly fast. Prudence prevailed. He picked up his coffee to go and got back on the road to New York.

God, how he loved New York. It was his favorite city, always exciting, always beautiful, always out of reach. Would he ever get to live there, in the style that he wanted to? Now that he was really acting on this going-underground plan, he was beginning to realize the enormity of the decision. His life had been quite good, even at the crappiest times. Did he really want to go and lurk in some hole for the rest of his life? What kind of life would that be? He'd surely get some fame and notoriety out of it, but these leakers and whistle-blowers always met unhappy ends. Exiled on foreign soil or imprisoned. Or dead.

He shivered. He still had time. He could step back and do nothing. His readers would eventually forget. He might not be the badass story breaker that he wanted to be, but at least he could come and go as he pleased, see the blue sky and green trees and pretty flowers. Stephen would definitely leave him alone. He had no incentive to unnecessarily rake up controversy. Maybe he could make a deal with him, Tyler thought. Offer to be his biographer! But Stephen's supercilious stare came to mind and ticked off Tyler once more. Never! He'd never make a deal with that prick.

Signs for New York started to pop in his peripheral vision. Soon the city itself rose in front. He drove down the west side and pulled into a parking garage near Lincoln Tunnel. The buyer of his Miata had instructed him to park there and meet him in the lobby of the apartment building around the corner.

An icy blast took his breath away as soon as he stepped out of the garage. He pulled on his wool cap and turned up the collar of his winter jacket. He was a Texas boy. Even Oregon, his adopted home state, had never been this cold. By the time he entered the building, even though it was just a few yards, he was red-faced and gasping. He removed his cap, stamped his feet to get the icy slush off his boots, and looked around.

The security guard at the front desk looked at him pointedly. "I am waiting for someone," Tyler replied and slumped down gratefully into an armchair as far as possible from the arctic blasts coming from the opening and closing of the front doors.

A few minutes later, an African American man came out of an elevator just behind where Tyler sat. He was a Socratic-looking man of sixty, with short gray hair and a spry beard. Even though the temperature outside was in the single digits, he wore cargo shorts, a white T-shirt and Teva sandals. He was in phenomenal shape. Tyler could see sculpted chest muscles under the T-shirt. His arms and legs were sinewy and well defined.

He stopped in front of Tyler and smiled. "Donnie Bell. David Tyler?" He sounded even better in person than on the phone.

Tyler rose. "Yes. How are you?"

"You look cold."

"I am. I can't feel my ass."

Donnie laughed. "There's a penthouse café. How about a cup of coffee?"

"That would be great."

They rode the elevator to the top. A Chinese woman got in halfway up, with a yipping little dog in her arms. The dog kept up an incessant yowling during the entire time it took for them to get to the penthouse on the sixty-second floor. When the elevator doors opened, a sudden tsunami of noise, coffee smells, and bright light washed in.

Tyler rushed out with a grunt of relief. A few seconds more and he would have smacked the dog.

They picked up coffee at the counter and went across the room to sit at a table near the floor-to-ceiling windows. Tyler looked around while he removed his jacket. The café was quite crowded. Young Chinese women and gay couples seemed to constitute 90 percent of the clientele.

"Here are two sets of keys. The papers are in the car. I'll show you when we go down." Tyler placed the envelope on the table.

"Thanks." Donnie stowed it away in one of the capacious pockets of his shorts. In return, he slid a cashier's check Tyler's way.

"You buying a new car?" Donnie asked.

"No."

"Going to live in the city, eh?"

"No."

Donnie sat back in his chair and laughed.

"What?" Tyler was annoyed.

"Sorry if I seem nosy. I've been on my own for too long. I am just happy to be among people again."

An ex-convict, Tyler thought in alarm.

Donnie looked amused. "No, no, nothing crazy. Actually, I used to be a bond trader."

Tyler hadn't expected that. But the man's hyper-educated accent should have tipped him off.

"Damn, those were the days!" Donnie thumped the table. "I made unholy amounts of money. Then came the divorce, and my wife took half."

Tyler was hooked. "I am sorry."

"Me too. I'd been working like a dog for years, under tremendous stress. And suddenly, before I had a chance to even count it, half my money was gone."

Donnie had gotten himself a large piece of cake, along with his coffee. He cut it in two and pushed half toward Tyler.

"It was a lot of money. Even in my absolute worst year, I made three million dollars." He nodded at Tyler. "Yup, that's the kind of money we are talking about. I was pissed. I walked out, cashed all my assets, and took off to Colorado, with my money literally stuffed in a suitcase. Crazy shit, eh?"

Tyler couldn't believe it. Donnie smiled. "Google me. Donnie R. Bell, Wall Street wunderkind, of Bear Stearns fame. The Bear went down in flames a few years after I left."

Lo and behold, there he was, in screen after screen on Tyler's smartphone.

"What did you do in Colorado?"

"I became a ski bum. I got a huge kick out of pushing my body to extremes. I jumped off cliffs, swam in rapids, climbed mountains without oxygen. There wasn't a mountain slope I couldn't ski. I was the Dos Equis man."

Donnie showed Tyler his knees and arms. "I have so many metal rods and screws in my body. I'll never pass airport security or get an MRI."

"How did you pay for all that?"

"All paid with cash—accidents, surgeries, rehab—no electronic trail." He looked at Tyler. "When I started my life in the mountains, nothing but the best would do. You know, Gordon Gekko and all that. After a few years, I became careful, and as the cash ran out, I slowly worked my way down the star ratings, all the way down to men's hostels and, toward the end, even sleeping in a park or church." He sat up and chugged a glass of water. "As long as I could ski, I didn't care. I also added ATVs, mountain bikes, and hang gliders to my toys."

He grinned at Tyler. "Then my gear started falling apart, and I didn't have the money to replace it. I was like the man in Somerset Maugham's story, the man who spent all his wealth in the pursuit of beauty and happiness, ready to kill himself when the money ran out, but when the time came to act, didn't have the nerve."

Donnie stretched with the luxurious extension of a cat. His T-shirt rode up, revealing a taut belly. "So here

I am, trying to reenter the workforce, barely a few years shy of the official retirement age. Because I don't have a goddamned penny to my name!"

He seemed positively happy. "My friend let me stay in her apartment for a few days and lent me the money to buy your car. She is away until New Year's. Once she returns, your Miata will be the only home I'll have."

"What will you do?"

"I will look for a job at one of these fancy wilderness shops that sell outdoorsy sporty stuff...you know mountain bikes, ski gear, trekking, and hiking. I am a fucking expert. There is one in Jersey. I was thinking of driving down to check it out. That's why I need a car. Jersey is relatively cheap. But I need to be close to the city to shake out my contacts and see if I can get a job, any job, in finance. I'd like to wear a suit again, you know. I kind of miss that."

Donnie's expression didn't match his melancholy words. He was happy, happy, happy.

"I desperately need health insurance right now—a job at Starbucks or Whole Foods or REI, one of those companies that pay for insurance. I need to check those out. Once I get the health-insurance situation straightened out, I can look for other options. But I am just too damned old. Nobody will hire me."

"How about your ex-wife? Won't she help?" What a stupid question, Tyler thought as soon as he asked. Tyler's ex would rather see him die of starvation than help.

"She blew through her money even faster. She goes in and out of rehab every few months."

"Do you regret doing what you did?" Tyler asked.

"Not for a second. I'd do it over and over again. I don't regret it for an instant. Perhaps if we'd had kids, but, no, pure joy, baby."

Tyler couldn't help saying what he said next. The question had been haunting him for the last few days. "Do you have a lot of experience surviving off the grid?"

Donnie paused and gave Tyler a strange look. "Listen, I am not some kind of weirdo survivalist or conspiracy theorist. I just wanted freedom to do what I wanted. I didn't break any laws. I wasn't on the run or anything."

"Of course not! I just wanted to know your experience. That's all."

Donnie was mollified. "It wasn't my goal to be untraceable. I wanted to keep my shit in a place where my ex couldn't get at it. But I knew many guys back there who did it as a matter of challenge or out of a distrust of the government. How can you live without leaving a trace in this day and age? That's nuts."

"Is it impossible? Did you know of anyone?"

"I knew several guys." Donnie subjected Tyler to another stare. "Listen, buddy, are you in trouble? If so, I don't want your car. I have enough problems as it is, without the feds chasing after my car."

"No, not at all." Tyler tried to reassure Donnie. He didn't have time to find another buyer. "I am a writer.

I like to collect unusual experiences to use in my writing. That's all."

"You sure?"

"Yes! Google me if you like." There were at least seven David Tylers who were writers, all in their mid-forties. It was a sufficiently common name.

"I'll pay you," Tyler added. "For your advice."

Donnie leaned forward. "Really?" He laughed. "Nah. You don't need to do that. A nice lunch will do." He shrugged. "I'd love a juicy steak at Quality Meats."

"You got it."

Donnie smiled once more. "OK. I'll tell you about a couple of friends of mine. You can figure it out from there."

He pulled up another chair and stretched out his legs on it.

"The first one was Simon. He was in trouble with the government. I don't know what kind. He cooked the books, I think."

Donnie shifted his weight to get comfortable. His knee seemed to be the source of trouble. He massaged it. "He sold his car, just like you did. He closed out all his bank accounts, just like I did. And shredded his credit cards, driver's license. He held on to his passport though."

He looked at Tyler. "I don't know what kind of money you have, but if you have any reasonable amount, I would recommend setting up a trust through a third party who can do transactions for you. Someone who you'd trust with your life."

"But you carried your cash around. I probably don't have a hundredth of what you did."

"That was stupid of me. I kept it in plastic boxes, stowed away in lockers and all kinds of stupid places. Even buried some in the woods, graveyards, mountains, streams. When I think back...it was insane. But I was too high to know any better. It all made sense. And I had a ridiculous memory back then. I knew exactly how much was in each of those boxes, stashed in over one hundred locations, all within two miles' walking distance of where I lived. Some of them were stolen, but I never kept more than a few thousand dollars in any one place, and I kept moving things around."

"What!"

"Yes." Donnie nodded happily. He pointed his fingers to his head and shot himself with an imaginary gun.

What's he smoking now? Tyler wondered.

"Anyway, the point is don't do that. When you need to communicate with the trustee, use public phones, Internet cafés, or plain old snail mail. That's what Simon did."

Donnie looked at his empty cup. "Mind if I get some coffee? Would you like some?"

Tyler shook his head. While Donnie was away, Tyler looked through his e-mail. Nothing special, just confirmation of his various appointments for the day. Just for kicks, he pulled up the Amtrak website to see where in the continental United States it could take him.

Donnie returned. Tyler put away his phone.

"Where was I?" Donnie asked.

"Put money in a trust."

"Yes. Then there was this Pakistani guy. Crazy fuck. He thought the government was out to get him."

"What was his name?"

"Don't remember. Probably not his real name anyway. Quite a rich guy."

"So why was this Pakistani guy hiding?"

"Not sure. You can never tell with these South Asian guys. Maybe he was fingered for a terrorist connection. Who knows? Funny thing is, he had a fifteen-year-old boy with him. Private tutor, homeschooling, and all that."

Tyler's ears perked up. Paranoid Pakistani? Fifteen-year-old boy? Could it be Sid Ali in some bizarre witness-protection program? But in Colorado? Why would you hide a brown-skinned man there?

"What's his name?"

"Who knows? First I thought he might have a thing for the boy. But I don't think so." Donnie was lost in his thoughts. "Nope, I don't think so. He was wacko but not a creep."

Tyler was disappointed. A name would have been nice, even a fake one.

Donnie sighed and sat up. "You know, do you want to come with me to the apartment? I might have a picture on my hard drive somewhere."

They picked up their trash and walked back to the elevator.

Donnie's borrowed home was a mess. It was a small one-bedroom apartment, filled with bellboy's carts loaded with outfits—dresses in all colors and styles. Hundreds of shoes were stacked in modular racks all over the place. It was like Imelda Marcos and Anna Wintour decided to share a crummy apartment and then had to fight over space.

Donnie and Tyler picked their way to a couch in one corner that Donnie had cleared for himself. A laptop and several drives sat on it.

"Let's see," Donnie said. Tyler was surprised at how organized Donnie was. His disk drives were labeled and indexed neatly. His suitcases and duffel bag were methodically stashed next to the couch. Donnie put on a pair of glasses and skimmed through his computer. With a professorial air, he identified the right drive and attached it.

"Here, look at this." Tyler leaned forward for a closer look.

A photo showed two men standing on the edge of a precipice, hands outstretched like birds in flight. Their feet were almost off the cliff, projecting well out. The men were trying to see how far they could go on the rim without falling into the abyss below.

"That's the Pakistani guy, on the left. The boy took the picture."

Tyler couldn't make out anything. The two men in the picture wore bulky ski jackets, caps, and gloves. There was ice and snow on the ground. Both sported beards and were dark complexioned. One man was a little bigger than the other, but that was all. It wasn't very illuminating.

"The guy had some injury. He couldn't do much. The boy helped him around. I think we did that stunt on a dare one day."

"That was in Colorado, was it? Where?"

"No, actually, it was near the Idaho and Montana border. The guy had some scheme...Mir! That was his name, Mir. He lived in Idaho, but his car had a Montana license plate. He said he lived close enough to the border that a Montana license was not suspicious, but it was untraceable in Idaho. He had paid for it with cash, had a fake driver's license and all. He was another guy who did everything in cash. I don't know where he kept his money though."

Donnie took off his glasses and closed the laptop. "That's all I got."

"Thanks. I need to leave anyway."

They took the elevator down to the garage.

A few hours later, after the promised lunch at the carnivore heaven, Donnie dropped Tyler off near the port authority bus terminal. He watched Tyler disappear inside the building.

Donnie smiled. He picked up his phone.

"I think he bought it," he said.

"Excellent," Neel's voice responded from the other end. "Your offer letter will hit your mailbox any second now. I just sent it out. Thanks, Donnie. That was nicely done."

"No problem. Thanks for the job, man. You saved my life."

"Nothing to it. Glad to be of help. Bye, Donnie." Neel hung up.

A FAREWELL

The snow came down in fat, fluffy flakes and softened Detroit's angles and dark corners. The highway was plowed clean. It slipped under the car with icy smoothness. They would be in Ann Arbor in less than ten minutes.

Wasim sat silently in the passenger seat. His sister, Fatima, was at the wheel. Doug was in the backseat, listening to Fatima.

"Wasim was the studious one, always reading, even at basketball practice. I was the slacker," she said to Doug in the rearview mirror.

Doug and Wasim had become even more busy after winning the election, trying to get Stephen's Washington team in place before Congress resumed its session in

January. They had decided to take a brief vacation before the swearing in and had been headed from DC to Hawaii, when Fatima called to say that Wasim's mother had been hospitalized. "Nothing serious, but you should come and say hello," she had said. So they decided to make a stop in Detroit on their way to Hawaii.

Fatima Roberts had surprised Doug. Contrary to his expectations, she was a big, brash woman. She was just a few inches shorter than Wasim. But unlike the slender, lithe Wasim, she was built like a linebacker, with big shoulders and a muscular body. She was an assembly line technician at a Ford factory, where, a few years earlier, she had met and married Frank Roberts.

"I'll drop you guys off at the hotel. We can see *Ammie* early in the morning. It's past midnight now."

She pulled up in front of Bell Tower Hotel. Wasim's eyes brightened as he looked around the familiar campus, where he had spent four of the best years of his life.

"I'll pick you up here tomorrow," she said. "Nice meeting you, Doug."

"Thanks, but don't bother, Fatima," Wasim replied. "We'll meet you at the med center. Text me the room number."

"I'll do that. Don't worry, Wasim," she said. "Ammie is fine. She needs some rest. That's all." She waved to them and drove away.

After checking in and leaving their luggage in the room, Wasim said, "Let's go out. I'll show you the campus."

Wasim was energized. It was snowing, but there was no wind, and everything was in soft focus, silent and muted. The students were crammed into libraries, restaurants, and other public spaces to study together in camaraderie.

The two men walked down State Street and around campus, checking out storefronts and pubs.

"We will go see the Big House tomorrow. It is the loudest, most incredible place during a football game. And the band!"

Doug laughed at his enthusiasm. Wasim replied, "I know you are not a football fan, but you need to see a Notre Dame or Ohio State game. It's insane—miles and miles of tailgating, the band, and the student section. It'll make a fan of anyone. You have to see it to believe!"

Doug smiled, happy to see Wasim perk up. He had been very quiet since the news of his mother's hospitalization.

After a while, Wasim's enthusiasm quieted down. They continued in silence through the cold, snowy night. Walls of plowed snow and ice rose on either side, like a tunnel.

"You know, one night when Fatima was in fourth grade...I was six years old at that time, but I remember it clearly...my father slapped my mother right in front of us." He spoke softly, as if to himself, but he looked at Doug from time to time to see his reaction.

"We knew that he used to hit her, because we'd hear her crying in the bedroom, and she'd look like hell the next morning. But he had never hit her in front of us before. I was terrified. I clung to Fatima all night. The next night at dinner, Fatima told my father, '*Abba*, I spoke to my teacher, and she said that you can go to jail for hitting Ammie.'"

He paused and then went on. "My mother and I sat aghast. Ammie tried to get up and shush her. But Fatima wouldn't back down. Even in those days she was big for her age, and she was naturally aggressive, just like my father."

Wasim sighed. "My father never hit my mother again. But he had other ways of getting back at her. Like yelling at me and calling me names—moron, son of a whore, bastard, some of the more gentle ones, those."

Doug listened without saying a word.

"I was determined to get the hell out as soon as I could. I knew he wouldn't pay a cent toward my college education. He could afford it. He has a lot of money stashed away…somewhere. I don't know what he intends to do with it. I applied for every job I could, every scholarship. I thought my heart would burst when I got a full scholarship from UMich."

He laughed a dry, brittle laugh. "Do you know why my mother's in the hospital?"

Doug shook his head.

"Because she stopped eating. My parents are moving to San Diego, because my father can no longer show his face around here, now that everyone knows I am gay. She wanted me to come home, to look around my childhood room and take my things, to see me one last time before they moved, but my father refused to let me enter the house. So she stopped eating. Fatima went to visit her and found her in bed, weak and lethargic, and admitted her to the hospital. My father hasn't visited her even once since she was admitted."

"I am sorry." Doug couldn't think of anything more meaningful.

"My mother won't leave him. I've asked her so many times. 'I'll take care of you; come live with me.' You know what she says?"

Doug shook his head once more.

"'Your abba's not that bad. He provides for us. He doesn't cheat. He's not that bad. Look at your uncle. He brought his mistress home!'"

Wasim kicked the snow. "That's her bar—he doesn't bring his mistress home!"

They had walked a full circle and returned to the neighborhood of the hotel. It blazed with glittering lights and fluttering flags just a few feet ahead.

"Sorry, for laying all this on you, Douglas." Wasim used the full moniker when he felt particularly affectionate.

Doug patted him on the shoulder. "Anytime, Wasim, I am happy to listen. There's not much else I can do to help."

They stamped the snow off their feet and went inside to the bright fire in the lobby.

The next morning was a blindingly sunny day. Harsh light bounced off the white snow and ice. The wind blew sand-like crystals of ice into their faces as they walked to the sprawling university medical center.

Ammie was in a semiprivate room, on the window side. The other bed in the room was unoccupied for now but was being prepared for a new patient.

"*Beta*!" She sat up when she saw Wasim. He rushed to her and hugged her. Fatima was already there with her husband, Frank. He was bigger and burlier than her, and he was blond and red cheeked.

Doug introduced himself to Frank while the Raja family huddled in a group hug.

"Ammie! You've become so thin!" Wasim said in Urdu.

"I am all right, Beta. Don't worry," she replied, also in Urdu.

While Wasim and their mother spoke, Fatima joined Doug and Frank.

"My husband is the foreman of the factory floor where we work. That's where we met."

Frank nodded. "I was trying to get her to join my congregation. Still trying." He smiled. "We have two little boys, twins. They were baptized a couple of days ago."

Doug listened politely. He was uncomfortable around overtly religious types, because religion was often a segue to "curing" him of homosexuality.

"Anyway, we need to leave now. I just wanted to say bye to you guys." Fatima interjected hurriedly and shook hands with Doug.

"Wasim, good-bye, my brother." She blew him a kiss. "Ammie, I'll stop by in the evening. Bye!" Frank waved to them and followed her. Doug turned away in relief.

Wasim left his mother's side and joined the couple to walk them to the elevator.

Doug was left awkwardly alone with Wasim's mother. They looked at each other for a while. Finally, he walked up to her and said, "Your son is a wonderful person."

She was a slight woman. Her skin hung loosely on her bones, as if still hoping for the missing flesh to grow back. Her wispy, long hair was tied in a bun and was almost all white. She must have been only in her midfifties but looked old and fragile. Her traditional *salwaar kameez* covered her arms and legs completely, but she wore no head scarf.

At the mention of Wasim, her tired face immediately broke into a big smile, and tears flowed down her cheeks. She waved him closer.

When he got near, she pointed him to the chair and said, "Sit."

He sat down. Wasim, where are you? Come back, he thought, in a slight panic now.

She looked at him for a long time, as if sizing him up. Then, she took out a box from under her pillow and gave it to him. It was the size of a small shoe box, made with a smooth, dark wood inlaid with silver filigree, with little claw feet made of silver. It was a work of art with beautiful craftsmanship, the real deal, not one of the cheesy, touristy knock-offs that Doug had seen so many of.

"Open, open," she said.

It opened on a hinged lid. The interior was padded with plush burgundy-colored velvet. On that regal bed lay six thick gold bangles, all bejeweled; a gold and ruby ring; and the coiled rope of a substantial gold necklace. He looked up at her.

"Wasim and you," she said.

"What!" He was shocked.

Wasim walked in at that exact moment. He looked at the two of them. "Ammie, what's going on?" he asked in Urdu.

She broke into a long explanation, tears streaming down her eyes. Doug couldn't understand much, although he had been trying to learn the language for the past few weeks. She spoke too fast, with no pauses between words.

"Ammie!" Wasim's heart was breaking. He sat down on the bed, near her feet, and looked at her with miserable eyes.

Doug waited for Wasim to translate.

Finally, Wasim looked away from his mother and said to Doug, "She has been saving her bridal jewelry for my future wife and daughters. She wants to know who she should give it to now."

Doug felt very uncomfortable. He didn't know what to do with the box that sat on his lap like a deadweight.

Wasim stood up and turned to his mother. This time he spoke in English, to include Doug in the situation. His voice was firm.

"Ammie, this is my life now. I know you don't understand it, and I can't make it fit with your expectations. But Doug and I are together. We are going to live together, in the same house, sleep in the same bed."

That's too harsh; take it easy, Doug thought in alarm.

"I don't know what our future will be," Wasim continued. "All I can say is I am not going to marry a woman and have children. That's simply *not* going to happen."

He stood with his hands folded across his chest and stared down at her. Ammie looked at him, puzzled, sad, and disappointed, all at once.

"Ammie," Wasim said in a milder tone. "Doug and I are happy together. He is going to be working for the newly elected senator as his chief of staff. I am going to study law at Georgetown."

He sat down and stared at her. "Remember, you used to say that I should become a lawyer? Well, I will become one, in three years. Doug is one of the main reasons I am doing it. Other than you and Fatima, nobody has ever done more for me. He saved my life!"

She glanced quickly at Doug and then back at Wasim.

"Ammie, don't you think we should spend our lives with people who support us and want the best for us? Would it be any use if I married some unfortunate girl and made her life, and my life, miserable?" Like yours, he wanted to add but stopped himself.

She shook her head.

"Well, this is my happiness. I need you to understand and believe it. Can you do that?" He pulled her toes and said, "Please, my good ammie, say yes."

She smiled at this reversion to his tried-and-tested childhood wheedling trick.

Wasim looked at his watch. He stood up. "I want you to take care of yourself. I will come and visit you in San Diego," he said.

She nodded, with tears gathering once more.

"We have to leave now; otherwise we will miss our flight," he said gently.

She looked at him, loathe to see him leave, her precious son.

"Fatima said she is going to show you how to Skype. We can see each other on the computer then. Every week."

Wasim signed to Doug that he was ready to leave.

Doug got up and placed the box near Ammie. "It was very nice meeting you, Ammie. We will take the box next time we meet. Please keep it safely with you until then." He shook her hand. "I will keep an eye on Wasim for you," he added, with a wink.

She laughed at that.

Doug walked out of the room to gather their bags, which were sitting in the hallway.

Wasim hugged his mother. "Give my *adaab* to Abba. How is he?"

"He's the same," she said. "Older."

"Ammie, I am glad that you are moving. You will be near Aunty Sara. It will be good for you to have your sister near you. You have no one here. Without his cronies around, you'll see that Abba will be a different man. It will be better for you."

"Beta, don't worry about me. I hope you know what you are doing with your life."

"I do, Ammie. Believe me. *Khuda haafiz*, Ammie."

"Khuda haafiz, Beta."

He stopped at the door and took a last look at her, at the woman who had so little joy in her life. Some of it was her own fault, an unwillingness to stand up for herself and brave the consequences, clinging instead to the shred of safety from a man who did not love or respect her, who used her cruelly, and some of the bleakness of her life was the result of a harsh tradition that denied education and independence to women, to ensure that they remained in place at the bottom of society, carrying its burden with their backbreaking drudgery.

He sighed and moved forward.

FEAR AND LOATHING

For the first time in almost twenty years, the James residence sparkled with life on Christmas Eve. Normally, the couple spent Christmas with Nina's parents in New Jersey. Before Nina came into his life, Stephen had made a point of being away during the holiday, sailing along some sunny shore. But this time around, Nina had insisted that they stay home. Her parents would arrive the next day, after finishing their own round of parties.

"We need to start doing this," she had said. "Otherwise our child will have no roots."

"On the contrary, she will have too many roots to choose from," he had laughed. But they bought everything on Nina's list—Christmas tree, decorations, lights—and had spent the day setting the tree up, in between answering the barrage of calls and e-mails for Stephen's upcoming Washington, DC, duties. Doug, his new chief of staff, was scrambling to put together Stephen's team.

Oddly, it was still just Nina and Stephen in that majestic house, no staff or help except for occasional visits from Mrs. Brown, the housekeeper, and the highly vetted cleaning crew that showed up once a week. They both liked it that way. It would have to change soon though, when the baby arrived. Deepa and Ravi had promised to help out, at least initially.

Nina looked up from the wreath she was arranging on the mantel and searched for Stephen, but he had been summoned by his phone once more. He was at the far end of the room, sitting in his favorite armchair, with his serious face on. He looked up at her and signed that he had to take the call, mouthed the word *sorry*, and turned away from her.

It was Neel.

"Stephen, can you talk?" he asked.

"Not really."

"Then just listen, and call me when you can."

"Go on."

"Tyler has returned to the United States. He has vacated his home, emptied out all his bank accounts, sold his car, terminated his phone services, and paid off all his debt."

"I see."

"He is going underground."

"And?" There had to be more, because Neel never did anything half-assed.

"And we are on it. We've planted a seed in his head. I am almost certain that he will take the bait. That might lead us to where he is going into hiding."

"Is George in on this?"

A pause. "Yes."

Damn, George. Stephen really didn't want his meddling help. But it was inevitable, sooner or later. There were too many secrets, and he would need George and his formidable machinery to deal with the fallout when the skeletons were dragged out of his closet, either by Tyler or some other obnoxious leaker.

"George is a friend, Stephen. It's good to have him in our corner."

Neel was right. It was a fine balance, this trade-off between necessity and principles to achieve a greater good.

"I suppose so." Stephen was reluctant to admit the truth.

"You know George better than I do, Stephen. He looks out for you."

"What's this evidence Tyler has gotten hold of?"

Neel sighed. "It's not good. Operation Cradlesnatch."

Stephen listened to Neel's account in stunned silence. Of all the secrets, that was probably the most damaging, and the one he regretted most. He had no qualms about how he treated grown men and women under suspicion. A whiff of doubt was enough, in his mind, to justify whatever means were necessary. Children were different, despite his brash claim that they were just collateral damage. He had known it was unconscionable at the time he had authorized the operation, and he had felt it even more acutely after Nina's miscarriage, and now, her pregnancy. But, at that point in time, that had been his best option to catch a vicious killer threatening to behead American hostages—blackmail the killer's associates by kidnapping their children, and demand his head as ransom.

"A photo, Neel?"

"Yes. You in that holding room."

"Fuck! How?" Stephen asked. The Agency had an official photographer but Stephen hadn't asked for one on that particular day.

"It's not an official photo," Neel said as if he had read his thoughts. "Looks like a pen camera."

"One of our own?"

"Yup."

That trash, Tyler! How did that picture fall into *his* hands?

Nina was wandering over with their treetop angel.

"I have to go now. I'll call later. Bye." Stephen signed off quickly.

He took the angel from Nina without a word and climbed onto the stepladder near the tree. She gave him directions: to the left, a tad more, no, no, the other way. He finally got the figurine to sit perfectly.

He came down the ladder and looked up at the angel. He had given it to Nina a few years earlier, when he had been under investigation after his expulsion from India. His future had been uncertain, and if it hadn't been for her, he would have seriously thought of following his father's example. He had the angel made in Nina's likeness, with her sweet smile and caramel complexion, dressed in a white silk sari with a red border, just like the one she had worn at their civil wedding.

"Help us," he muttered under his breath.

"Everything OK?" she asked.

"I'm fine." He managed to smile and went back to sit in his chair. A drink would be perfect right about now, just what he needed, but he stopped himself.

Nina walked over and looked at him. Something was off. She sat down in the sofa next to his chair.

"Who was that on the phone?" she asked.

"Nobody."

"Are you in trouble?"

"No, not at all, Nina," he replied, this time with a genuine smile.

That seemed to satisfy her. She tried to get out of the low-slung sofa, but her belly got in the way. He laughed and helped her up.

We'll deal with it, he thought. We have the best surveillance technology—crawlers that can scan millions of computers in a split second, supersophisticated face-recognition software, voice recognition that can put the human ear to shame. That was what his company specialized in. He and Neel were part of an elite group of experts in extreme electronic surveillance that left no fingerprints. They could handle Tyler.